DEATH CARD

A Novel by

Nick L. Sacco

CCB Publishing
British Columbia, Canada

Death Card

Copyright © 2013 by Nick L. Sacco
ISBN-13   978-1-77143-105-7
First Edition

Library and Archives Canada Cataloguing in Publication
Sacco, Nick L., 1957-, author
Death Card / by Nick L. Sacco. -- First edition.
Issued in print and electronic formats.
ISBN 978-1-77143-105-7 (pbk.).--ISBN 978-1-77143-106-4 (pdf)
Additional cataloguing data available from Library and Archives Canada

Contact Nick L. Sacco through his website: www.acephantom.com

Back cover artwork credit: Police Brutality Clip Art from Vector.me (by liftarn)

Publisher: CCB Publishing
              British Columbia, Canada
              www.ccbpublishing.com

Acknowledgements

To my long time friend, Bill Thompson, who shared his knowledge and technical expertise as an Air Force veteran. Bill helped me plug holes in the technical areas of the book.

To all of my friends and family for their support and confidence.

My biggest thanks is to my smoking hot girlfriend, Marcy, who was by my side every step of the way while I wrote *Death Card*. She gave me both positive and negative feedback, listened to my ideas and endured my rants. She spent hours pouring over every word of my book looking for typos, making suggestions, and laughing, when I was witty enough to trigger her sense of humor.

"You see dictators on their pedestals,
surrounded by the bayonets of their soldiers
and the truncheons of their police ...
yet in their hearts there is unspoken fear."
- Winston Churchill

Chapter 1

A thunderous sonic boom rattled Washington, D.C. Throughout the city, people panicked as windows shattered and car alarms blared. The undetected supersonic aircraft raced away after dropping its deadly package. Specifically designed to carry nuclear weapons, the B-2 Stealth Bomber was miles away before the carnage erupted on the city below. Its precision-guided warhead detonated directly above the White House.

Chapter 2

Maggie Kerr was struggling with mixed emotions as she steered her yellow Jeep Wrangler toward the White House. As an ambitious young reporter, she was eager, yet hesitant, to attend this press conference. She felt this assignment might be just what she needed to move up at the *Washington Post*, where she had been working for nearly five years. During this press conference, Maggie hoped she might get a seat close to the front, among the other media big shots. She imagined the scenario now: The speaker, spotting her raised hand in the sea of other reporters, would motion for her to rise. Uncrossing her shapely legs to stand in her four-inch heels, she would toss her long red hair over one shoulder. Her green eyes smoldering, with notebook clutched to her ample bosom, she would shout a question so significant, so life-altering, that it would be repeated on every news outlet for weeks to come. Maggie had rehearsed it a hundred times...in her mind. In reality, a more experienced reporter would beat her to the punch. Maggie suspected the speaker would be a listless government drone, holding the mundane title of Assistant to the Assistant for the Department of Mad Cow Research.

As Maggie drove down Connecticut Avenue, she thought back to the text she had received earlier in the evening from her assignment editor. The recognizable sound of the Darth Vader theme song tipped Maggie off that her boss was sending her a message.

Duty calls. Press conference 10 p.m.
WHITE HOUSE. DON'T BE LATE.
Anything good? Write it up and e-mail it to the news desk ASAP.

Maggie had been looking forward to curling up on the couch with her favorite guy, Puma, a six-year old Calico she had rescued as a kitten, a big bowl of popcorn, and two hours of her favorite home makeover show.

Now, nearly ten o'clock, she drove through the dark along Independence Avenue. She felt jittery and anxious. It seemed strange to be summoned to a press conference at such a late hour. The traffic seemed about as normal as any Washington evening. Suddenly, Maggie spotted a motorcycle cop pulling into the upcoming intersection, his red strobe lights flashing. Though she had the green light, the officer raised his arm ordering her to stop.

Maggie peered out her windows, but didn't see an accident or a DUI checkpoint. For a second, she considered flashing her press credentials and mentioning something about being late for an important mad cow news conference. Maybe she would undo a couple of buttons on her blouse and thrust her chest forward at the cop. She would say, "Officer, these babies have an appointment at the White House." Her humorous thoughts vanished quickly when a convoy of military trucks, Humvees, and armored vehicles suddenly barreled through the intersection just feet from her car. Maggie could see soldiers in full battle gear. She noticed that nearly every vehicle had a staffed, menacing-looking machine gun on top of it.

"The boys sure are playing army late tonight," Maggie thought to herself. A shrill whistle sounded. Maggie looked up to see the motorcycle cop waving rapidly at her to keep moving. She hit the gas and gave a small wave at the police officer as she passed. He ignored her and didn't wave back.

As she neared the Capitol, she noticed police officers in reflective vests and more soldiers in their fatigues busily setting up barricades. It must be another political protest following the recent presidential election and the authorities were getting prepared, Maggie thought to herself. For the past several months, protests had grown more frequent and violent. A dozen different antigovernment groups, including the Tea Party, had been demanding everything from changes in policy to the removal of President Marcus Barakat. As more factories and businesses closed, the unemployed swelled the ranks of the protesting crowds. There had been bloody clashes with Washington police and mass arrests. One famous evening news anchor said the current protests seemed like a combination of the 1968 Democratic riots in Chicago and the World Trade Organization riots in Seattle. Now, as the oath of office neared, violent clashes were erupting all across the nation.

Two blocks from the Capitol, Maggie was stopped at her first checkpoint. An armed man dressed in all-black battle dress utilities leaned into her window. "National Security Force" was stitched over his left pocket. In a firm voice, he ordered Maggie to turn off her radio and asked for her press credentials. He then vanished into a nearby military-style tent while two other NSF agents holding rifles and sidearms stood staring intently at her car. Quite suddenly, Maggie felt extremely uncomfortable. She couldn't put her finger on it, but something was definitely wrong with this situation. She self-consciously ran her fingers over the buttons of her blouse making sure nothing was exposed. She continued to wait, getting more nervous as time went by, feeling like she might have diarrhea or even throw up, as the NSF agents continued to stare at her. Finally, the first man reappeared from the tent. He pointed a finger down the street. "Do you see those lights?" Maggie turned her head and saw a scene of flashing light bars and flickering road flares further down the street. Maggie thought it looked like a ten-car pileup accident scene.

"Drive toward those flashing lights and park where you are directed," he ordered, stepping away from her car.

"Mad cow disease? Bullshit! I was definitely dreaming when I thought that," Maggie whispered to herself, shifting the car into gear and driving toward the chaos ahead.

A block down the street a pattern of burning road flares on the ground forced Maggie into a single lane. She wondered how many people had suffered convulsions or migraines from the flashing strobe lights as she slowed her car to a crawl. Finally, a soldier waving two orange-coned flashlights similar to someone directing an airplane to the gate, guided her toward a line of parked cars. To Maggie it seemed like a bizarre street carnival. Glancing around, she realized that all the streets near the White House were barricaded and filled with military, police, and the black-clad NSF troops. Immediately after lowering herself down from the driver's side of her Jeep, a soldier directed her toward an immense green military tent erected in the street outside the fence that surrounded the White House. A line of people were snaking their way toward the tent entrance, a cordon of armed troops on either side. She began to recognize faces from the various media organizations like CNN, NBC, FOX and ABC.

As she got in line Maggie looked up ahead and saw it was barely moving. A reporter she recognized from another network was in a heated argument with two men in dark business suits. The reporter was demanding to find out why no electronic devices or cameras were allowed in the press conference. He wasn't getting an answer. In response, the two men shoved past him, seized his camera equipment, and added it to a stack of others.

As the line began to slowly shuffle forward, Maggie could feel a tension building in the air. She glanced over her shoulder at the reporter who was now screaming in protest, as his camera operator stood silent with a confused look on his face. "Since when are cameras not allowed in a press conference?" Maggie asked herself.

The tent was huge and dark, not like any press conference she had attended in the past. She could barely see. As her eyes adjusted to the dark, she noticed the room was filled with rows of folding chairs, and a small podium stood on a stage at the front of the tent. Behind it hung a huge smiling image of President Marcus Barakat. The first three rows of seats were already filling up with reporters. As she looked around, a hand suddenly grabbed her elbow. Maggie, who had attended a self-defense class, jerked her arm away and began to assume a defensive position. Looking up, she recognized her assailant as Charlie Ashman. Charlie was Maggie's close friend, who worked as a political events blogger. Maggie smiled and gave Charlie a big hug.

"I almost kicked you in the nuts, dude," Maggie said with a laugh. "Never sneak up on me."

"I was just trying to get your attention before you sat down with some other good looking guy."

"What the hell are we doing here, Maggie? We should be playing darts and drinking beer," Charlie said, flashing a flawless smile and a playful wink. Maggie liked Charlie . . . and the way he looked. He was a "man's man." He had dark hair, cut in a short military fashion. A "battle cut," he once said it was called. He wore khaki colored cargo pants that had more pockets than Maggie could count and a blue denim shirt, the sleeves rolled up so high she could see the Army Ranger tattoo on his muscular bicep.

Charlie was an incredible writer who preferred the freedom of working for himself. His freelance articles were engaging to his large audience and backed by some wealthy advertisers. Charlie had built himself a good relationship with the Washington media. He and Maggie, while not officially dating, spent many hours at their favorite bar or coffee shop. They could talk about anything from the most mundane topic to items of great seriousness.

"Follow me," Charlie said to Maggie, taking her hand and leading them to a pair of seats at the end of a row. They were close to, yet just behind, the big-name media faces who occupied the area of importance within throwing range of the podium. Charlie looked toward the front row and then turned and gave Maggie a comical, pouty face. He began to march in his chair, swinging his arms and raising and lowering his feet. "I want to sit up front and be a macher," he said, using a Yiddish term for a big shot or someone of importance. Maggie laughed whenever Charlie said something in Yiddish, even though she understood very little of it herself. At one point in Charlie's life, he had been dating a beautiful Jewish woman whose strict Orthodox father hated any guy his daughter brought home, especially goys, or non-Jewish men. So, to win his approval, Charlie came up with a plan. For two weeks he had studied the Yiddish language, memorizing hundreds of the old Jewish words. Finally, ready and confident, Charlie launched his stunt at the height of a Shabbat dinner at the house of his girlfriend's parents. "I just love shtuping with your daughter," Charlie said smiling from one parent to another. Charlie would later relate that the first sign of trouble was the sudden silence that seized the room. Slowly raising his eyes from his plate, a fork full of food balanced at his open mouth, Charlie realized that both parents and a younger brother were staring at him as though lobsters were suddenly crawling out of his head. For a moment, Charlie had considered slicing his wrists with the butter knife, but he didn't want to ruin the beautiful white lace tablecloth. Dinner was cut short, and Charlie did not get to enjoy the mother's wonderful challah bread. He was personally escorted to the door by the father, who offered up some new Yiddish words for Charlie.

"You're a schlemiel and a nudnik. Now you go look those words up, mister smart ass," the father said, glaring and slamming the door in Charlie's face. The following day Charlie received an angry phone call from his now ex-girlfriend demanding to know why he had so proudly told her parents he liked screwing their daughter. A quick check of his Yiddish dictionary revealed that Charlie had mistakenly used the word for sex when he meant to say shmooze, or to talk or chat. Charlie Ashman's attempt at speaking the Yiddish language to impress the girlfriend's father had ended in disaster.

Charlie stopped his mimicking and leaned close to Maggie. "Something's going on here, Maggie," he whispered quietly to her. "Just before I left home, I got a phone call from Sarah Palmer. Her husband, Andy, is the managing editor at CNBC. Some government-looking guys in a black SUV showed up and demanded he go with them. They said he was needed at some important meeting, but wouldn't say anything else. They just took him and left. Then on my drive over here, I get a text message from someone I know at FOX. Same story about his boss being summoned to a private audience. Now we're here. I don't know what's up, but I have a bad feeling."

Maggie began to respond when a rustling of movement brought everyone's attention to the front. Four men in suits and sporting earpieces had come into the tent. To Maggie, they looked like Secret Service agents on steroids. With their arms at their sides, they stood in a line, their eyes darting over everyone in the audience. Charlie squeezed Maggie's hand and nodded his head, indicating she should look behind them. Slowly and calmly, Maggie glanced over her shoulder and spotted a half dozen dark-suited men standing at the rear of the tent. As Maggie began to whisper into Charlie's ear, a woman stepped onto the stage.

Maggie recognized her from television. She held some minor role in President Barakat's cabinet. Small in stature, wearing a red pantsuit with matching pumps, her face shining with perfect makeup, she looked like the epitome of a female politician. With her close-cropped brown hair and big eyes, she flashed a thin-lipped smile at the audience.

Maggie had never attended a press conference where the speaker held no notes or flash cards. This woman was completely empty-handed.

"Evening, y'all. My name is Donna Koontz," she said with a thick, southern drawl. Leaning against the podium, she looked out over the audience of media people. "I'm the new press secretary for President Marcus Barakat. I'll just jump right to the point of why y'all are here tonight. The president and his staff feel that all the recent nationwide discontent has impeded the progress of the goals the president has made for the American people. So, effective immediately, there's gonna be a whole bunch of important and profound changes. Guess what?" she said, spreading her arms out wide like a TV evangelist and smiled. "It all begins right now."

Immediately, an aide handed Koontz a thick, red-covered booklet. She held it high over her head and shook it for everyone to see. "From now on, the government's gonna begin directing all the daily operations of the media. Newspapers, television, radio, even you bloggers," she added, singling out those like Charlie.

"This is your new Bible," she said, holding the book like a model displaying a new product. "It tells you how to write and report anything and everything. You will adhere to it . . . religiously," she emphasized, dropping the book on the top of the podium with a thump. "It's real simple, folks. Follow it to the letter of the law, just like you would your own personal Bible, don't deviate from any of the rules, and we'll all get along wonderfully," Koontz said with a fake laugh.

"Many of you in the media have reported the news in a positive way toward President Barakat and his administration this last term," she continued. "However, others of you have tried to slant the news reports against President Barakat. Any negative news reporting will STOP immediately." Maggie and Charlie turned and stared at one another in openmouthed shock. Before either could say a word, a loud voice brought their attention back toward the podium. It was *Associated Press* reporter Phillip Elliott. He stood up to address the new press secretary.

"Ms. Koontz," Elliott said, "are we to understand that the White House is going to begin dictating and censoring the content of the news?" A chorus of voices could be heard around the room. Other reporters started shouting questions and raising their hands. Koontz began motioning for everyone to quiet down. She turned her attention back to Elliott.

"I think I speak for everyone here," he said, waving an arm above the murmuring crowd. "This is a complete violation of the First

Amendment to the Constitution. Since when does the government of the United States decide it's going to change one of our most basic and important freedoms?"

Elliott crossed his hands in front of him, calmly awaiting a response. A chilled silence fell over the room as the other reporters waited for an answer.

Donna Koontz let out a deep sigh of frustration. "Since right now," she snapped back with anger. Turning to one of the black-suited men behind her, she shrugged her head toward Elliott. The man hopped off the stage and crossed the distance to the still-standing reporter in less than two seconds. As the other reporters watched in horror, the black suited man pulled a handgun from his concealed shoulder holster, and in one swift, practiced motion, raised his arm and blasted a nine-millimeter bullet into the forehead of Phillip Elliott.

The discharge of the gun in the small space of the tent sounded as though a cannon had been fired. There was a surreal moment of time as Maggie watched Elliott's head jerk backward violently before his body crumpled to the floor.

Some of the reporters who had served as combat correspondents in danger zones immediately took cover. Others jumped from their seats and tried to flee, but the exits were already blocked by the dark-suited men.

"Get down," Charlie yelled, dragging Maggie below the seats beside him as the room erupted into cries and screams. He held a protective arm across her shoulders as Maggie's mind tried to comprehend the violence she had just witnessed.

"GET BACK IN YOUR SEATS!" the men in black suits began ordering the terrified reporters. Charlie looked around cautiously before taking his seat and then guiding Maggie up beside him.

The acid stench of gunpowder filled the air. All the seats around the dead body of Phillip Elliot had emptied. A cloud of blue smoke lazily floated above the room. One of the black suits began wrestling away a cell phone from a tall thin woman who was trying to record a video of the carnage.

"Quiet, please. Quiet, please," Donna Koontz, said, as if directing a class of second-graders. "Please take your seats. Anyone else who attempts to take any cell phone pictures or video will be arrested," she said, leaning across the podium.

Calmly, and, as if unaffected by what had just happened, Koontz moved in front of the podium to tower above the crowd of terrified press officials.

"This ain't your daddy's government anymore," she said sternly, her dark eyes taking in everyone in the audience. "The old ways, well, they just aren't working anymore, so the President, his staff, and the American people are going in a new direction. The president wants everyone to jump on board and help him build a new nation," Koontz said cheerfully with a forced, toothy smile.

"However," she continued, arms now crossed, the smile gone and an air of foreboding in her voice, "do not underestimate the determination of our president and his new staff to reach our goals and lead our nation toward a new future. Dissension will not be tolerated and that's the truth," Koontz snapped.

She turned and began to walk toward the curtain of the tent when she suddenly stopped and turned back, as if just remembering something. "I'm sorry, y'all, but in the excitement, I failed to tell you that all electronic communications – you know, cell, telephone, television, and Internet – are suspended for 48 hours. It's what y'all might call a news blackout. Tomorrow at noon the president is gonna address the nation. Don't miss it. Trust me, it's gonna be exciting! Don't forget your new guidelines," she said, pointing to a pile of the red-covered books on the stage. "You're gonna need 'em."

A small-statured, wimpish man met Koontz as she strode out of the tent. "Ms. Koontz," her aide said, shaking, "what about . . . you know . . . him." He nodded the way she had come, to where Elliott's body lay.

Koontz stopped to adjust an earring before answering, "Send flowers to Mrs. Elliot," she said, smoothing the front of her jacket. "Then have her killed, too," she replied coldly.

As if on cue, four of the black suits surrounded the press secretary, and the group began to walk away together.

"But, Ms. Koontz," the aide stuttered loudly, pointing toward the tent. "How do we handle . . . him?"

Without breaking stride, Koontz yelled over her shoulder, "They're called landfills, Andrew," and continued walking, leaving her assistant behind.

Maggie was in complete shock. Shaking and fighting off panic, she turned to Charlie in disbelief. As she looked up into his eyes, she saw that his face was a mask of fear and confusion. "Oh my God, Maggie. Let's get out of here, NOW!" he said, pulling her close for a second, and then turning to leave.

Chapter 3

Some of the reporters walked to the podium, carefully picking up the red books like they were poisonous snakes. Some wept, some whispered among themselves; but most just stood in shocked disbelief.

Charlie briefly left Maggie's side and snatched two of the books from the stage. Putting his arm around her, he guided her out of the tent entrance and into the night. It seemed that the number of security and military people had tripled during the press conference.

After parking Maggie's car in a nearby fast food restaurant parking lot, Maggie and Charlie silently drove away from the Capitol in Charlie's vehicle, the sights and smells of the press conference execution repeating in their minds like a clip from a horror movie. With a white-knuckled fist, Charlie squeezed the steering wheel of his older, black Saab, his right hand clenched on the gearshift between the seats.

At one point Maggie turned on the car radio, but all the stations simply played a loop of the same three Bee Gees songs. No DJ to be found, no jingles, no commercials. Some stations, off the air, simply played static. She tried her cell phone, but there was no signal. When she tried to call the service carrier, an automated voice instructed her to try again later due to unexpected high call volume.

Tossing her useless cell phone into her purse, Maggie finally broke the silence. "What the fuck is going on? They just murdered someone in the middle of a press conference, Charlie. Shouldn't we be doing something?"

Charlie drove another block without responding. He guided his car onto a side street and stopped. He rubbed his temples, eyes closed, pulling his thoughts together. "A government has to control the press, Maggie, to control the people. Whatever this new government plan is, they want to make sure the public hears only what President Barakat wants them to hear, and nothing else."

"I'm not a big history person, Charlie," Maggie said, turning in her seat to face him, "I never have been. You, however, are quite the historian. What do you think is happening? Because, frankly, I'm scared shitless."

He turned and reached across the seat for Maggie's hand. "I had a social science teacher in high school named Mr. Renkin. He said, 'Never trust a government that is critical of, or wants to control, the press.'"

He paused to look out the driver's window. "What we witnessed tonight, Maggie," he said, pounding the steering wheel with his fist, "screams of Stalinism. We just saw a news reporter, a human being, get his head blown off simply because he questioned a government official."

"But they can't *do* this, Charlie," Maggie pleaded. "It's a crime. We just had front row seats to a murder. The American public isn't going to sit back and allow this."

Checking his mirrors, Charlie began to pull back onto the street. He glanced at Maggie as he shifted gears. "The American public will never hear about what we saw tonight," Charlie said sternly. "Phillip Elliott will simply vanish. This press meeting tonight with that bitch Koontz, will never be revealed to anyone. It will be as if this never happened."

"We can tell people," Maggie answered, sitting up straight in her seat. "We should go to the nearest police station right now and report what we saw."

Charlie jerked his right hand up as quickly as a snake striking and pointed his finger sternly at Maggie. "If you say anything about tonight to anyone, even the police, Maggie, you'll wind up just like Phillip Elliot," Charlie warned. "They wasted Phil and he was a big name in the media. You think they'll hesitate to make a third-string reporter or an Internet blogger disappear?"

"No offense," he added, patting Maggie on her leg.

"None taken," she replied, crossing her arms and looking out the window into the dark.

We should go by my office," Maggie said suddenly looking at Charlie. "Maybe someone there has more information on what's happening."

For a moment Charlie drove without speaking. A large white fire

13

truck, lights flashing and siren wailing, passed them going the other direction. "Good idea, Maggie," he said, flashing a subdued smile.

As Charlie steered his car toward the office of the *Washington Post*, Maggie suddenly remembered the booklet that Press Secretary Donna Koontz had ordered them to take and read. She reached into the back seat and retrieved one, looking at the front cover title for the first time.

PRESS PROTOCOL AND PROCEDURES

Maggie went directly to the table of contents and began to read.

1. Prohibited and Illegal Media Reporting Acts
2. News Story Structure and Guidelines
3. Live Television and Field Reporting Directions and Regulations
4. Interview Questions and Techniques
5. Violations, Penalties and Punishments
6. Banned Content

"We're almost to your office," Charlie said, bringing Maggie's attention back to the present.

Maggie tossed the publication into the back seat as if it were an old catalog. "There's some really scary stuff in there, Charlie," she said quietly, "and I'm just talking about the table of contents."

"You think that's scary, Maggie," Charlie said, nodding out the front window, "look up ahead."

Maggie turned to face forward and felt her heart flutter. The multi-floor office of the *Washington Post* was as dark as night. The normally busy and bustling 24/7 news building was black and empty. The only lights she could see inside were red EXIT signs.

Even worse, there were huge concrete blocks set up on the sidewalk, like the ones used on highway construction projects, that formed a barricade around the building. Bright lights, usually seen at an emergency or accident scene, lit up the street. Maggie counted at least twenty heavily armed soldiers, their rifles held at the ready, standing around the building. They looked serious and eyed Charlie's car suspiciously as he drove by.

"Stop staring, Maggie," Charlie ordered, focusing his attention out the front window.

Maggie suddenly felt a knot building in her stomach.

"Does this mean I'm out of a job, Charlie?" Maggie asked, turning to look out the rear window.

"It might," he replied, glancing quickly at Maggie. "I'm purely speculating, but after what we've seen tonight I'll bet money that when President Barakat addresses the nation tomorrow, he's going to impose martial law. Why else would half the US military be out in the streets?"

"He can't do that, can he?" Maggie asked, fishing in her purse for a hair tie. She began to put her long red hair into a ponytail. "Doesn't he have to get approval from the Senate or Congress or friggin' someone?" she asked, looking at Charlie for answers.

"Maggie, the only thing that stands between a free country and a dictatorship is a leader with a conscious. We both know President Barakat has been under attack from the Democrats and the GOP for a long time. And lately, it seems he hasn't been afraid to show his anger when questioned about his failure in his domestic and foreign policies."

Charlie pulled the car to a halt.

As Maggie looked up, she saw they were parked outside their favorite neighborhood bar. "Oh good, you must have read my mind. I really need a drink," said Maggie. Charlie and Maggie had been frequent customers of Brothers, an Irish-themed pub, for about four years. It was the perfect little place, surrounded by step-up apartment buildings, and was home to some of Washington's professional elite. Charlie helped Maggie out of the car and they began walking down the tree-lined sidewalk toward the entrance.

Near the door, Charlie pulled Maggie into the shadow of the building and whispered quietly to her. "Don't mention anything about what happened tonight, Maggie," he said. "Now is the time to be cool and calm and simply keep our ears open. Understand?" Charlie asked in a deadly serious tone. She nodded silently.

Outside the entrance, two men in suits stared at their smart phones, grumbling loudly to one another. "They should find these hackers and cut their nuts off," said one, a short, chubby man with a terrible comb-over. His friend grunted in approval, held his cell phone over his head and began turning in a wobbling circle, seeking better reception.

Maggie could smell an attorney a mile away, and both these guys reeked of legal briefs and out-of-court settlements.

As was usual for a Friday evening, the pub was noisy and full of customers. The clinking of glasses and silverware added to the drone of voices and conversation. A young waitress with a long black ponytail draped over one shoulder immediately recognized them. Smiling and waving a pair of menus over her head, she motioned them to follow. They navigated through the front area of the restaurant, eventually passing pool tables and people playing darts.

Two drunks at the bar were causing a scene. One hefty man wearing a hockey jersey was berating a short, stocky waitress who stood, arms crossed, staring at him with a look of disdain on her face.

"This isn't tonight's game," he slurred, pointing a buffalo wing at the big screen televisions mounted on the wall behind the bar. "I'm telling you, that's last week's game."

Puffing out her chest, the waitress stepped closer until she was nose-to-nose with the drunk. "I know it's not tonight's fucking game," she half screamed. "I heard you the first fifty times. There's something screwed up with the satellite signal and WE. . . CAN'T . . . FIX . . . IT." She turned on one heel and, with a huff, stormed away.

The drunk watched her walk away with glassy eyes. "It's not tonight's game," he mumbled at her retiring figure, pointing his beer bottle toward the television as if it were a remote control.

Charlie and Maggie were led to a booth in a dark corner of the restaurant where the walls were adorned with sports memorabilia. Sliding into the booth, Maggie realized everyone seemed relaxed and normal. People laughed and drank. A younger man pointed a french fry at his giggling date, emphasizing something important and witty.

"What's going on, Sally?" Charlie asked the waitress as she flipped open her ticket book and poised her pen. "My phone and TV are both acting weird," Charlie lied, fishing for information. "Don't think I'm behind on a bill or anything."

"Don't have a clue," Sally replied. "About an hour ago, the Lakers game is on, then the satellite just goes off. When it comes back on, last week's game is playing."

"What about the other channels?" Maggie interrupted, purposely fishing for more information.

"What other channels?" Sally replied with an innocent giggle. "Most of the channels are off the air. I'll bring you some water. Do you guys need some more time to decide?"

"Yeah, Sally, give us a few more minutes." As the waitress turned and headed toward another table, a customer at a neighboring table leaned over to Charlie and Maggie.

"Sorry to eavesdrop on your conversation," the older, well-dressed gentleman said, peeling off some dollar bills and laying them on the table. "I spoke with a cop at the intersection outside when I was parking my car. He said the word going around is that hackers have crashed everything. He said it was causing a huge mess," the man said, opening his hands out wide for emphasis. "Probably the Chinese. Whoever it is, I just hope they fix it quick. I get grumpy when I miss my reality shows," he said, letting out a laugh and heading toward the door.

Maggie reached across the table and tugged on Charlie's wrist. "Finish what you started to say in the car about the president."

Charlie began to fidget with a salt shaker, switching it from hand to hand. Raising his dark blue eyes to meet hers, Charlie began to speak in a hushed tone.

"All the rights we enjoy as American citizens can be taken away in a second, Maggie. President Barakat doesn't need a national emergency to impose an executive order to suspend the Constitution. However, if something does happen or an incident is created, then he looks less evil. You know, the incident sort of justifies his actions."

"Why does this sound familiar? Refresh my memory, Mister History Wizard."

For a moment, Charlie stared at Maggie with a look of stunned silence, his mouth hanging open. Then, placing the tip of two fingers under his chin, he deliberately, and in a very animated manner, began to push his mouth closed.

"Did you have mono and miss history class as a child?" Charlie asked sarcastically.

"History wasn't one of my strong subjects or interests," Maggie said, pointing a fork threateningly in Charlie's direction. "That's why I went to journalism school. I keep you around to tell me what famous dead people did in the past."

Charlie looked around, taking an inventory of the people near them, before speaking. "In 1933, Adolph Hitler employed the Enabling Act, which immediately gave him dictatorial powers. It would be the same if the commander in chief were to act on an executive order. It is basically the same thing. On paper, activating the executive order makes the president a dictator by eliminating our democratic process and putting the kibosh on the Constitution."

Charlie paused for a moment to give Maggie a chance to think about what he had just said.

Maggie took a drink of water, the glass shaking in her hand. "You are right, Charlie. Now I really am scared to death. I mean, look at what's happened. That Koontz woman gave us our new Bible, ordered the public execution of a well-known journalist, and now Washington is beginning to look like an armed camp."

Charlie's intensive gaze on Maggie was suddenly drawn past her to the sound of loud voices inside the front door, where a small crowd had gathered.

"Stay here," Charlie ordered. He walked to stand at the edge of the small crowd. One man seemed to be the center of attention, waving his arms and speaking loudly.

As Maggie watched Charlie stand, his hands folded, she felt some degree of safety. Charlie wasn't just some desk jockey like other guys she knew who spent their days on the phone and in front of a computer. Charlie belonged to the 1 percent of Americans who had served in the US military. He had been an Army Ranger before being wounded in Somalia several years before. Maggie met him when he was a war correspondent embedded with an infantry unit in Iraq. It was during the invasion and then occupation of the war-torn country.

Charlie, camera running, never hesitated to follow a squad of battle-hardened soldiers as they raced from a burned-out car to the alleyway of a building. Charlie would turn the camera on himself and give a cool account of the action, a wall pockmarked by bullet holes as his backdrop.

Charlie had been home preparing for a new assignment in

Afghanistan when a horrible life-changing event happened in Charlie's life. His young wife, Kathy, a nurse in the neonatal unit of a pediatric hospital, was tragically killed by a drunk driver. She was driving home after an evening shift at the hospital when the other driver, who had more DUI convictions than most people had socks, blasted through a red light. Kathy had barely held onto life, sinking into a coma on the way to the hospital. The drunk, however, had stumbled from the wreckage of his piece-of-shit pickup truck with a broken nose. His blood alcohol content was four times higher then the legal limit, and the floor of his rig was scattered with beer cans and empty whiskey bottles.

Kathy had lingered in the ICU on a breathing machine for weeks. Maggie had sat quietly with Charlie at the hospital until the fateful day Charlie made the decision to turn off the life support. He had sat alone in her room long after the doctor and nurses had gone. Maggie waited outside the hospital for Charlie for hours but finally left, deciding Charles wasn't going to leave the hospital anytime soon.

Maggie was waiting in the wings when Charlie decided some months later to step out of the shadow of his wife's death and return to his life and career.

Charlie was still standing on the fringe of the circle of people as the man continued to rant and rage. Several people in the crowd, including Charlie, asked questions. Finally, Charlie began walking back toward Maggie, a look of deadly seriousness on his face. As Charlie threw some money on the table, he motioned to Maggie that it was time to go. Grabbing her purse, Maggie joined him as they elbowed their way back through the crowd and onto the sidewalk.

"That guy is a limo driver, and he just came from picking up some big shot at Dulles. Says they're shutting down the airport. No flights in and no flights out. He also said the airport is surrounded by armed troops."

"What? Why would the armed forces surround the airport?"

"I have no idea. But it's not just the army, Maggie. Homeland Security is on the streets as well. And who are those guys with the National Security Force? I have never heard of that agency before."

"I hadn't heard of them either until I ran across those NSF agents at the checkpoint," Maggie said.

"So what now, Charlie? What's the plan?" she asked, clutching her purse close.

"I think it would be safest if you stay at my place tonight. Then tomorrow we can listen to the president's speech, just like that crazy woman Koontz told us to do. The president's speech will hopefully clear this whole mess up. I just hope it doesn't confuse things even more. In any event, we will know where we stand."

As they walked through the dark toward Charlie's car, a police helicopter hovered just a couple of blocks away. Its bright spotlight flickered back and forth illuminating the street below. A voice blared over its loudspeaker warning people to remain in their homes.

Chapter 4

"MESSAGE," the voice said loudly. Startled, Charlie opened his eyes but remained motionless on his oversized couch, still wearing his clothes from the evening before. The light filtering through the living room window of his apartment told him it was early morning. "MESSAGE," the voice repeated, but louder and with more annoyance in its voice.

Charlie sat up straight, rubbing his eyes with the heels of his hands.

"MESSAGE!" screamed the voice, clearly pissed off this time. Charlie reached out and snatched his cell phone off the coffee table. He couldn't remember why he had chosen such an annoying message ring tone, but it sure did the job.

He began to eagerly read, hoping for any bit of information about what was going on.

TUNE INTO YOUR LOCAL TELEVISION OR RADIO STATION AT NOON EASTERN STANDARD TIME FOR AN EMERGENCY MESSAGE FROM PRESIDENT MARCUS BARAKAT. LIVE STREAMING VIDEO OF THE PRESIDENT'S IMPORTANT ANNOUNCEMENT AVAILABLE AT HTTP:// WWW.WHITEHOUSE.GOV.

Charlie lay back on his couch and covered his eyes with his forearm. He still couldn't believe he and Maggie had witnessed the killing of Phillip Elliot. Charlie had hoped it was just a bad dream. It wasn't.

Charlie had dabbled in the journalism profession for years, beginning as the editor of his school newspaper and yearbook. He liked to write, taking thoughts and ideas and creating colorful, visual stories for others. It was true some stories, covering a track team awards ceremony and such, were dull. He often thought of the time he was scolded after covering a National Honor Society luncheon. *"Goody Two Shoes Gather for Crumpets,"* was the headline he had created that earned him a trip to the principal's office. Later in life, Charlie would describe himself as the ranking school nerd because he carried a 35 mm SLR camera everywhere. He took pictures of teachers, sporting events, and other students. One day, during homeroom, Charlie spotted the school bully sitting across the room busily picking his nose. Like most other students Charlie had been victimized by the bully. He had been pushed, shoved, and verbally abused. Silently, Charlie reached into his camera bag, retrieved a zoom lens, and waited. Charlie began to click pictures the second the bully had his finger stuck up his nose past the first knuckle. The following morning, Charlie spotted the bully in the hallway where he was teasing a younger girl about her clothing. The bully began to smile as he made the girl cry. Marching up to him, Charlie presented the bully with an 8 x 10 glossy photograph of him sitting unconcerned, picking his nose. Paper-clipped to the picture was a note from Charlie that read, "Bully anyone else and this picture goes in the yearbook."

After that, the tough guy began to leave everyone alone. Charlie saw the impact that photography could have when the bully never made eye contact, nor spoke to, Charlie Ashman ever again.

Early every morning as other students played dodge ball in the school gym, Charlie worked in a converted bathroom under the bleachers developing film and printing pictures. Charlie was smart and figured out a way to make money. He would take action pictures in the afternoon of the high school jocks playing sports. He would then develop the film and print the photographs in the morning. He sold the black-and-white glossy 5 x 7 prints to the jock's girlfriends during school. The young, love-struck girls would buy all of Charlie's pictures and he, in turn, would use that money to finance his growing collection of cameras, lenses, and accessories.

As a junior, Charlie worked his way onto the local newspaper in his small town in Maine. The editor, Percy Pascoe was an old-school, hard-nosed newsman who cut his teeth at the *Chicago Tribune* before moving to Charlie's small town to buy the *Custer Free Press.* Though the town and readership was small, Percy Pascoe rode his news staff hard and edited every article and story like it was a big-city publication. When Charlie brought Percy Pascoe a story on a suspicious business fire, Percy returned it with a large red rejection stamp on the cover page. This only served to make Charlie work harder. He began seeking out story ideas and kept submitting them to the hard-nosed editor. Sometimes he got a rejection letter back, often weeks later, and other times he just heard nothing. Finally, Charlie broke through the tough exterior of Percy Pascoe when he researched and interviewed everyone he could about the possible failure of a local dam. Charlie had come home from school to find that his mother had received a phone call from Percy Pascoe. He had skipped through the small talk with her and simply left three questions he wanted Charlie to follow up on for his story. He was on the job the next morning. Charlie rewrote the article with the requested interviews and delivered it to Percy Pascoe in person. There was no fanfare, in fact the editor, Percy Pascoe, a large man, sat scanning the manuscript, ignoring Charlie who sat across the desk from him. Finally, tossing the story onto his desk, he looked sternly at Charlie.

"I'm not paying you for this story, but I will give you a byline."

Charlie nodded, stuttered his appreciation and, once out the door, raced home with his good news. As promised, his article, *"What if the Dam Breaks?"* was the front-page story the next morning. For a week people on the street, his teachers, and even other students, complimented Charlie on the story. Charlie finally found the catalyst he needed to keep writing, and fell into a good rhythm in his storytelling. This "Charlie rhythm" helped him succeed in publishing more articles and closed the gap in his relationship between him and Percy Pascoe.

One day, as Charlie was sitting in Percy Pascoe's office, he noticed an index card taped to the bulletin board on the wall among pictures and newspaper clippings. Written upon it were the words, "Six Million." Charlie got up the courage to speak and asked about its significance.

"Six Million stands for how many Jews the Nazis murdered during World War II. I keep it there as a reminder of the evils of man."

Percy Pascoe continued talking about his experiences in the war. His infantry company had liberated a German extermination camp and he had seen first hand the living skeletons peering through the fences at him. The editor explained that he saw bodies piled six high and open trenches filled with the dead.

Charlie and Percy Pascoe never talked about the atrocities again.

Two years later, Charlie decided to take a hiatus from the journalism field to pursue a career his father, the missionary, was staunchly against. Charlie joined the army. His dad had thrown out several objections, most reinforced with detailed Bible scriptures.

Charlie soon found himself in basic training at Fort Benning, Georgia. Here, he shed his camera for an M16A1 rifle and concealed his nerdiness with olive green fatigues. The army suited Charlie well. When he was young, he traveled with his missionary parents and his younger adopted sister, Shade, to places where they often went without food or struggled to find a place to stay. His father always reminded the family that it was God's plan and that their needs would be provided for by God. In the army, Charlie found that he usually had three hot meals a day, a rack to sleep in at night, and a roof over his head. These luxuries changed when Charlie applied for and was accepted into the Army Ranger program. Out in the woods and swamps around Fort Brag, he slept in the rain, warded off bugs the size of poodles, ate C-rations, learned the art of combat, and earned the Ranger badge.

Charlie got his first taste of battle in 1989 during the invasion of Panama, that ousted dictator Manuel Noriega. Panama was a fairly easy operation for Charlie's unit. He and a company of troopers had choppered in and captured a small airfield the CIA thought Noriega might use to try to escape. When a convoy of Panamanian Defense Forces – really, Noriega's thugs – arrived, Charlie's squad tore them to pieces in an ambush of rifle and grenade fire. The survivors threw down their weapons and ran into the surrounding jungle faster then a raped ape.

In 1993, Charlie experienced his second and bloodiest combat action in a corner of the world barely known to most people, Somalia. In a botched snatch-and-grab operation targeted at war lord Mohamed Farrah Aidid and his lieutenants, Charlie was one of eighty wounded in a night-long battle against Aidid's followers. The battle would later be the subject of the movie, *Black Hawk Down*. Charlie would refer to it as the night an RPG rocket tried to blow his balls off.

Raising his arm up, Charlie was checking the time on his watch when a voice interrupted him.

"They already shut the cell service down," he heard Maggie say. He turned to find her standing beside the pocket doors going into his bedroom. She wore one of his light blue button-down shirts, her legs long and bare.

"I'm sure we . . . well, probably every American . . . got the same message blast right before they flipped the switch back to off," Maggie said, snapping her phone closed. She looked at Charlie staring back at her, and it took a moment for her to register her lack of clothing.

"I'm sorry," Maggie said making a playful curtsy. "I'm a very bad guest. First I steal your bed, leaving you on the couch, and next I'm helping myself to your shirts. Soon I'll be asking to borrow your debit card."

Charlie rose with a smile, and walked up to her, leaning close. For a moment she held her breath and crossed her arms over her breasts, thinking Charlie was moving in for a kiss. "One hell of a time to begin acting romantic," she thought to herself. However, typical of Charlie, he merely reached around the open door and stepped back, holding a bathrobe he apparently had hung on the bedroom wall. It was three times bigger than Maggie's thin frame, but at least it covered her up completely. "This should keep you warm," he said. While it seemed a gentlemanly thing to do, Charlie was not only trying to protect Maggie's modesty, but also eliminate the temptation for him to stare at her sexy figure.

Maggie slipped her arms into the robe and followed Charlie into his kitchen, tying the belt into a loose knot. As Charlie began making coffee, Maggie crossed to the living room window and looked out onto the street below. Charlie's second-floor apartment gave him a bit of a view, but there wasn't much to see. The normally busy street was ominously empty. Further down and across the street was a bus stop where a small group of people sat on a bench or stood around waiting for the next bus. Some were talking with others. One man, holding a gym bag and wearing bright red sweat pants and a hoodie, kept looking at his watch. He would then lean across the curb and look down the street, waiting for the appearance of his bus.

"Black with a little cream, if I remember right," Charlie said, placing a mug of coffee on the table next to her.

Maggie gave a "thanks" and then turned her attention back to the people at the bus stop. She saw a big, black SUV pull up next to them. Maggie noticed its black-tinted windows and counted six different radio-type antennas sprouting from its roof.

Red sweat suit guy approached the driver's door. The SUV was between Maggie and the man so she couldn't see the occupants. But she could see that red sweat suit was being told something by the driver. The man began shaking his head, as if irritated, and as the vehicle pulled away, he turned and kicked his gym bag across the sidewalk. He began talking to the other people at the bus stop and then, picking up his bag, began to walk down the street. Maggie sipped her coffee, watching the others slowly disperse, until the bus stop sat empty. A loud thumping began, the distinct sound of a military helicopter's rotator blades cutting through the air. Charlie walked over to the window and stood next to her, their eyes scanning the sky as the sounds came closer. Suddenly they came into view, a flight of four Black Hawk helicopters flying in perfect formation just above the trees. Just as quickly as they appeared, the four heavily armed machines crossed out of sight behind some trees.

Maggie and Charlie both sat silently for a moment before Maggie spoke. "Are we at war Charlie?" she said, sitting back and crossing her arms.

Charlie took a sip of coffee from his mug, which sported a big US Army Rangers logo. He sat, thinking. Maggie felt it was time for her to stop throwing questions at her friend and let him come up with some answers. Maggie knew Charlie well enough and was aware of his thought process. The military man in him was assessing the situation, putting the pieces of the puzzle together. Maggie understood all too well. Her father was a retired navy officer. As a SEAL, he had led men in combat in Vietnam and later during the invasion of Grenada. Throughout the years of her childhood, her father had always had the same philosophy. "Get the facts, remain calm and make a quick, prudent decision," he had instructed Maggie a thousand times. Charlie was doing the same thing now.

"It's something big Maggie, that I can assure you," Charlie said, his tone serious. "My first thought was a government coup. That can't be right because President Barakat is addressing the nation at noon, so that means he's still in power."

"How does the nightmare we witnessed last night play into all of this?" Maggie asked, shaking the spoon from her coffee cup at him.

"Historically, whenever there is an overthrow of a government or a grab for power," Charlie began to explain, "the first thing that is done is to seize and control the media. That way whoever is taking power can limit the news and information the citizens receive. Last night was a warning to us, the media, that this is a whole new playing field, and the government isn't fooling around."

Maggie began to nod her head in agreement. "I had a teacher in high school," Maggie said, folding her arms, "who said to worry about anyone or any group who doesn't like the media or who wants to censor it."

"Your teacher was right on the money," Charlie began to say, when someone began pounding on the apartment door. Maggie and Charlie stared across the table at one another. The pounding grew louder and Charlie, pushing away from the table, headed for the door, Maggie close behind.

It seemed as if the person knocking was determined to bring down the door, threshold and all. Charlie had just turned the knob and was trying to crack the door to peak out, when it suddenly burst inward, shoving Charlie aside and almost knocking him off his feet. A black, female police captain stood panting above Charlie. She quickly scanned the room, stared at Maggie for a moment, and then turned to quickly shut and lock the door behind her.

"What the hell, Shade!" Charlie snapped. "You almost knocked me on my ass." The policewoman ignored Charlie. She moved toward the window, peeked out, and looked both directions as if she thought someone was following her. Then she quickly grabbed the heavy cloth curtains and pulled them shut. Standing beside the window, she rested her back against the wall, eyes closed, catching her breath.

Maggie's mind was racing as she noticed Shade's bizarre, paranoid behavior. Shade could get wound up but was typically afraid of nothing. Maggie and Shade had often sat together at the hospital when Charlie's wife was in the Intensive Care Unit.

When Charlie was growing up, his parents were missionaries

traveling to some of the unknown parts of the Third World, including countries in Asia, Africa, and South America. Charlie was a little boy when they traveled to Nigeria to perform work for their church. His parents had returned home from the African nation with two reminders of their trip – Malaria and his new baby sister, Shade.

Events had been put into place weeks before Charlie and his parents stepped foot on the African continent. An aging priest, the spiritual leader of the jungle region, had rescued the sick and malnourished Shade from a village devastated by the deadly Ebola virus. Other nearby villagers had alerted Father Russo of the epidemic and even led him within sight of the huts and outbuildings. However, none would come near. In the same manner their fathers and forefathers had prevented the spread of disease outbreaks, they had sealed off all paths to the village with piles of logs and then set fire to the brush and trees outside the hamlet. A scorched-earth policy had always worked in the past, so they continued it into the present.

Father Russo had squeezed through an opening in the logs that the local men had created just for him. He had barely stepped through it when a noise made him look over his shoulder. The passageway was already being sealed behind him. The village was only three hundred feet away. A small haze of smoke from the brush fires encircling the village made it difficult to see. Father Russo wondered which saint he should pray to when facing a deadly disease zone. He continued to walk forward and remembered the square cloth surgical mask a nun had placed in his hand as he had left the mission. He dug it out of his pocket and tied it over his mouth and nose, not really knowing if it provided much or any protection from the invisible germs ahead.

As he neared the village, Father Russo saw the first line of bodies lying in a neat row near the dirt path as he entered the maze of run-down buildings. Smoke rose from them and the odor of burning flesh assaulted his senses. Someone, at some point in the early outbreak of the disease, had tried to burn the bodies of the dead. The priest quickly crossed himself and walked beside a rough, wooden picket fence and into the heart of the village. He came to an abrupt stop, taking in the sight before him. For a moment he stood silent. The priest tried not to think about the vultures that fluttered overhead. It was as if everything in the priest's world had suddenly come to a stop. He heard dogs barking in the distance, fighting over something.

Father Russo placed a hand over his cloth mask and looking right to left, estimated a hundred bloated bodies lying in the sun. As his hearing suddenly returned, Father Russo became aware of the din of millions of flies whirling around the bodies like a gray cloud. Sickened by the nightmare scene before him, Father Russo slowly began to back away down the path he had just come. He turned and began to walk faster away from the bodies, when he heard the cries of a baby. He stopped, trying not to breathe in the death-filled air around him. He stood silently listening . . . nothing. He began to take a step when he heard it again, the unmistakable sound of an infant. Father Russo began to look around him, and then his eyes settled on the open door of a cinder block shanty to his left. He walked to the entrance and tried to peer inside, but the small room was black and frightening, with the horrible smell of death emanating from within. As he finally gathered the courage to take a step inside, he saw the body of an older woman who sat with her back against the wall at the entrance. A trail of dried blood ran from her eyes down her cheeks, and from her ears and mouth. The baby cried again in the dark, bringing the priest's attention from the dead woman back to the dark doorway.

He could barely see, but it was almost impossible for him to miss the shapes of the dead on the floor. The stench of the rotting corpses caused him to retch, but he continued to slowly thread his way among the bloating bodies of Shade's family. A stiff forearm stuck out from a tattered sheet on a mattress inside the doorway. The rest of the victim lay covered. Several others lay upon the earthen floor where the deadly virus had ended their lives. Trying to hold his breath, Father Russo crept deep inside the cinder block windowless hovel, his heart beating as if it were going to leap out of his body and escape the nightmare on its own. Stepping over and around the bodies in the dark, the priest focused on the faint noises radiating from a far corner. There, he found the filthy baby, lying on the floor wrapped in an old, dirty blanket, barely breathing.

Making his way back to the barricade with the baby, Father Russo found himself facing another serious problem. The village men were furious when they learned he held a survivor from the desiccated village in his arms. Most of the men ran away terrified, but one large black man would not back down. It was obvious from his angry demeanor and gestures that he wanted the baby dead. He even motioned menacingly at Father Russo with a machete to go back, pointing at the village and making a stabbing motion with his weapon.

Father Russo wasn't to be intimidated, not after the hell he had just been through. To the old priest, the bundle in his arms was the reason God had sent him to the village. As Father Russo stepped toward the man who now held the machete raised high over his head, the priest spotted the look of terror on the villager's face as his eyes locked on the crying infant. Father Russo suddenly jumped toward the man, holding the baby out like an offering. With a scream, the man turned and fled down the path away from them, as if he were being chased by the devil. Father Russo, with the dying baby cuddled in his arms, began the walk back toward his church.

Father Russo and the nuns in the convent hospital treated and tended to the frail baby. The priest spent the first night sitting beside the old bassinet the nuns had pulled into the room. He stayed awake all night, praying beside the small baby, stopping only to change a dirty diaper or to hold her in his arms while she nursed hungrily on a bottle. Father Russo saw the concern on the nun's faces and knew deep down the small infant would probably not survive her ordeal. Perhaps she already carried the Ebola virus. The priest himself might have possibly contracted the deadly virus, especially after his risky visit to the village. "What happens is God's will," Father Russo had whispered to the baby, kissing her softly on her forehead. He gave a quick thanks, realizing that the baby's head was cool, and not burning with fever, like the other virus victims.

The nuns finally persuaded Father Russo to leave the bassinet and get some rest. He had been sitting with the baby for nearly thirty hours. The nuns assured him they would take good care of his favorite patient. If anything changed, someone would summon him immediately.

The call came nine hours into his sleep. A young boy, Abeeku, an orphan who lived at the convent and did odd jobs for the nuns, stood shaking the priest's shoulder. "Come, Father, come quickly," he said, flipping the blanket off the priest and grabbing Father Russo's forearm, helping him to stand. As Father Russo put on his glasses and slipped on a pair of sandals, Abeeku handed him his robe. Father Russo struggled to put it on with one hand as Abeeku, holding his other, earnestly began to lead the priest down the steps from his room, toward the hospital.

Silently, Father Russo mumbled a prayer, as he was led toward the hospital. "Another grave to dig," he thought to himself, picturing the white crosses in the field near the chapel. Once at the hospital, he was surprised to see the atmosphere wasn't one of sadness or loss. Several nuns met Father Russo with a smile and a bow. Abeeku led the priest to where an older, small-framed Benedictine nun, Sister Nutina Grace, sat rocking the baby in her arms. Wearing the traditional black and white habit of her order, she looked up with a huge smile.

"God has sent us a miracle," Sister Nutina said quietly to the priest in French. "He has snatched a beautiful soul away from Satan and given her to us."

Bending down, Father Russo placed a hand upon the baby's forehead. It was cool. The baby made a smacking noise, but continued to doze.

"God spared this angel. There is no fever, no disease," Sister Nutina said, rocking the baby slowly. Father Russo patted the nun's small hand and let out a long breath. Stepping out into the cool African air, he made his way toward the chapel. Abeeku held a heavy wooden door open for him and then stepped back into the dark. Inside, the candles were burning on the walls, and the altar in front sent shadows dancing across the rows of pews. Father Russo sat, and in the silence, gave a prayer of thanks. He wondered what would happen to the baby now. The nuns had decided to name her Shade, which meant "singing wind" in African. "After all, Father," one nun explained, "if she hadn't been singing, you never would have found her."

The answer to Shade's future would come a few days later, when Charlie and his parents paid a visit to the convent and met Father Russo and his staff. Charlie's parents fell in love with the small baby in the nun's care. His mother rocked and talked quietly to the baby for a long time before she held the little bundle out to Charlie. "Go ahead Charlie," she said smiling, "why don't you hold her? See if she grows on you."

Shade did grow on him, and Charlie was thrilled when his parents told him that his new baby sister would be joining their family, and traveling back to the U.S. with them.

Growing up in the U.S., Shade blossomed from a near-dead victim of the Ebola virus to a tough, "see the hill, take the hill," type of woman. In school, her mind worked like a sponge, soaking up everything she saw and read. She aced every test and exam. Charlie remembered her throwing a fit in high school when she received a B+ on an exam. She acted as if the world had ended. She didn't take crap from anyone and never backed down from a fight, even taking on the school bully in a brawl that left both of them bruised and bloody. Shade was as sharp physically as she was mentally. She lettered eleven times in track and basketball and challenged the school board until they let her compete on the "boys only" wrestling team.

After graduating high school, Shade immediately applied to the police department. She easily breezed through the exams and physicals, and once in the Academy, found her calling. She worked the streets, kicked doors down at drug houses, fought drunks twice her size, and worked her way up the career ladder, landing in an officer position in the Criminal Intelligence Division.

Now, visibly disturbed, Shade began to pace around Charlie's apartment with her arms crossed. "Sit down, guys," she suddenly ordered. Maggie and Charlie sat together on the couch, as Shade pulled a kitchen chair into the room and sat in front of them.

Shade, looking down at the walkie-talkie on her gun belt, turned one of the knobs, and the sound of police traffic went silent. Facing them again, she jabbed her index finger threateningly and scooted forward to the edge of her chair. "Listen up, both of you. What I say here, what I tell you, everything is top secret and never, ever leaves this room. Do you understand?" Shade asked, looking at both of them. Maggie gave a short burst of nervous laughter, realizing that her world of reality had been turned on its side and things were somehow never going to be the same.

They both anxiously nodded in agreement, and Shade began to talk in a low voice, the same tone she used when sending a warning to some young hoodlum on the streets. "There is serious shit going down. Bad stuff, and I only know part of it. Last night, they called in all the command staff, everybody, on duty, off duty, on vacation, *everyone*,"

Shade emphasized, poking her index finger at the palm of her hand. "The word is that the U.S. is under some kind of cyber attack, and that martial law is being put into effect. We are supposed to keep doing our jobs, but now the army and the National Security Force is in charge."

"That's bizarre," Charlie said to Shade, leaning forward on the couch. "So, what do you think is going to happen?"

"It's total bullshit," Shade snapped. "First, cyber attacks don't hit on this kind of scale and affect this many areas of communication. Even our IT guys at the station were shaking their heads and asking questions. Second, why do our police radios still work, and the 911 lines still function, but no one can make any inbound or outbound calls? Here's the major clue that something rotten is going on behind the scenes. Our guys saw military convoys on the move *hours before* this alleged cyber attack ever happened. We were getting directions from the command staff to help the army set up road blocks and clear the streets right after rush hour."

"Oh my God, Shade. This whole thing is really weird," Charlie said.

"We're under orders not to say anything to anyone. If a citizen asks what's going on, our response is supposed to be the cyber attack crap line. On top of that, our patrol people are to keep everyone off the streets, with no group assembly of any kind. If anyone starts asking questions, we are supposed to say it's for their own safety. If they push the issue, we arrest them," Shade said, tapping the handcuff case on her gun belt.

"Wait a minute," Maggie chimed in suddenly. "Your commanding officers are telling you this? Does the chief of police really think this is a cyber attack? What do these restrictions on the public have to do with it?"

Shade began shaking her head, and then looked at Maggie with a smirk. "It's not the chief giving these orders, or our captains, majors, or anyone else in the command staff. It's the earpiece guys."

"Who . . . what are the earpiece guys?" Charlie asked, leaning closer toward his sister.

"Good question, big brother. Seems it's a government agency we've never heard of. That is why I don't believe this national emergency is anything more than a smoke screen. At about six

33

o'clock, when all of this stuff started happening, all of our division commanders were sitting in a meeting room. Nobody knew anything, and the chief and his staff were sitting like statues. Then, all of a sudden, these three big goony dudes, wearing black battle dress utilities and sidearms, like the SWAT guys, come in, followed by a dozen armed soldiers. They have no insignia, except a patch on their shoulders. The chief was acting really weird, almost as if he was scared. He said the men were with the National Security Force. The National Security Force, kids. Have you ever heard of them?"

Maggie and Charlie looked at one another, confused, and shook their heads in unison. "We might have heard of them, Sis," Charlie added.

"I'll break it down for you," Shade said. "These guys work directly for the president. They outrank everyone, including the military. They say, 'jump,' and we say, 'How high?' The leader of the National Security Force tells us that the president has enacted martial law and suspended the Constitution until this emergency is under control. Period. End of story."

"This is crazy," Maggie said, raising her voice angrily. "Someone should have challenged them or voiced an opinion. Instead, you all just agreed?"

Shade rolled her eyes, before answering back. "Oh yeah, several people protested, Little Sister, and every one of them got their asses arrested on the spot."

Charlie stood looking down at his sister. "So the chief really arrested his own people, Shade . . . really? How does that work?"

Shade walked over until she stood in front of Charlie, and began poking him in the chest with her index finger. "We didn't arrest them, Big Brother, they did. These National Security people have their own jails, and they are playing by an entirely different set of rules. We had everyone from lieutenants to majors getting cuffed and hustled away today, just for speaking their minds. I'm telling you that big shit is happening on the reservation."

Charlie ran his fingers through his hair, thinking, but before he could answer, Maggie came and stood between him and Shade. "Tell her what happened last night, Charlie," she urged him in a soft voice. "Go ahead. Tell her."

"What happened last night?" Shade asked, shifting her eyes from Maggie back to Charlie. "I put my ass on the line telling you what I know, now you better spill the beans, Brother."

Maggie retreated to the bathroom to get dressed and freshen up, while Charlie sat back down on the couch, and explained to Shade the terrible events that happened at the press conference. Maggie came out in time to hear Charlie asking his sister, "What prison ships?" She stood in the doorway of the bedroom listening, suddenly wanting to know what they were talking about.

"One of our guys has a brother who works at the ship yards. He says they've been turning some old navy ships into floating prisons. It was real hush-hush stuff. They were told the ships were to be used to hold terrorists prisoners from the Marine base at Guantanamo Bay, Cuba. That was the story. Then last night while all the shit was hitting the fan here in D.C., those ships were being lit up and going active. Sounds like an awfully weird coincidence, Charlie, don't you think?"

Charlie stood thinking for a moment, and then suddenly turned toward Shade. "If martial law has been put into place and the military is on every corner of the street, then how did you get here?" Charlie asked.

Without taking her eyes off Charlie, Shade reached inside her white uniform blouse and retrieved a laminated photo ID, attached to a lanyard around her neck. "This is how, Bro," she answered. "If you hold certain positions within the police department you get one of these 'do not go to jail' cards. With this card, I can move through checkpoints and travel around the city freely."

Charlie examined it and with a smile he said, "You always could get past the rules, Shade."

For the next ninety minutes, Charlie and Maggie sat on the couch pouring over their copies of the new *Media Rules* that Press Secretary Koontz had handed out, moments after having Phillip Elliott murdered. Shade, who had been up all night, was taking a nap in Charlie's bedroom. Charlie had promised to wake her in time for the president's news address.

The *Media Rules* covered everything from writing a news story to creating an article for the Internet. Occasionally, Maggie or Charlie would direct the other to a certain page and bring something to his or her attention. The common theme throughout the guidebook was strong advice to never question anything said by the president and administration, to never say anything negative about the president and administration, and, if it came out of the White House, the information was to be treated like the word of God. The last chapter went into great detail about how any reporter or newsperson would be dealt with for violations of the rules. "Indefinite detention without cause or trial," Maggie read aloud to Charlie.

When the television suddenly came on, both Charlie and Maggie jumped. Charlie had turned the flat screen on earlier, and cruised through all the channels, finding nothing on them. He had left the channel on one of the major networks in anticipation of it eventually coming back to life.

"Shade, get in here," Charlie yelled.

The screen was immediately filled with a graphic image reading "AMERICA UNDER ATTACK" featured with powerful broadcast background music. Grabbing the control, Charlie quickly flipped from one news channel to another. The exact graphic and music was on every channel.

Shade came into the room, rubbing sleep from her eyes, and threw herself into a big, padded chair near the screen.

After about fifteen-seconds, the graphic faded to show Brian Williams facing the camera. At first he appeared normal as usual, but anyone watching could quickly detect a sense of tension. Unbeknownst to the U.S. citizens watching the newscast, there were a dozen armed NSF agents making sure Williams didn't deviate from his prepared script. Williams began explaining how the United States had suffered the worst cyber attack in history. For the next sixty minutes, Williams explained that all communications had been shattered by a massive assault by unknown suspects. His broadcast was interrupted several times by interviews with alleged experts, explaining intricate details about cyber crimes, and field reports, reassuring the viewers the military and government had the situation under control. Williams kept reminding the people at home that a presidential address was coming on at the top of the hour. In one breath, Williams soberly stated the attack was caused by a foreign government, but then in another, he left open the option it was domestic terrorism, accusing members of the far right, the Tea Party and white power or Nazi groups.

Finally, Williams told the viewers they were going live to the White House with President Barakat, and the image changed to the press conference room, with the large seal of the White House in the background. President Barakat, wearing a dark suit and red tie, came to stand behind the podium, the US flag standing to his right.

"Listen to that," Charlie said, turning his ear toward the screen. "No cameras clicking, no sounds of people sitting down. All I hear is total silence. The press isn't even there."

Maggie and Shade both looked at each other and nodded in agreement.

The president looked into the camera and began speaking in his clipped tone. "Ladies and gentlemen of the United States. Much has transpired in the last twenty-four hours. A group or nation, still to be determined, committed a brazen and nationwide cyber attack upon our great country. Everything, from cell phone carriers to the Internet and the media, was completely crippled by this unpredicted assault. I am happy to report that, due to the efforts of this government, in partnership with communications experts across the nation, disaster has been averted. We are recovering quickly, and, even as I speak, law enforcement, especially the NSF, FBI and CIA, are searching and gathering evidence to find and deal with the cowards who attacked us."

"I must report that preliminary evidence shows that this cyber attack was committed by a foreign nation, we suspect a Middle Eastern country in collusion with the assistance and aide of high-ranking, ultraconservative members of our own government. Sadly, several respected members of Congress and the Senate, including the Speaker of the House, have been taken into custody. They will be questioned and, if guilty, brought to justice."

"Every citizen of this country must understand that it is my goal and responsibility to protect you and this nation. Changes are being made that some of you may not understand. Many of you may think of these changes as negative, but you must remember, my friends, these changes are for your own good and safety."

"I know that we as a nation will triumph against these enemies, both foreign and domestic, and we will come out of this a stronger people and a stronger nation."

"Last night, after learning of the scope of this attack, I ordered that martial law be imposed. This was not an easy decision. This difficult choice was made after an emergency briefing by national security officials. Once I am assured that the security of this nation is guaranteed and the situation is stable, then martial law will be rescinded, and life as we know it will be restored. Until then, my fellow Americans, I ask that you work with me and your government. This administration will be putting programs into place and taking measures that many of you may question or not agree with. Again, let me remind you that these changes are for the good of the nation."

"I have ordered the borders with Mexico and Canada closed. Travel into or out of the country is forbidden until this emergency has ended. I've also ordered the US military mobilized to assist and reinforce local law enforcement and emergency services. Please cooperate with these brave men and women and stay out of their way so they can do their jobs."

"Finally, listen carefully to what I'm about to say. In the face of this attack on the United States, treason or aiding or abetting the enemy in any manner will not be tolerated. It will be dealt with swiftly and gravely. Enemies of this nation, take note that we are watching you. To my fellow citizens, I urge you – no, I *implore* you – to immediately notify the police or the military if you suspect anyone who may be a subversive, or anyone who may attempt to rebel, or who challenges our government. I'm relying on you to help us find and bring to justice anyone you suspect of these actions."

"I also want to report that my cabinet has been preparing for just such an emergency. Several days ago, we started a new, specially trained and equipped government agency, the National Security Force, which will be taking over management of this crisis. All other government agencies, including the FBI, CIA, and the NSA, will be taking orders and direction from our new security force. I'm sure everyone will rest better knowing these special officers are on the job."

"Be assured that the situation is well in hand, and your welfare is my utmost concern. We will overcome. God bless you, and God bless the United States."

With that, the screen switched back to Brian Williams, who began repeating the speaking points of the president's message. Charlie pointed the remote at the television and began flipping through channels. All the channels were back to normal broadcasting. Two women were screaming at one another on a courtroom program. A QVC speaker was hawking a set of cookware. Sigourney Weaver was battling an alien on an old movie channel. Paula Deen was stirring something in a mixing bowl and talking about southern cooking.

Maggie looked down at her phone, and then at Charlie and Shade. "Cell phone signal is back. I'll bet the computers and telephone are up and running again as well."

Charlie stood with his hands on his hips, looking down at the two women. "I guess it's time to get on with the day but be prepared for some major changes," Charlie said. "Shade, you're our best resource for inside information, but you have to be so careful because you are really in the hornet's nest. I think we all need to listen to everything and say little to anyone. I'm suspecting the government will have moles inside every place, everywhere. Do you guys agree?"

Both women nodded in agreement.

"Shade, would you give Maggie a ride back to her car? I'm going to start surfing the web to see what I can find. Let's meet here later tonight and compare notes."

Meanwhile, at the White House, a cameraman signaled President Barakat they were off the air. Immediately, Donna Koontz walked up, tipped her head to one side and gave President Barakat a toothy grin, red lipstick showing on her teeth. "Excellent, Mr. President," she chimed in a birdsong voice. "Just excellent."

President Barakat started to shake her outstretched hand when he spotted a man standing in the shadows behind the stage. The president walked right past Koontz as if she didn't exist, and she lowered her hand, completely embarrassed.

Koontz didn't like disrespect, and she felt mortified that the president had just shunned her in public. She knew this was not the time to rock the boat so she just kept smiling, the same way she had her entire career.

Thirty-five years earlier, Donna Koontz had thrown her hat into the political arena, easily sliding into a city council position for a small municipality outside of San Francisco not far from Berkley where she had graduated from college. Koontz had left Berkley with a degree in political science and a mind crammed full of liberal thinking. Like a cookie-cutter image of so many other radicals, Koontz was raised in a setting of wealth and privilege. Her family had moved from the deep south of Alabama when she was still young. Koontz's father owned several thriving computer technology companies in the Silicon Valley. Her mother spent her days at the gym or on the tennis court at the exclusive country club where they belonged. Nothing less than a BMW sat in the driveway of their two million dollar home.

Yet Koontz admired socialism and communism, two systems of government that vilified the way of life her parents lived. In her junior year, during summer break, Koontz traveled with a small group of other like-minded radicals to Nicaragua for their first taste of a socialist regime. In jeans and a tube top, a bright red bandana in her hair, she fit right in with her radical friends. Of course, she was simply visiting and had a pocket full of cash from her parents. She wasn't out working in the fields twelve hours a day, and Daddy was just a phone call away. She was just visiting. From Nicaragua, they traveled to China and then to Vietnam where the communists had defeated the South Vietnamese and raised the flag of victory in 1975. Again, Koontz was just a visitor looking in on socialism, not actually participating in it.

Yes, Donna Koontz was jealous of the socialist and communist governments. She dreamed of a day the United States government would be transformed. The wealthy would be toppled, and every citizen would be equal. It didn't even bother Koontz if a few thousand innocents had to be sacrificed for the cause. Koontz was sure of one thing. Whether it was a socialist takeover or a communist victory, Koontz was going to be among the politburo, the ruling elite. She knew she would never stand in line for eight hours to buy a pair of shoes or a loaf of bread.

Donna Koontz had learned in her study of socialism that change had to start at a grassroots level. Koontz believed being elected councilwoman was a great place to start.

Just a few months into her new job as councilwoman, Koontz began to push for a gay-and-lesbian themed city park, complete with a fountain pool encircling a statue of two men embracing. The council didn't seem alarmed or even opposed to the park. One of the councilmen thought the statue might be pushing the theme a bit much. The other councilmen tabled Koontz's plan, citing a lack of funding for the project. "If you can come up with the funds, Ms. Koontz, I'm sure the council would gladly reconsider your proposal," the mayor suggested, not realizing the trouble he had just set into motion.

The next day, against a backdrop of barking and howling dogs, Donna Koontz toured the city's animal control facility. Her questions to the staff seemed innocent enough. How much did it cost to board a stray dog for one day? What was the cost to euthanize a cat? Koontz went from room to room and looked into every cage with the animal shelter staff in tow. She would pause at a cage and ask a few question of the employees. She busily scribbled on a note pad, pausing often to glare disapprovingly at one of the noisy caged animals. Koontz returned the next morning with two lists. The first list consisted of the animals to be euthanized. The second list was made up of the animals to be sold to a research lab. With no sense of emotion whatsoever, Koontz notified the stunned Animal Control Director that someone would be coming to pick them up.

"We can't do that. There's a thirty-day holding period for every rescue," the kennel director stammered.

"Not anymore," Koontz ordered, walking away. "I want these animals taken care of today," she shouted without looking back.

Donna Koontz had thoroughly and coldly calculated the cost of housing a rescued animal, including food, water, supplies, and man-hours, and compared it to the expense of having the animals euthanized. Koontz had calculated that death was the cheaper option. After a few calls to some dubious animal research labs, Koontz determined that if the animals were euthanized, she would have the funds she needed for her park statue within sixty days.

"Any means to achieve the end," she had defiantly thought to herself.

Before Donna Koontz had even started her car, the animal control director and employees were furiously making calls. After they called the mayor and several San Francisco television stations, Koontz's plan to acquire her park money at the cost of the kennel's pets came to a

41

screeching halt. Word spread quickly and the media descended on city hall and the animal control center like hornets. Behind them poured hundreds of angry people who filled the parking lot in protest. Like a mob chasing Frankenstein, the outraged crowd demanded retribution for Donna Koontz's actions. The mayor, completely blindsided by Koontz's evil scheme, assured the media a complete investigation was in progress and that no animals would be harmed. Koontz's actions achieved a secondary result. The animal control shelter was transformed into a "no kill" facility within forty-eight hours.

Newspapers and television stations ran the scandalous story complete with Donna Koontz's non-smiling DMV picture. By the end of the nightly news, Koontz had become the most hated woman to darken the state of California.

Koontz couldn't believe the public's reaction. She fumed with anger during her drive home. She had been planning to have the director and staff of the animal control center terminated. "I'll teach those loudmouthed fuckers a lesson," she thought to herself. However, Koontz found herself the one fired at an emergency session of the city council. The meeting was so crowded that it was standing-room only. Nearly everyone wore a T-shirt with Koontz's picture on it and the words: "*Euthanize Koontz*." The city council fired Koontz in record time with a unanimous vote. As the audience of pet lovers stood and gave a standing ovation, Koontz stormed out of the meeting chambers.

A small group of protesters were already waiting for Koontz when she pulled into her street. A half-block from the chanting crowd, a man in a black suit stepped off the curb, right in front of her car, forcing her to a jolting stop. Stepping beside the driver's door he motioned for her to roll down her window. Koontz reluctantly did so, expecting the man to draw a gun and shoot her. Instead, he handed her a folded piece of paper and walked away. Koontz quickly read it.

"Love your spunk. Want to work for me? I need people like you."

Attached was a business card from a politician she was unfamiliar with. After a couple of phone calls and a face-to-face meeting the following day, Donna Koontz became an aide to little-known Democratic Senator Marcus Barakat.

Now, President Barakat dismissed Koontz for the tall man wearing a dark suit barely covering his muscular physique. He stood straight and tall, his dark eyes almost hidden below his protruding forehead. His hair was cut short, and his entire demeanor oozed cloak-and-dagger.

Neither man shook hands with the other, nor offered a warm greeting. They stood for a silent second, until the president finally spoke in a low voice. "How is Operation Stalin going, Mr. King?"

Max King tilted his head, sharply right and then left, emitting small popping sounds from cracking his neck, before answering. His demeanor was very serious, yet cocky, in front of the most powerful man in the world. "Everything is going according to plan, Mr. President," he replied. "The Joint Chiefs of Staff have been arrested and are being held in secure locations. Our own hand-picked people are being placed in command of all four military branches and the Coast Guard. We have blockaded all the major ports, closed down the airports, and are taking control of the major U.S. cities, especially those on the coasts – such as, Miami, San Francisco and New Orleans. We are telling the foreign press that a plot to have you assassinated was foiled and that is the reason for such a lockdown. The media will be reporting the same story beginning tomorrow morning. I feel confident in saying that Phase One of Operation Stalin is nearly complete."

"Keep up the good work, Mr. King," said the president, as Secret Service took up positions around him. "I'm going to expect a lot out of you," he said, walking away.

"Any means to achieve the end, Mr. President." As the president walked away, King pulled a smart phone out of his inside coat pocket and quickly dialed a number. A moment later a voice answered, "National Security Operations."

"This is King. Begin the roundups now," he said without emotion.

"Yes, sir," replied the voice.

Max King shoved his phone into his pocket, and tossed a breath mint into his mouth before walking out of the room.

A ring of Secret Service agents escorted the president outside to his motorcade. Climbing into the vehicle, President Barakat settled into the comfortable padded seat. Donna Koontz slid in the back seat behind him and took her usual position.

"Wonderful speech, Mr. President," Koontz said smiling broadly.

"Really moving."

Barakat nodded his head and looked out the window as the motorcade began to pull away. His mind began to drift. He thought about his beginning and how far he had come.

President Barakat's father, Jean-Pierre, had immigrated to the United States from Algeria at the height of the conflict between Islamic revolutionaries of the National Liberation Front and French colonial rulers in 1958. His father, a low-level French government official who sympathized with the NLF, had met his mother, Ginny, at a small sidewalk cafe. She was an intellectual and active member of the French Communist Party in Paris. The scathing articles she had written about the French policy in Algeria had brought her onto the radar of the French government. She had left before the French authorities could pick her up and later returned to the turmoil in Algiers when bombings and terrorism were daily events. Barakat's parents shared a love of communism and anarchy. They had even considered moving to the USSR, but Barakat's mother had issues that kept her in Algiers, and Barakat's father was important to her goal. Her four brothers were active terrorists with the NLF. A fifth had already been killed in a failed attack on a French police station. The remaining four were operating a secret bomb factory, and that's where Barakat's father was needed. With his position in the government he was able to channel money from France into Algeria and ultimately into the coffers of the NLF to buy guns, ammunition, and explosives. For more than a year, the arrangement worked well. Barakat's father helped the NLF spread a campaign of terror, while showing fake anger at the bloodshed that he himself helped create. However, the family's secret support behind the scenes came crashing down following a French commando raid on the bomb factory. Two of Barakat's uncles were shot dead, one was captured, and another escaped into the night. President Barakat's mother and father knew it was only a matter of time before French interrogators broke her brother down and he would reveal their names leading the police and army to look for them.

Gathering up what little belongings and money they could, President Barakat's parents fled from Algeria to the United States where they sought and were granted political asylum. At the time, there was tension between the two countries, so getting accepted into their new country came fairly quickly and with little scrutiny. With the United States becoming increasingly mired in the unpopular Vietnam War, and protests and violence surging stateside, President Barakat's parents found themselves in the perfect environment for their leftist agenda. President Barakat's mother quickly began teaching at the University of Chicago while his father found a quiet job teaching French.

The seeds of revolution would be planted in young Marcus Barakat's mind while researching a simple homework assignment about the history of French colonialism. When he questioned his mother how the NLF could justify killing eight million Algerian civilians to gain freedom from France, her answer had been very matter-of-fact. "Terrorism creates fear, and fear creates change. If you want to overthrow a government, you have to be brutal and without remorse. It doesn't matter if it is 800 innocents or eight million. Whatever means to achieve the end." Barakat would never forget this piece of deadly advice.

Eventually, in 1968, Ginny Barakat's surviving brother would escape to the United States, along with news that her other captured brother had been tortured and executed by the French army. In the United States, Ginny's brother burned off his anger by joining the Weathermen, a revolutionary force that fought for the overthrow of the United States government. Barakat would be greatly influenced by another life event in the summer of 1968. As secret members of a Marxist anarchist group, Jean-Pierre and his brother-in-law were busy assembling a bomb in the basement of a Chicago tenement building, its target an army recruiting station. However, something went wrong. A spark as minute as static electricity triggered the pipe bomb, killing both men instantly and setting the building ablaze. In the next few days, Barakat watched as the police, arson investigators, ATF and the FBI came to their home, questioned his mother, and searched high and low for evidence tying her to the blast. Ginny Barakat remained silent like stone to the investigators and denied any involvement or knowledge of her husband's or brother's radical actions. When asked why she had communist newspapers in her possession, she calmly defended herself by saying she was an intellectual and that she was not breaking any laws. Later, when Ginny was alone with her son, she

45

simply said, "Sometimes you must hide in plain view of your enemies." A month afterward, after being allowed to travel again, she and Marcus moved to Los Angeles to continue their lives.

Marcus excelled at school, especially when it came to running for a school office or heading up a campaign. College was even easier. Barakat graduated with a degree in political science and found a job immediately with the American Civil Liberties Union, writing flyers and newsletter articles. At the same time, he began working on the election staff of a leftist-leaning California representative of East L.A. In this role, Barakat was able to make contacts, earn friends, and, most importantly, learn about the ways of government and the election process.

During Barakat's run for the California Senate, his mother committed suicide after taking a handful of pills washed down by a bottle of vodka. Barakat, though saddened and now parentless, didn't hesitate to use the loss as a way to gain more votes. He described his mother as a woman who had been oppressed by government and society and who had made her own way. Secretly, Barakat was glad she had taken her own life, particularly before the election. During all of his election campaigns, when asked by reporters about his parents' revolutionary thoughts and actions, Barakat simply pleaded ignorance. Regarding the death of his father, Barakat explained to reporters that his parents had been separated and that he hadn't been in contact with his father in many years. Barakat assured the reporters that he never really even knew his father.

Barakat used the advice his mother had given him, "Sometimes you must hide in plain view of your enemies," and he looked at democracy as the enemy. So he perfected hiding in plain sight. Even though he was a hard-core atheist like his parents, Barakat attended an inner-city Protestant church. He volunteered, shook hands, smiled, and charmed people. He read scriptures and bulletins to the congregation while holding down the bile in his throat.

To Marcus Barakat, political parties were just names, Democrat, Republican and Independent. He ran as a Democrat but only because his liberal leanings would be less suspect and more easily accepted.

During his election campaign, Barakat walked the blighted streets and crime-ridden neighborhoods and listened intently to the people as they spoke. At every opportunity, Barakat pointed the finger of blame at the rich politicians in government. Barakat explained to the people that the rich politicians in government were the ones keeping down the poor in the ghettos. Oh, yes, Marcus Barakat was on their side and promised change if he could just make it into office.

His plan worked, and when he ran for a U.S. Senate seat, he and his staff saturated the same depressed neighborhoods. They went door-to-door and corner-to-corner signing up voters. It didn't matter if they were met at the door by a meth head with a crack pipe or a gun as long as the voters could sign on the dotted line. On Election Day, Barakat even sent a fleet of vans into crack-house neighborhoods, outside liquor stores, pay day loan offices, and pawn shops shuttling voters to the polling sites. His plan worked, and Barakat was easily voted into office, the youngest senator in the history of California. Barakat also happened to be single, never married. He had considered a wife, but neither a wife nor children were a part of the big picture. He thought about using a family as a tool to draw more votes, but he had done just fine without them so he was happy to play the part of the handsome, young bachelor.

Barakat's charismatic personality and openly liberal reformist platform gained him a wide audience, and it wasn't long before supporters within and outside the Democratic Party were urging him to run for president. Initially, Barakat put on a face of complete disinterest at the notion, feigning little notice at all. In truth, he saw the presidency as the opportunity to slowly foist changes on America and lead her down the path to a powerful socialist nation.

During his run for election, Marcus Barakat used every trick in the book and promised anything and everything that would sway a vote. For the illegal Mexicans flooding the Southwest, he pledged immigration reform and told the illegals that the immigration agents were the villains. For those on welfare, he explained their plight was a conspiracy of the deplorable rich. He told them those who had all the money had to share their riches or pay penalties to subsidize the people on welfare. While playing dumb, Marcus Barakat fanned the flames of class warfare just enough to swing the votes his way. The liberal media and high-minded Hollywood voters jumped on his bandwagon. It really didn't matter if he pledged false promises. As his

47

mother had taught him, "Any means to achieve the end."

Barely sworn into office, President Barakat started making changes. In his mind, things would play out smoothly and as planned. He believed one of his rabid supporters would present a bill on immigration, gun control, or one of the other several controversial issues that polarized the nation. His fellow zealots would push it through the House and Senate and that would be the end of that. At first, it appeared that was exactly how it was going to go. Then the veil of smoke and mirrors began to dissipate. The changes that President Barakat were making became more noticeable. For the first time in history, he began seizing large corporations and manufacturing companies and nationalizing them under government control. To the public, he swore with a smile it was a temporary measure to help boost the economy. However, the promised recovery didn't come, and the economy continued to plummet. More homes went into foreclosure. More jobs were lost. More people filed bankruptcy. President Barakat quickly sidestepped any criticism of his failing economy and instead misdirected the American people with more changes.

If Marcus Barakat were ever to bare his soul to a trained psychiatrist, he would be diagnosed as a narcissist with a dangerous and raging God complex. Barakat believed he deserved privileges above all others. He felt he was better than anyone else. He thumbed his nose at the rules of society and loathed the American Constitution. Barakat believed the American Constitution was just a stumbling block to keep him from his goal of creating a socialist or Marxist society, which was Barakat's plan for the United States. President Barakat believed he never made a bad decision or a wrong decision. He never regretted a decision. Very simply, President Barakat knew he was smarter then anyone else in the United States, and he knew what was best for the mindless occupants of HIS country. In the self-absorbed, narcissistic mind of President Barakat, no task or goal was out of reach. He had listened to his mother's advice while also secretly studying Lenin, Marx, and any other communist reading he could get his hands on. Marcus Barakat wasn't afraid to use force to accomplish his goal. As his mother had once said: "It doesn't matter that innocents have to die as long as you come out the winner. Any means to achieve the end."

So in his grand scheme, President Barakat planned every detail. First he needed to surround himself with like-minded people he could trust completely. Donna Koontz was one of the first. Barakat was drawn to her like a moth to a flame. Anyone who would execute every animal in a rescue organization to earn money for a park had the type of mental attitude Barakat was seeking. He quickly recruited Koontz and gave her a quiet desk job until her name was no longer a daily word in the news. Max King was the second like-minded person and the most important. King was a cold-hearted mercenary who fed on power and would follow any order, no matter how harsh or cold-blooded it might be. In Barakat's mind, Max King was the bayonet he would need to achieve unchallenged power. Like an attack dog, he only needed to point Max King toward his target and drop the leash. President Barakat had conducted secret meetings with both Koontz and King in which he had outlined his plans and explained their roles within his new empire. Both were immediately on board. Donna Koontz had smiled with satisfaction while Max King had coldly nodded his head. After the meeting, both Koontz and King were sent out to assemble a custom-tailored cabinet of cutthroats like themselves.

President Barakat and King had outlined plans for declaring the fake emergency that would give him the authority to impose martial law and send the US military into the streets of the nation. However, the military officer in Max King knew that the military would only obey orders for so long. At first there would be no questions, but, eventually, troops trained and equipped to fight foreign armies would grow weary of policing their own country's citizens. So Barakat and King created the blueprint for President Barakat to establish his own private army separate from the US military, with power over all branches of the US Army, Navy, Air Force and Marines. This private army created and commandeered by Max King would be under direct command of the president. They chose to name the new army the National Security Force because it sounded less threatening to the civilian population, and the sudden mobilization of the NSF after a nationwide emergency would be seen as welcoming. By the time the US people realized the true purpose of the NSF, it would be too late.

Max King stuck to President Barakat's playbook, selecting ranking officers with a blind allegiance to President Barakat and his socialist views. These officers then began filling the ranks with the same. Within weeks, these new black-clad troops began showing up across the nation and at large military bases. In every case they carried orders to train without question or harassment. As more troops began to arrive and weapons and armored vehicles poured in, the rumors started flowing that they were a new, ultra-secret anti-terrorism unit. Regular military troops could only look on as the new NSF agents trained directly under their noses. No one was allowed to speak with them and the NSF agents openly ignored the soldiers who hosted them.

When the time came, Max King issued orders to the new NSF troops to leave their staging camps and report to their assigned areas. Thus began the plan of turning the United States into a police state that would have made China's Chairman Mao proud.

"Operation Stalin" was put into effect by Barakat, Koontz, and King. It was well-planned, with the right people, all for the same cause. They were quiet, didn't bring attention to their plan, and didn't cause alarm. King and Koontz clearly understood the consequences of failure, but President Barakat in his psychotic mind, much like Adolph Hitler, considered himself and his plan flawless.

Chapter 5

The next day, most of America discovered that big changes were taking place. Washington had turned into an armed camp overnight. Military vehicles stood at every intersection, and armed troops operated barricades at every train station, airport, and harbor. While police and military choppers crisscrossed the sky, navy and coast guard vessels met and searched every ship, whether commercial or pleasure, that entered US waters.

What the public didn't learn was that thousands of US citizens were being rounded up nationwide, most on the same vague charge of conspiracy against the United States. These U.S. citizens were not allowed to face a judge, post a bond or get a court date. They were simply being detained for the sake of being detained.

Off the East Coast of the United States, several navy ships floated, which had now been converted to prisons. They began getting new detainees every day, hundreds of them being former critics or opponents of President Barakat.

What the public also didn't know was that early in the morning of the President's speech, a line of over a dozen gray prison buses bounced and banged down a rutted, gravel road into the countryside. The buses were packed with nearly every member of the US house and senate, over six hundred men and women. The buses stopped, and heavily armed troops herded the frightened and confused people out into a light rain, until they were standing beside a long, freshly dug 8-foot deep trench. Across from them, two large yellow backhoes sat beside a berm of earth dug from the pit. Many of the group had obviously been taken from their beds as they still wore their robes and pajamas. Others were partially dressed, being rushed out of their homes in the early morning hours.

Donna Koontz, wearing a long trench coat, stood at the right end of the trench. She held a brightly colored umbrella over her head to deflect the rain. "When your name is called, please step forward," she said nonchalantly. Koontz lifted up a sheet of paper in a black-gloved hand and began to shout out the names of nearly seventy-five senators and members of congress. Many were powerful individuals, including the Speaker of the House. Most obeyed, stepping toward the ominous hole, their faces showing a mix of fear and confusion. In a few cases, soldiers elbowed their way into the crowd to drag a reluctant victim forward.

As if on cue, two dozen troopers stepped between the selected group and ushered the relieved and uncalled people back several steps. Suddenly a group of black-clad men, armed with machine guns, poured from a large SWAT van behind Koontz, and spread out in a line between the soldiers and the group at the edge of the trench. They all looked toward Koontz for a moment, waiting. A tall man had joined her. Max King, a cigarette hanging from his lips, nodded toward the men, who immediately turned, raised their weapons to their shoulders in a swift, well-trained motion, and began to spray the backs of the men and women with high-powered bullets. A chorus of cries went up from the crowd in the back, as the victims began to crumble to the ground or into the trench before them. The gunfire seemed to last for hours. The sight and smell of gunpowder lingered in the air, and shell casings covered the ground. The murderous gunfire continued until King waved his hand and ordered the group of executioners to cease fire.

Moans and cries came from the survivors. Many fell to their knees, while others looked away or buried their faces in their hands. A woman fainted. One man vomited.

Donna Koontz walked calmly until she was standing in front of the terrified group. She raised her hands wide over her head. "Quiet, please. Everyone, please settle down." Koontz continued, like a schoolteacher talking to fifth graders. She scanned the crowd of survivors until she felt the eyes of the men and women on her.

"The president and his administration will not tolerate traitors or those who create road blocks to his progress. Your cooperation is not asked for; it is expected. If any of you cause waves or create dissension, you'll be joining your friends in the ditch here," Koontz said coldly, pointing at the ditch full of dead bodies of the members of the Senate and House of Representatives.

"Some of you in the crowd are replacements," she continued. "We expect you to do a better job of, let's just say, 'collaborating' with the President, than your predecessors."

Koontz looked over the crowd before her, smiled and gave a friendly wave. "Y'all have a great day," she said with a fake southern drawl. "Go home, have some breakfast, and then get back to work." She made the last statement while swinging her arm and fist upward, in a "go get 'em" sign. She then turned, and walked back to Max King, who stood, unmoved, surrounded by the black-clothed men who had just committed the mass murder.

The soldiers began herding the weeping survivors back onto the prison buses for their ride back to Washington.

"God save the King," Max said to Koontz, tossing his cigarette butt onto the ground. "Do you have any more of these scheduled?"

"Not today," Koontz replied back coolly, looking into a small make-up mirror while checking her lipstick and brushing back a wisp of hair.

Minutes later, the buses began driving back down the dirt path, away from the kill zone, bouncing across the ruts in the hard-packed earth. Koontz, King, and his execution squad followed in four large black SUVs. As the caravan disappeared into the forest and out of sight, a figure, lying undetected in the brush, carefully raised his head. Face concealed with camouflage paint and clothing to match, the figured glided through the brush with the movement of a professional soldier, hunter, or both. The man aimed the lens of his video camera toward the clearing and continued to record the actions of the backhoes, pushing dirt onto the pile of bodies in the ditch.

"Let's see you fuckers explain this," former Army Ranger, Charlie Ashman, whispered to himself.

Chapter 6

Eight months later . . .

Winding down the roads of southern Missouri, the brightly painted bus stood out like a beacon. Large and flamboyant, the passenger bus looked like it should be carrying a group of senior citizens on a cross-country tour. It only took one glance to see that this bus was a rolling billboard. A huge rainbow flag painted on the side ran from nose to tail. As it trailed off two-thirds down the bus, an image of four smiling children emerged. A momentary glance revealed a small white boy, a black girl, an Asian girl, and, finally, an Arabic-looking boy, all appearing to be around nine or ten years old. Arms around one another, they smiled at the passing traffic. *"Drive for Diversity"* was painted in eight-inch tall letters below their images.

Ten men and women sat in various seats on the bus. Their ages ranged from as young as 19, to as old as 56. The group leader, Regina Mitchell, seemed to be the only one awake. Forty-one years old, Regina busily typed out a text to her wife and partner back in Boston. She had been raised in a strict Pentecostal church. Regina had even married once, and was a mother of a twenty-something daughter. But twelve years earlier, Regina's life had taken an abrupt detour. It began with a simple friendship at work with another woman. Her name was Samantha, but everyone called her Sam. She drove a forklift in the warehouse, and everyone knew that Sam was an open and out-of-the-closet lesbian. In fact, Sam's favorite thing was stealing straight women away from their husbands or boyfriends. She jokingly called it "poaching," and, unknown to Regina at the time, Sam had set her hunting sights on Regina. Sam was the stereotypical lesbian: boots, jeans, flannel shirts, and hair cut so short people often mistook her for a boy straight out of army boot camp. Regina was the complete opposite, looking like a poster girl for a traditional office secretary, always wearing a dress, heels, and makeup.

As their friendship became more intense, they started to hang out more often. Regina began spending more time with Sam and less time with her husband, Antoine. Sam started taking Regina to country music concerts and bars. Regina liked the attention from Sam and felt a weird excitement every time they spent time together. Regina started to feel emotions for Sam that she had never felt for her husband, Antoine. She quickly changed from wearing high heels and dresses to adopting the same clothing style as her new secret lover. Eventually, she just quit coming home, despite the fights it caused between her and Antoine. She would stand in the kitchen, her husband hovering at the end of the counter from her, arms crossed, a look of anger and confusion on his face, demanding to know why she hadn't come home, called, or returned his messages. Eventually, her stories of falling asleep at Sam's while watching a movie began to grow old.

One day, while her husband was at work, she and Sam came to the house and packed up all of her things. She left a pathetic "Dear John," or in this case, "Dear Antoine," letter in the kitchen and went to live with Sam.

After buying a farm together in the countryside near Oklahoma City, they decided Regina should be in charge of paying the bills. Of course, it only took Sam nine months to start pouching another man's woman. This new relationship would last less than nine months. One day when Sam was at work, she secretly packed her things and moved to the big city of Boston, where she easily blended into the gay and lesbian community. What Sam didn't know was that Regina had stopped paying the bills, including their mortgage, months before. By the time Sam realized the depth of the betrayal, Regina was long gone, and the bank was taking the farm.

In Boston, Regina became a roaring liberal, fighting for every gay cause she could find. She put all of her energy into making gay marriage legal in the state, and, while doing so, met her current partner, Kris. Together they began to volunteer with the ACORN organization and the Democratic Election Committee to get liberal presidential candidate Barakat elected.

They had hardly stopped celebrating their victory of Barakat's win when Regina heard about a new movement that President Barakat had personally created. It was entitled *"Drive for Diversity."* Barakat created twenty different teams to complete his goal of introducing diversity and change to the United States citizens. In truth, the objective of the program was to teach those unwilling to participate in his changes, to start participating.

Regina applied for and was awarded one of the coveted positions, and was quickly promoted as leader of her particular team. Now, for three weeks out of the month, she and her crew traveled the country putting on speeches and skits, handing out DVDs and pamphlets, and bullying everyone they met into accepting the President's diversity ideas. This was simple brain washing, whether the people wanted to accept it or not.

Now, as the sun began to set, Regina's team was headed to what they privately called a "Hot Spot." A Hot Spot was an area that had come onto the administration's radar due to noncompliance of the president's agenda. Regina and her assistants would have to lean on a few people or groups until voluntary or non-voluntary compliance was met.

Each of the twenty separate groups were given the authority to call public meetings, school assemblies, and work place gatherings, so they could tout the government's message and spread the propaganda they had been carefully trained to use.

Members of their audience would often sit sullenly, while Regina and her team talked or sang. Their message, that all Americans should become more liberal in their thinking and stand behind the president, was often ignored. While some of her group talked or "rapped" their message, Regina would stand off stage and scan the crowd, making a mental note of anyone she detected reacting negatively – the sideways shaking of a head or a ridiculing laugh. These people would often be called out later for special one-on-one counseling.

Problems usually arose at the end of their presentations when the members of the audience were given loyalty forms to sign. The official government document asked for their names and other personal information. There was a signature line at the end of the document asking them to pledge their complete allegiance to the president's plan. Regina and her team were also authorized to educate the American citizens that President Barakat was to be addressed as "President for

Life." Regina would listen to the groans of protest from the audience. Not all gratefully signed and returned the paperwork. Sometimes, the loyalty forms were often crumpled up and thrown on the floor. That was when Regina would feel the anger creep over her body. Her dark eyes would narrow, she would purse her lips, and prepare to do battle for her president.

Unbeknownst to the general public, Regina's team, as well as all the other teams, had been given a vulgar amount of power by the president. Small groups or individuals could and would be singled out for private discussion. Often, Regina would have a squad of National Security Officers on hand to enforce her orders. Out in the sticks, she would have to rely on the local good-old-boy cops, and even they knew better than to question her orders, even if it meant rounding up people they had known for years.

She tried, at first, to be friendly and cajole the holdouts to accept the president's call for nationwide teamwork. However, if that didn't work, she had absolutely no problem switching into bitch-mode. She could make a few calls, and someone would be suspended from work without pay. She could and would direct Family Services to separate children from parents while a straw investigation was conducted. She could and would freeze bank accounts, impound cars, and, in some cases, have men or women detained on new and far-ranging domestic security laws enacted by President Barakat.

It didn't bother Regina to deal with the intricate details of her mission. She was more than willing to do whatever it took to accomplish the mission the president had trusted upon her. Word quickly spread that certain leaders of the teams, like Regina, could simply make a phone call back to Washington, and school leaders were suddenly replaced for lack of cooperation. People were fired for no cause. Expensive fines were levied against business owners, who weren't working hard enough. It was the business owner's responsibility to persuade their employees to accept the president's message of change and sign their loyalty agreement to his administration.

As she sat on the bus and texted Kris, Regina hoped things would be easy at the next backwoods town where they were heading. While she was passionate about her job and the president's message of change, and his program to enforce it if necessary, Regina was ready to get back to Boston and be with her partner. Pulling her hoodie around her, she sent her final text message of the night and then put her head back and began daydreaming.

Not every one of their stops went smoothly. She had recently quit counting how many times she had some protester removed from the audience. She always asked the people to come quietly but if they put up a fight, she simply called security. She came to learn that the small towns were the worst. Her muscle had to be enforced by the local cops and they tended to be less physical when dealing with someone they were related to or someone they knew. In the bigger cities, especially those close to DC, she had the new National Security troops to do her bidding. These guys were bad-ass, not like the local yokels. At a moment's notice, they would drag someone, man or woman, screaming and fighting off to a private interrogation room while five hundred other people looked on with open mouths. They, like Regina, had been given great power by the commander in chief. They could and did use excessive force without fear of repercussion. Several times in the stairway of a building, behind stage or in private, Regina had looked on unsympathetically while four or five security officers beat and stomped a member of her audience who dared question the president's call for change and cooperation. She hated the conservatives and, like her president, considered them an obstacle to his plan of a community more accepting of everyone.

When she was alone with someone who showed any defiance to her message, she shed the friendly mask she used on stage. She became cold and heartless. Regina had no problem tearing families apart. The children would be taken to a state-run facility while the parents would do some time in an "educational reform" center. Years before, the Communist Chinese, North Koreans, and North Vietnamese called them reeducation camps. While the president agreed completely with the purpose of these camps in the Communist nations, he didn't want to scare the public by stealing the same title from his socialist cousins. But Regina knew the truth. Anyone sent to the camp would receive a heavy dose of indoctrination to the new belief system. Holdouts would be denied food and sleep, and physical torture was not out of question. In some cases, people in the camps would simply disappear. They would be walked to a remote area, sometimes forced to dig their own graves, and then simply shot in the head by a member of the guard force.

Even after parents had gleefully accepted their government brainwashing, they would not be reunited with their children. The children were kept in a state facility so that the indoctrination of the president's way of thinking would become their life choice. They were trained to become perfect citizens in Barakat's government, never to see their parents again.

Yes, Regina had a dark side . . . a very, very dark side. She would stand calmly, an infant in her arms and wave innocently as the mother, screaming and crying, was dragged away by security officers. Recently she had taught herself a new trick. She would take the small hand of the child she held and wave it in a good-bye gesture to those being dragged away. "Say 'bye' to mommy," she would say with a smile, or daddy or whoever was being taken away.

Regina was determined to accomplish the president's mission regardless of who got hurt or killed along the way. She would always urge the members of her audience to report those who appeared to be an enemy of the country. Secret tip hotline phone numbers were always advertised and at the conclusion of a meeting pens or key rings with the hotline number imprinted on them were handed out to everyone so that they could report neighbors, family, and friends.

Just twenty minutes before Regina started daydreaming, the driver of the bus, an old hippie they called Cheech because of his long gray ponytail and love of smoking weed, had pulled the rig off Highway 44 in Southwest Missouri. They were now on a two lane secondary road leading into farmland, heading toward their next destination. As tall oak trees passed by outside the windows, the rest of the team continued to nap and sit quietly. Regina silently hoped they could find a decent restaurant in the next town and a place to stay with hot water and comfortable beds. She had just stuck her cell phone into the pocket of her jacket and had began to relax when the sudden slowing of the bus shoved her roughly into the seat in front of her and brought her back to reality.

"Holy shit," Cheech said loudly, as the air brakes of the bus made a loud whooshing sound. Regina quickly slipped her feet back into her pink clogs, and began heading toward the front of the bus. She grabbed onto the seats for support as the quickly stopping bus swung her 200-pound frame from side to side.

"What's happening, Cheech?" she asked, coming up behind him and leaning to look out the huge front window of the bus.

Cheech set the air brake of the bus and pointed an old weathered finger at an object on the ground, lit up by the headlights of the rig. "Look what some stupid redneck has done," he spat with distain. Regina peered forward, letting her eyes adjust. Suddenly, she saw what had Cheech so exasperated. Sitting on the black top was a large cardboard box. The words, "free kittens," were written across the side in large black letters.

"Get me out of here and back to civilization, Cheech," Regina said, opening the door of the bus. "I'm so tired of dealing with these inbred, white trash lowlifes. They need to be spayed or neutered just like their stupid pets." Cheech grunted in agreement and then began to pull a small, thin doobie out of the pocket of his denim jacket. He figured he might as well take some tokes while the boss checked out the obstacle in the road.

Stepping onto the black top, Regina began to stomp her way toward the box, while the rest of her team watched from inside. Trees dominated both sides of the road, and a chorus of crickets echoed in the dimming light as she walked. "Thank the lucky stars there isn't any traffic coming. This box of kittens would become roadkill instantly if Cheech didn't see it," she thought to herself, finally reaching the container.

Pausing, she peered into the box and then let out a sigh. Bending down, she scanned the ground before standing and holding the box high over her head. With the opening of the box facing toward the bus, she showed the rest of the passengers who watched her that it was empty. Cheech, a smoking marijuana cigarette clenched in his lips, flashed his middle fingers of both hands, as if to say, "fuck the world," as the others began to move slowly back to their seats in the dimly lit interior of the vehicle. Regina had just turned her back to the bus, and was in the process of tossing the empty box into the ditch, when a deafening roar and blinding flash of light shattered the night. Buried beside the road the IED, improvised explosive device, created with one hundred pounds of fertilizer and diesel fuel, lifted the bus like a toy three feet off the ground and flipped it onto its side in the ditch. In a microsecond, the blast wave slammed into Regina, knocking her head-over-heels like a rag doll down the road. She bounced painfully through the gravel and onto the edge of the road, finally landing in a heap of blood and torn clothes while her pink rubber clogs bounded off the pavement like rubber balls. In shock, with her ears ringing, it took Regina several moments to register that the air had suddenly become filled with the sounds of gunfire.

Sitting on her scrapped ass, Regina began to scramble backward like a crab, propelling herself on her heels and the palms of her hands. Illuminated by the blazing inferno of the bus, she began to spot dark clothed figures coming out of the trees, firing fully automatic rifles into the burning hulk of the bus. One of the men with an assault weapon stood calmly at the front of the bus, firing measured bursts of gunfire through the shattered front window where the body of Cheech hung like a broken doll over the steering wheel. Suddenly, the shrill sound of a police whistle sounded over the loud crescendo of the shooting. The firing ceased immediately, and Regina heard the shouted sounds of orders being given. She staggered to her feet, staring at the flaming shell of the bus and listening to the pop and crackle of the fire that consumed it. At least a dozen shooters ran to the front of the bus, and formed a circle facing outward. Several began changing out the clips on their rifles, their eyes trained outward, never looking down, like specially trained military members. Their movements were determined and professional.

In complete fear and shock, feeling as if she were going to vomit, Regina stood on rubbery knees and turned to run the opposite way, when a tall, dark, figure suddenly appeared in front of her. A scream tore from her throat, but the wraith seemed unmoved. Suddenly it raised an arm, and a black-gloved hand extended something small and shiny toward her. For a second, she stood frozen with fear, until the figure shoved the object into her hand. Then, just as silently, it calmly strode past her and disappeared into the dark beside the road.

Regina looked back over her shoulder toward the destroyed remains of the bus. The circle of figures had also vanished just as silently as the one she almost ran into moments before. She jerked back around and then looked into her hand to find she held a playing card, the black Ace of Spades. She didn't know what it meant or why the figure had given it to her. Dropping to her knees, she began to dig into the pocket of her hoodie for her cell phone. Regina was shaking so badly it took her three tries before she successfully dialed 911. She held it to her face with trembling hands as her eyes darted left and right for any signs of the people who had attacked her bus.

A moment went by as the phone dialed, and then she heard a woman's voice ask, "Nine-one-one, what is the nature of your emergency?" Regina never told the police dispatcher the reason for her 911 call. She didn't say what had just happened or even where they were. At the exact moment she opened her mouth to speak, a bullet, fired from a concealed sniper rifle tore through the cool night air. It sliced through the darkness at 1,600 feet per second, hitting the rear of Regina's smart phone. The energy of the projectile shattered her device into a hundred pieces of plastic and circuitry, passed through her open mouth, clipped off the top of her tongue piercing, severed her spine and exploded out the back of her throat in a spray of blood.

Regina Mitchell, eyes locked open in panic, collapsed forward onto the roadway, dead before her head hit the pavement, the Ace of Spades still clutched in her left hand. Behind her dead body, the bus burned unchecked, sending its flames up into the quiet country sky.

Chapter 7

There was a deep sense of dread in the meeting room of the White House. Several aides and staff sat around a long oak table scribbling on legal pads or tapping away on the screens of their smart phones or tablets. Donna Koontz, appropriately dressed in black, calmly sat reading the contents of a file folder, her reading glasses perched on the end of her pointy nose. Max King sat opposite her, listening to someone on his cell phone. He concentrated without speaking, occasionally grunting a reply. As the door opened and the president strode in, King hung up and slide the phone into an inside coat pocket.

"Good morning, Mr. President," Koontz said, with a somewhat nervous smile that seemed to stretch the edges of her mouth across her face. A few others offered greetings to the president as he took his place at the head of the table. President Barakat folded his hands on top of the table and leaned forward, scanning everyone in the room. He did not smile or offer an acknowledgement to anyone. When he spoke, his voice was gruff and direct.

"So tell me, people," the president said, folding his arms tightly, "what is so important that I was woken up at 5 a.m. to attend this meeting? This had better be good."

There was a chorus of mumbles, but Max King was the first to respond.

"It appears, Mr. President, that not everyone is willing to hold hands and sing Kum Ba Yah together just yet." Max lifted up a printed sheet of paper and, leaning back in his chair, began to read. "Last night, six of your *Drive for Diversity* buses were attacked and the team members were killed. The buses were located in Missouri, Arkansas, Alabama, Colorado, and two in Oklahoma." King paused to let the news sink in before continuing. "All were destroyed in coordinated attacks using IEDs, gunmen, or a combination of both. In two cases, survivors of the initial attack attempted to surrender but were executed instead."

The president leaned forward with his face in his hands. After several moments he sat up straight and looked toward King. "What other information do we have on the attacks?" the President asked.

"Not much, Mr. President," King responded. "Five of the attacks were committed in the middle of nowhere and were only seen by the cows standing in the fields. Any human witnesses came onto the scene long after the assaults had taken place and had no helpful information. One diversity team was gunned down in the lobby of a fast food restaurant. It seems the employees had been locked in the cooler by several masked men wearing camouflage clothing just a minute before the bus had stopped."

The president glared at Max King with obvious anger. "So who did this, Max? How did this happen? How did these people just vanish like a fart in the wind?"

"Mr. President, I say again," replied Max King, "these attacks were well-coordinated. Whomever planned these operations knew the routes of the diversity team. This wasn't just the work of some single, pissed off guy. They had information and the intelligence to carefully plan these attacks."

Pushing back his chair, the president suddenly stood up and began pacing, hands on his hips. "So what are we doing about it?" the President asked, stopping suddenly and glaring at Max King.

"For now, Mr. President," Donna Koontz, chimed in, "we have recalled the remaining three diversity teams to the Washington area, where they will be heavily guarded by security personnel while the investigation into these attacks continues."

President Barakat, fuming, stared at the wall for a moment, before finally turning back to face the group. "I want every town within fifty miles of these attacks shut down," the president screamed, leaning over the table, his face flushed. "I want them closed off. Nobody gets in and nobody gets out."

The president leaned across the table, staring at Max King. "Mr. King, I want your intelligence people to question every citizen in these cities, and I mean everyone who isn't shitting in a diaper or in a coma. I want answers. Teach them that collaboration with domestic terrorists isn't going to be tolerated. Drag them out of their nice, comfy homes and stick these people in some tents behind barbed wire for a while.

Better yet," the president said suddenly, snapping his fingers, "let's use our new prison trains. There have to be rail lines close to these areas."

Max King nodded his head in agreement as the president continued his rant. Several months before, as the president was planning his grab for power, he had ordered Max King to have ten thousand specifically designed railroad cars secretly built. Each car was its own jail holding cell on wheels, being forty feet in length, with shackles welded to the inside walls and floors. One unit could hold up to one hundred prisoners, even more if you needed to cram them in like canned sardines. Each sealed car had one single sink and toilet. The president and his design team were specific that the comfort of those locked up inside was totally irrelevant. After being built, they had been concealed and stored at navy shipyards on the East and West Coasts, until they were needed. President Barakat had just decided that time had come.

Quickly, the president turned to face Donna Koontz. His movement was so fast that the press secretary jerked in her seat, as if bitten. "I want these attacks announced on the news as acts of domestic terrorism. Make these people look like a bunch of crazies, firing guns and throwing bombs," the president spat. "I don't want the American public to have any idea how cohesive and organized these people are."

"As you wish, Mr. President," Koontz said, smiling and bobbing her head.

Max King rose from his chair and turned to everyone at the table, except Koontz, barking, "Get out!" He pointed a finger at Koontz. "We need *you* to stay!" There was a moment's hesitation, and then the room began to clear until only King, Koontz, and the president remained.

"We have bigger fish to fry, Mr. President," King said. "I received a phone call right before this meeting and we need to discuss it immediately."

With that, King opened his laptop and pulled up a YouTube video. As the video was loading, Max King showed the president and Donna Koontz that the video had been viewed over 12 million times. After a moment, a video image appeared. It was immediately obvious that the person filming the video was lying down in some foliage. The first few seconds showed two yellow backhoes busily digging a trench. Pink flags attached to two-foot-tall pieces of wire marked the boundaries of the project. What appeared to be a supervisor, dressed in a reflective vest, white T-shirt, and blue jeans, walked back and forth between the two earth movers, waving his arms and giving directions. The video had been edited, but anyone watching got the picture that a long, wide hole was being dug. The video continued but was now showing several gray prison buses driving down an earthen path toward the videographer. They were followed by three large black SUVs. The vehicles passed closely in front of the person filming, making it apparent that the videographer was well-blended into the brush and had not been seen. The president leaned back in his chair, his hand covering his nose and mouth. Koontz leaned forward, holding her face in her hands, peering through an opening in her fingers at the images on the screen.

No one in the room spoke. Finally the sounds of automatic gunfire and screams emitted from the screen. "Shut it off," the president ordered, with anger in his voice. Still leaning back in his chair, he looked coldly at King and then at Koontz. "So, which one of you fucked this up?" he demanded coldly.

"Mr. President," Max King answered firmly, "we never felt a need for security. For God's sake, only a handful of people even knew about this operation."

The president turned his head and stared at King. "In that case, finding the source of the leak shouldn't be difficult, should it?" Turning to the press secretary, the president said, "Do whatever you have to do. Shut down the Internet, I don't care. This video had better die here."

"I'm afraid that ship has already sailed, Mr. President," King responded. "This video has already gone viral. I just showed you it has been viewed over 12 million times. Every news source in every country is showing this, and now the UN is making noise."

Glaring out the corner of his eyes, the president took in the new information, without looking away from Koontz. He leaned closer to her and lowered his voice. "Get your media machine rolling, and impeach this video as a fake. Make it look like some right-wing group created it. Better yet blame it on the Jews. Get somebody. Anybody.

Torture a confession out of them until they agree they work for the Israeli government. Blast it on every television station and then make this dupe vanish."

"That's fine, Mr. President," Koontz said, flashing her fake smile, "but there will be those who won't believe the video is fake."

"Remember what Adolph Hitler once said, Ms. Koontz," the president said, as if reading from a book. "People will believe a lie if it's big enough and they hear it often enough. I'd urge you to remember that while your people clean up this mess."

Again, Max King responded to the president's suggestion. He aimed the control at the screen and fast-forwarded to near the end of the YouTube video. The cameraman had used the telephoto lens on his camera to focus on King and Koontz standing together, a smoking cigarette hanging out of King's lips. "I'm not doubting the fine abilities of our press secretary," Max King said sarcastically. "How do we explain Donna Koontz and I standing together at the end of this massacre? What happens when John Doe Public notices his senator has suddenly vanished off the planet?"

The president stood and glared at King and Koontz and it seemed that he might explode. "This wasn't an accident, you know. Some asshole out hiking in the woods didn't just stumble onto this. Whoever made this video was waiting in the exact right place and at the perfectly right time," the president's voice boomed. "We have a leak somewhere," he said, looking from Koontz to King. "I want you to find out who the leaker is and find out now!" the president ordered. "It appears that your incompetence has forced me to move forward more quickly in my time schedule. Shut down everything that will spread this fucked up video for at least ten days," the president barked at Koontz. "Maybe we'll get lucky, and the entire world will forget this happened. You two start planning some damage control," the president snapped, as he stood to walk out of the room.

Donna Koontz sheepishly raised her hand. "Mr. President, one last thing please."

The president stopped and gave her an irritated look. "What?" he asked.

"Umm . . . you're basically launching a pogrom against the Jewish people, Mr. President. Something like this hasn't been done since

Joseph Stalin. How should I handle the response from Israel?" Koontz asked nervously.

"Fuck the Jews," President Barakat growled. "That's how you handle that!" He then walked out of the meeting room.

Chapter 8

Max King sat in his office at the White House. He had tossed his suit coat over a chair and loosened his tie, trying to free himself of the stifling feeling his phony attire gave him. King was much more comfortable wearing cargo pants and a button-up camp shirt. The suit and tie gig wasn't for him. He'd rather put on BDUs (battle dress utilities) and sturdy boots anytime.

He needed time to think, a luxury not afforded him in his past professions, where life-or-death decisions were often made on the fly. King had started his military career on a path of honor and service as a United States Army officer. King's life started out as rocky as hell. His father was a Detroit auto plant worker, and his mother moonlighted as a cocktail waitress at a dark, smoke-filled hole in the wall near the automobile manufacturing area where his old man worked. Max was very thankful that he was an only child. There was never enough of anything to go around for him as he was growing up. Having to share what meager things he had with siblings would have made the bad situation even worse. His dad would head off early every morning and spend the day at his mundane job, installing windshields in new cars they could never afford to own themselves. To make matters worse, his father had expensive hobbies that ate up a great amount of his take-home pay. While other fathers found enjoyment in golf or bowling, his alcoholic old man picked riskier diversions. Those hobbies were much too run-of-the-mill for him. He liked betting on the dogs or rolling dice with a dozen losers like himself in the back alley behind his favorite bar.

Because of his home life, Max limped along in grade school. He didn't fail, and he didn't excel. He had no parental support. His mother would make the mandatory parent/teacher conference, and then retell what she learned to his uninterested father, who stood in the kitchen, scratching his ass, in his dirty boxer drawers and a stained blue work shirt, his sweat socks hanging limp around his ankles.

His mother, while far from being Mom of the Year, tried to show interest in Max, but she always had a constant battle on her hands with his drunk and pissed-off dad. Fights would begin in the evening and drag late into the night. The subject of the fight never changed. His mother would scream at his father who, while drunk, had stolen the last of her cash she was saving for items like milk and bread. Sometimes, she would outsmart him by stashing the small amount of cash from her paycheck where he couldn't find it. That always brought on the biggest fights. His old man would always start off nice, trying to sweet-talk her out of enough dough for some drinks. Then he would be reduced to begging. Finally, his anger would take over, and he would become a dangerous, wild animal. He would throw his mother against a wall or choke her until she almost passed out. Many nights, a young Max King would hide in the dark in the back of his closet, while three or four Detroit police officers stood in the living room of his house, refereeing another domestic fight between his parents. However, no matter how mean or violent his father got, his mother always refused to press charges. The cops would listen with no emotion, make a veiled threat of what would happen if they got called back by another concerned neighbor, and then take off.

Max, being only nine or ten, noticed how several of the policemen looked at and spoke to his mother. It made sense to him later when he was older. While his father was a grimy, drunk loser, his mother was beautiful. She was slim and tall, with long blonde hair and piercing blue eyes.

When he had just turned eleven years old, the fighting between his parents abruptly ended, and Max's future changed. He was walking down the tree-lined sidewalk toward his apartment when he saw the police cars. He knew they were at his house. They always were. As he got closer, he even recognized one of the policemen standing at the gate that opened into his yard. Yes, on this day, his mother had found the courage to tell her alcoholic husband that she was leaving and taking Max with her. At first, his father had taken the news well. He didn't explode in anger or break anything, which he had often done in the past. Instead, he pulled a cheap .38-caliber, pawn shop revolver from his dresser drawer and shot his mother through the heart, killing her instantly. He then calmly walked into the kitchen, sat down at the dinner table, and fired a second round into his open mouth, blasting the back of his skull all over an auto union calendar pinned on the wall next to the refrigerator.

For almost two weeks after the incident, Max languished in the foster care system. He was angry at his rotting father and disappointed his mother hadn't had his father arrested years before. Things did improve, for the most part, when his grandparents came and took him back to live on their farm near Topeka, Kansas.

He didn't know his grandparents very well because his father had hated his in-laws and had forced his mother to cut off contact with them when Max was very young. They were full-time farmers, and Max quickly became a full-time farm hand. His grandparents were kind but strict. He learned to drive a tractor, buck hay, and tend to the livestock. Most importantly, Max went to school where he excelled like never before. He studied hard, made good grades, and went to college at Kansas State in nearby Manhattan. It was at K-State that he entered the ROTC program. Max needed the discipline and direction offered by the ROTC program. He would go on to graduate from officer training school, bid farewell to his aging grandparents, and take his first post as a green second lieutenant in a rifle company along the DMZ in South Korea.

The military was the perfect environment for King. He was a cold and calculating leader looking at his troops not as friends or buddies but as tools of the United States government. King trained these men into highly skilled killing machines. He drilled his NCOs (noncommissioned officers) who, in turn, drilled their troops. Lieutenant King proved he had the abilities the army needed, with the biggest attribute being his ability to follow orders. If he was told to take the hill, he took the hill. If he was told to march his platoon into a rice paddy, he marched them into a rice paddy. Max King understood the importance of following orders. It wasn't that he accepted every order as being right or sound; it just wasn't his job to question his superiors. It was his job to get the mission accomplished. Second Lieutenant Max King was so devoted that if his superiors had ordered him to lead a charge into the Soviet Red Square, he would have done so without so much as a shake of the head.

King's superiors noticed his efforts, and he quickly rose through the ranks to become Captain King. Soon after, he received new orders, and found himself back in the states, in jump school at Fort Benning, Georgia. Captain King soon made an acquaintance with one of the instructors, Staff Sergeant Ralph Westcott, a bull of a man who didn't take shit from anyone, especially some lowly "leg" in his training program. Westcott and King clicked, and after King had completed his jump school and received his wings, he and Westcott became drinking buddies.

Westcott was a Korean War veteran. He had been in what soldiers called a real "shooting war," but, unlike himself, Westcott hated the army, the boredom, and the routine. Westcott liked fighting, plain and simple. To him, it was the biggest adrenalin rush a man could experience. In the heat of combat, as hundreds of screaming Chinese troops rushed up a hill toward his platoon, Westcott found his drug of choice. As his own men panicked and screamed and the Chinese troops blew blaring bugles, then-Private Ralph Westcott became cool and calm. While other men fired wildly, some burning through a clip of ammunition in seconds, Westcott calmly aimed his M1 rifle at the charging communists, picking them off one by one. For whatever emotional reason, Westcott developed a huge erection in the heat of battle, and every time he squeezed the trigger he felt his penis jump in his pants. When the enemy came close, Westcott snapped his bayonet onto the end of his rifle and charged into the fray, stabbing and slashing like a man on drugs.

Eventually the Korean War ended, and Westcott found himself back in a boring civilian job. One day he met Hans Doggendorf at a social club in Chicago frequented by military veterans. Westcott soon learned that Doggendorf, who had served in the German army, was recruiting mercenaries to fight in Africa. Sitting in a dark booth, Doggendorf explained to Westcott that he was seeking experienced, fighting men to join him and his private army in the Congo. Westcott was mesmerized by the offer, three thousand dollars a month in gold coin, paid travel – all to kill a group of jungle bunnies that he didn't give a rat's ass about. Where did he sign up?

Now, back at the bar, Captain Max King listened, and hung on every word that Westcott said. He listened to Westcott talk about the small African governments he had helped overthrow, the corrupt individuals or militia leaders he had been paid extra to assassinate. Westcott had made a lot of money while fighting in Africa, even though he had squandered it all on liquor and women.

Captain King soaked in every tale that Westcott shared with him. Thinking about a life as a mercenary became all consuming. He began to read about the history of mercenary fighters from the time of the Roman legions to the present. King was in complete awe. He knew then that he would become a mercenary.

The road to achieving this goal would open when U.S. troops invaded Iraq in 2002, and King and his unit were deployed. Here, King really found his calling, commanding troops in combat. He would kill Al Qaeda terrorists, or the Taliban, or any other Arab who happened to be in his gun's sights.

Max King led his troops into combat with cold determination. He really hit his stride in the heat of battle with bullets flying and RPG rockets blasting so close that King was showered with gravel and debris. King knew that he couldn't show fear or indecision in the face of the enemy. He always remained cool and calm and became the rock his troops could depend on.

King had thought back to old movies he had seen of the British army, in the thick of battle with Zulu warriors in Africa. Vastly outnumbered, the English officer or ranking NCO would calmly direct his troops.

King found this demeanor to be natural for him. He would quickly size up the situation, direct the tactics and fire of his troops, and get the job done.

Like in any war, King suffered deaths and casualties in his company, but he never showed grief or anguish to his troops, nor did he think of the casualties again. To Captain Max King, the men in his command were simply killing machines. Sure, they had wives and families and sweethearts who would grieve for them, and that was good enough. They were simply tools that allowed him to get the mission finished. If a few got crippled by fire from an AK-47 rifle or blown to bits by a rocket or grenade, so be it. Compassion was not an attribute of Max King. While being raised by his grandparents on their Kansas farm, King never felt one bit of remorse or hesitation about killing and slaughtering a head of livestock. This emotion didn't live within him.

So when Max King watched one of his own troops being loaded into a body bag, or a cluster of dead, innocent civilians on a blood-splattered street, his compassion level never deviated. The worst thing about having one of his own troops killed was having to write a phony letter to the closest relative back home. "Dear so-and-so, your son, Private John Doe, died bravely in battle . . . blah, blah, blah." King would have preferred a form letter where he simply filled in the name of the dead and the date of death. Then the rest of the letter would simply explain that their loved one had died because he had done something stupid.

On a humid, dusty day, Max King's dreams would take a step toward reality when an unmarked Humvee pulled into his compound near Basra, Iraq. A khaki-clad figure wearing a biker-looking doo-rag, climbed out. Max stood watching as three other men, all heavily armed, took up positions with their backs to the Humvee, with their rifles pointed at the ground. The biker dude came directly toward King. He seemed to be about King's age and wore a Kevlar vest over his shirt and an automatic handgun strapped to his thigh in a black nylon, tactical holster. Aviator sunglasses concealed his eyes. The man offered a firm, calloused handshake to King and introduced himself simply as "Doug."

"We need to talk . . . in private," he said, looking suspiciously to his right and left before focusing back on Max King. In King's quarters, a small building of plywood and camouflage built by Navy Seabees, the two sat across from one another at the table.

"Let's cut the bullshit and get to the facts," Doug said, pulling a manila folder from inside his shirt. He opened it, scattering the contents on the table between them. King immediately spotted a photograph of himself in uniform, paper-clipped to the top sheet. Whoever this guy was, he had a dossier on King. Max King thought this guy might be Army intelligence or CIA.

"Captain King, I work for a company called Blackwater," the man said, thumbing through the paperwork he picked up from the table. "You were recommended to us, and that's why I'm here."

King knew that Blackwater was a huge, private security contracting company that worked mostly in Iraq and Afghanistan, providing protection for high-ranking diplomats. Blackwater's largest client was the U.S. State Department. The company, situated on a seven-thousand-acre private compound in North Carolina, ran a very cloak-and-dagger operation. Not only were the ranks of Blackwater made up of the best – CIA, Navy SEALS, and Marine Force Recon – they privately trained the best of the best from these elite military units.

Captain King's new friend, Doug, came completely prepared to the meeting with King. He held the clout to have King transferred from the army and onto Blackwater's payroll within 48 hours. All he needed was a decision from King.

"If you want to stay here trading shots with these towelheads, that's okay by me," the man said, lighting up a cigarette. "However, Captain King, Blackwater gives us the authority to pursue some of the higher-ranking Islamic big shots." He paused to blow a cloud of cigarette smoke toward the ceiling. "Oh, and our rules of engagement, well . . . let's just say, they're much more liberal than usual. In your current situation, Captain King, you will often have to call HQ and beg permission to engage the enemy. That is not how we work. Think of us like a fine surgical instrument. When we make a move, the bad guys never see it coming, and the bleeding heart liberal politicians, who are so terrified of collateral civilian damage, never know what went down. If they did, they would shit themselves. Blackwater operations gives a new name to silent but deadly."

King quickly evaluated the information he had just heard. "I'm in," King said, rising to his feet. The deal was immediately closed with a firm handshake across the table.

"Secure your gear, Captain," Doug said, putting his dark sunglasses back on and heading toward the hatch of the building. "I'll send a vehicle to get you tomorrow. Be ready to ship out."

Max King stood in the doorway and watched Doug quickly cross the dusty grounds toward the Humvee. He made a circling motion with his right hand over his head, and the men standing guard around the vehicle immediately joined him and jumped inside. A minute later they were gone.

Three days later, Max King was on the job in the ranks of the Blackwater organization. He no longer had to wear combat fatigues and a Kevlar helmet. Khaki cargo pants and a ball cap took their place. He still wore the hot, protective body armor over his torso, an assault rifle slung across his chest, and a 9 mm pistol on his hip. Now, instead of the weight of commanding troops, his responsibility became guarding someone who needed his degree of protection. His days consisted of scanning crowds of strange Iraqi citizens, looking for one who might be hiding a weapon or trying to get close enough to detonate a suicide vest. His orders were very clear to not let that happen. If he felt someone in a crowd was acting in a threatening manner, King's orders were to simply blast a hole through them, thus ending the perceived threat. If he was wrong and accidentally shot the wrong person, the State Department would handle the damage control with the press and make a hefty restitution to the family of the dead. King didn't think twice about these people, because to him, it was all about the business. He was paid to guard one person, and that is what he did. If he was sent out in the dark of night to snatch a suspected terrorist or insurgent leader out of their bed for a few days of waterboarding and other interrogation, then he did that as well. To King, it was all part of his job.

It was during one of these bodyguard operations that Max King met a young senator from California by the name of Marcus Barakat. The lawmaker had come to inspect the situation in Iraq for himself. Barakat was openly against America's involvement in the war. A cunning, hard-core liberal, Barakat devised a strategy of directing his fake promises toward the untapped, yet very vocal and motivated voter, the minority.

Whether they were undocumented Mexican workers, the black communities, the inner city poor, or the gay and lesbians, Barakat came across as a friend to everyone. Whenever he could, and he found reason every day, he condemned the rich and pitted those who had against those who didn't have. His message to his would-be voters never touched on the fact that the majority of the rich he chastised owned companies and firms that provided jobs. He kept his message focused on the haves versus the have nots.

Barakat pushed for gun control, embraced same-sex marriage and touted any other belief that would earn him the liberal vote. His strategy worked, eventually winning him the presidency. A political reviewer once said that Marcus Barakat would screw a dog if it won him votes from perverts who liked fucking their poodles.

Now he was just another senator, grandstanding in Iraq in front of the cameras, and Max King was the armed thug, laden with the responsibility of keeping him from being killed by some extremist with a grenade and a dream of dying a martyr.

During his three days of promoting himself in Iraq, Senator Barakat often spoke with his tightlipped bodyguard. The conversations were interspersed with questions from Barakat to King about Iraq and the war and King's take on America's involvement. During these times, King would answer with complete and informative answers. Barakat quickly discovered that his no-nonsense guardian was quite different from most guards – he was smart and seemed to know how things worked. Barakat was impressed with Max King's intelligence and attention to details.

While traveling from one junket to another, their chauffeured SUV bouncing along on one of Baghdad's poorly maintained roads, Senator Barakat and Max King sat in the rear seat chatting about current and past events. Both, as it turned out, had a mutual interest in American history. Even though Barakat was still a child during the Vietnam War, he had strong feelings about the United State's involvement. Barakat told King, without any hesitation, that he felt the conflict in Vietnam, which claimed thousands of American lives, was just another imperialistic war created by the United States. When Barakat mentioned how hard it must have been for the U.S. soldiers to fight in such an awful war, King's response was quick and direct.

"Soldiers do what they are ordered to do. Wars are never won by soldiers disobeying orders," King responded coolly. "Wars are won when troops are disciplined to such a degree that disobeying an order doesn't even cross their minds."

Barakat nodded in response to King's view. Barakat thought for a few moments and then looked toward King, who sat, machine gun across his lap, his eyes on constant alert, watching the front and side windows.

"So, Mr. King, let's take this one step farther," Senator Barakat said, looking intently toward him. "U.S. soldiers massacred over a hundred women and children in the village of Mei Lai under the orders of Lieutenant John Kelly. How could those troops do that?"

Max King replied, without looking toward the senator or pausing from intently scanning the sides of the roadway for threats.

"Because the soldiers of that platoon were following orders from their higher-ups. They didn't get their orders from the villagers, and none of those villagers signed their pay checks." King turned and looked directly into Senator Barakat's eyes. "Soldiers are trained to follow orders. That, Senator, is why those troops did what they did."

Feeling that Max King had successfully passed the secret test Barakat had thrown at him, Barakat didn't offer a rebuttal. He smiled to himself and made a mental note that Max King could become a great asset someday.

Later, once he was safely at his hotel in the "green zone," Senator Barakat conferred privately with his top aide. "I want you to learn everything you can about this Max King . . . I mean everything," Senator Barakat said, putting his arm around his assistant. "Keep tabs on him. I want to know where he is at all times and how to reach him."

The aide nodded his understanding and then scurried away to begin his research.

Senator Barakat and Max King's paths would cross again. He found in King the man he would need to carry out any orders without comment or question.

Chapter 9

"This sucks," the thirteen-year-old girl growled from the back seat of the minivan. "I want to be with my friends. "Where are we going again?" she demanded.

Her irritated mother turned from the passenger seat. "For the tenth time, Autumn, we're going to register our family. If you ever took your nose out of your phone and stopped texting for one minute, you might have a clue about what's going on in the world," her mother snapped. Her freckled, redheaded daughter mumbled under her breath, never taking her eyes off her cell phone, as she busily typed a message to another of her moody thirteen-year-old friends.

"It's all good, Jessica," her husband, Bill, said, patting his wife's knee, condescendingly.

"No, it's not all good," she replied, turning back to face the front window. "Explain to me again, Bill, just why we have to do this. What's the purpose of having a census? Doesn't that give the government the family information they need? At least when the government is taking a census, they send someone to your door or mail you out a form to complete. They don't make you drive halfway across town."

"This is a good thing," Bill Booth replied, stroking his beard. "You've seen the news. With all that's going on, the government is just trying to protect us. We're helping them make us safer."

Jessica, an attractive brunette (a MILF, according to some of Autumn's male friends), stared at her husband as if he was crazy. "Bill, I realize you're an educated college professor, but I think you are way off on this one. Doesn't any of this bother you? When the first terrorist attack happened, I sort of understood that the entire country needed to be put under temporary martial law. That's been months ago and we're still under lock down. My sister can't even come see us because of all the checkpoints and searches of her car. Seriously, how dangerous can a soccer mom, an eight-year-old, and a toddler be?" she asked sarcastically.

"I'm just an educator, not a security specialist," he replied without taking his eyes off the road.

Crossing her arms, Jessica continued to think about what was happening. She remembered that the announcements had been broadcast, first over the news and then in specialized press briefings from the White House. Then came the e-mails and text messages that no one had the power to ignore or block. The announcements were very clear. Everyone had to report to his or her local Department of Motor Vehicles office. However, instead of registering a car or renewing a driver's license, everyone had to register . . .themselves. To Jessica, this seemed strange and suspicious, but others, like her husband Bill, thought the government was doing the right thing. Just a few nights before, when Bill and Jessica were having dinner with a group of friends from the college where Bill taught literature, the topic had come up. Six of the eight in the group chatted enthusiastically about the announcement over wine. Of course, Jessica had seen the same TV coverage as everyone else. The press secretary, Donna Koontz, or as Jessica liked to refer to her, "Old Lipstick Face," had droned on about a nationwide registration of all citizens. She rambled on about the benefits, how it was for the safety of the country, blah, blah, blah. People whose last names started with A through D would have to register by this date, E through H by this date, and so on. On a last note, Old Lipstick Face reminded everyone that failing to register was punishable by law. All Jessica could think about while watching the press secretary stand at the podium and rant on and on was one thing. Did the woman own any clothes other than a red pantsuit?

Reaching their destination, Bill pulled into the parking lot of the DMV. It was packed with people circling, trying to find a spot. Jessica had never seen it so busy at the DMV, even when she had to renew their license plates. As usual, there was a heavy security presence, but Jessica was getting used to that. At least one Humvee sat in the parking lot, a soldier standing on its top turret, operating a menacing looking machine gun and looking bored. A dozen others like him stood in pairs near the front sidewalk, rifles slung over their shoulders, watching everyone who arrived.

As they neared the front of the building Jessica felt a tinge of apprehension. It wasn't the soldiers so much as the new National Security Force that President Barakat had put into place. While the army troopers looked scary, the NSF agents looked even worse. She spotted the first one inside the front entrance of the door. They all wore the same black battle dress utilities, the ends of their trousers bloused over black leather boots, a black beret, and black web belts that held their sidearms and handcuff cases. To Jessica, they were a cross between cops and combat troopers, but, oddly, she noticed that none of them wore rank. No chevrons sewn on their sleeves or bars on their collars. They just had a patch on their left chest that read "National Security Force," and a pin sporting the presidential seal.

Inside the door, Jessica and her family saw the same security. It reminded her of the type of security seen at an airport. All bags went through an X-ray machine, and Jessica noticed with some concern that a metal detector had been installed for everyone to pass through. Of course, her husband's belt buckle set off the alarms like it always did, and an NSF agent trotted over. The NSF agent quickly scanned him with one of the hand-held wand devices. As she cleared the security checkpoint, Jessica heard someone in the line ahead of her make a joke about being strip-searched. Nervous laughter followed.

The line that snaked its way toward the front row of agents wasn't that long, but Jessica noticed that it wasn't moving quickly. Each individual or family who moved forward to one of the dozen agents operating the desks was taking a long time to be processed.

As she waited in line, Jessica, like those around her, was a captive audience to several flat screen televisions, which ran a government-produced video. A well-groomed man and woman smiled at the camera and explained the importance of what they called the "National Registry," and how it was going to protect the American citizens. After about the fourth time of watching the film, Jessica figured the repeating loop was about five minutes long. She also noted that, toward the end of the clip, the two actors, teeth gleaming, reminded the audience that the National Registry was mandatory. Providing false information was a violation of the new National Security Protection law. Jessica was all for the security and protection of her family, but this seemed just a little too creepy.

A booming voice suddenly made her jump back to reality.

"TURN THAT OFF!" an NSF agent yelled, rushing toward her and pointing. Jessica looked behind her. Autumn stood holding her phone to her chest. She had obviously been texting while she stood in line. Her face was full of fear as the female NSF agent stormed toward them.

"NO CELL PHONES IN HERE," she said in a loud voice, her eyes locked on Autumn. "What's wrong with you? Didn't you read the signs at the door?" she said in a scolding voice.

Jessica quickly pulled a now-crying Autumn close to her as she struggled to shut off her phone. Jessica locked eyes with the stern NSF agent. Bill stood speechless with his mouth open, but made no effort to interfere.

"She made a mistake," Jessica said, still holding Autumn protectively to her, with her eyes still on the NSF agent.

For a moment, Jessica and the NSF woman stood staring at each other in what seemed to be a Mexican standoff. Finally, the NSF agent pointed at Autumn's phone. "Put that away now," she said, before turning and walking away. That's when Jessica realized the entire room was deadly quiet, and all eyes were locked on them.

"Thanks for the back-up, Bill," she said sarcastically, still holding Autumn close as the line continued to inch forward.

Jessica looked at her watch and calculated they had been waiting for nearly fifty minutes. They had reached the head of the line and now waited to be called. From here, Jessica could see and hear the clerks at their desks. All were busy in front of their computer screens asking questions and typing away at their keyboards. They didn't smile and didn't seem to be friendly. It was like the worst government clerk worker having a really bad day.

A middle-aged man sitting at a desk to Jessica's left turned and looked in her direction as the clerk typed away on her computer. Jessica quickly read the front of his ball cap, "Proud to be an American," before he turned back around. She bit at her lip, her mind turning. Something about his hat got her thinking. Jessica began to scan the room with her eyes. Without attracting attention, she looked to where a pair of NSF agents stood. She studied their uniforms. Jessica finally figured out what was missing from their uniforms. "Where are the American flags?" she asked herself. Normally they hung in every government building, but there were no flags here and no patches on the uniforms of the NSF troopers. There was, she noticed, a large smiling portrait of President Barakat high up on the wall looking down on her.

Jessica felt a chill of concern and was leaning in to whisper to Bill when loud voices, obviously in an argument, stopped her. It was the man in the flannel shirt at one of the desks. He was obviously pissed.

"It is none of your business how many guns I own," he replied in a loud voice. "What does that have to do with anything?"

The overweight clerk looked at the man coldly. "I asked if you owned a weapon, and you said yes."

Before she could continue, his denim-wearing wife interrupted. "Is it even legal for you to ask that question?" she said, straightening up in her chair.

The irritated clerk glanced at her. "Yes, I can ask you that question, and, yes, you have to answer it. I need to know what kind of weapons you own, sir," she continued, now looking at the husband.

Before he could answer, an NSF agent suddenly appeared from behind the clerk, who sat looking at the couple without any emotion.

"Is there a problem here?" the agent asked, pushing past the clerk to stand towering over the couple. Jessica thought that the clerk must have pushed a button to summon help, because the man came out of nowhere and seemed ready to fight.

"What's the question?" the NSF agent asked the clerk, without removing his eyes from the husband and wife.

"Do you own any guns?" she said with a smirk.

The NSF man crossed his arms and stared. "So, answer the question. Do you?"

For a moment, the man looked at his wife and then, in a stuttering voice, began to answer.

"I'm sorry, I didn't understand the question," he replied smiling. "I thought she asked if I owned any guns . . . ever. I don't anymore." His wife gave a nervous smile and nodded her head in agreement.

"Nope, no guns in our house. Too dangerous," the wife added.

For a moment, Jessica felt the tension in the air until the clerk and the NSF agent looked at one another, unconvinced. The clerk even raised her painted-on eyebrows as if to say, "Bullshit."

The NSF agent was still towering over the couple, intimidating them. "You realize that providing fake or fraudulent information during this interview is a serious offense," the NSF agent said to the couple. They both answered, "Yes."

The agent studied them for a moment and then before turning to walk away he leaned down to whisper to the clerk, "Tag them both." The clerk nodded and turning in her chair, opened a drawer of her desk, and took something out.

Jessica silently watched the events unfold in front of her. Apparently the intimidation by the NSF agent had worked because the couple sat quietly during the rest of the interview, giving quick yes and no answers to the clerk. There was only one time when Jessica saw them hesitate at the end of the interview, when the clerk gave them a form to sign. They both studied the paper and then talked quietly to one another. The woman turned, and Jessica could detect a look of deep concern on the woman's face as she directed her husband's attention to a paragraph on the sheet with her index finger. But after a few seconds, Jessica watched them both sign and return the forms to the clerk.

"Hold out your right wrists," the clerk said to both of them. Jessica leaned to the side trying to see what was happening, but the couple blocked her view. A moment later they both rose from their chairs and stood to leave. It was then that Jessica saw they were both wearing red bands around their wrists, the kind millions of people wore every day to show their support for different causes.

"Next person," the clerk said, looking toward Jessica and her family, as she ran her fingers through her short cropped blonde- and pink-streaked hair.

Jessica and Autumn took seats in front of the clerk's desk. Bill had to go grab a third chair from an empty table before joining the family. The clerk looked at them blankly and then began to read a prewritten statement. It was obvious that she had directions to read this to everyone who sat across the desk from her.

"Before we begin your individual security interview, I must warn you that it is a federal offense to provide false or fraudulent information during this inquiry. Do you understand?" the clerk asked.

Jessica, Bill, and Autumn all answered yes, but for the first time,

Bill glanced at Jessica with a look of hesitation on his face.

The clerk started with Autumn. Her questions were fairly innocent and basic. Name, address, date of birth, phone numbers including her cell phone and e-mail address. As Autumn answered, the clerk quickly typed onto her keyboard, never taking her eyes off her computer screen. It was evident she was filling in the blanks on some computer program. The only question she asked Autumn that caused both Jessica and Bill to look at one another, was, "What is your Facebook address?"

Autumn hesitated and looked at her mother, confused.

"If I wanted to visit your Facebook page, or friend you, sweetie," the clerk said, with a wisp of a smile, "what e-mail address would I use? Is it different from the one you gave me? Do you use any other e-mail address?" she asked, tilting her head, like she was speaking to a five-year-old.

Autumn quickly answered her. "My e-mail address, the one I gave you," she said softly, "it's the same as my Facebook address."

"See how simple that was?" the clerk said.

The clerk shifted her attention to Bill next, and her course of questions began exactly the same as those she had asked of Autumn. When asked his profession and where he worked, Bill happily shared that he was a professor at the local college.

"How nice, an educator," the clerk said, and for the first time since they had sat down, she actually seemed pleased. However, after the basics, including the Facebook information, the clerk's tone took a much more invasive tone. The first of these questions asked his political affiliation.

"I'm sorry, but what was the question?" he asked, leaning forward in his chair.

"I'm asking if you vote Democrat, Republican, or Independent," she said inserting a pause between each of her words.

"Oh, huh, well, I normally vote for who I feel is best for the job," he almost stuttered.

The clerk typed and then spoke without looking at him.

"So you're an Independent then," she said matter-of-factly, as she continued looking at her computer screen. Now the clerk paused and looked directly at Bill, her fingers poised at her keyboard. "Did you vote for the current president in the last election?"

Bill thought a moment before slowly answering, "Yes, yes I did."

"So, does that earn us a discount on our federal taxes?" Jessica asked sarcastically, her arms folded disapprovingly.

The clerk ignored her sarcasm and continued tapping away at her keyboard.

"Do you own any guns, and, if so, what type and caliber? I also need to know where you keep them in your house," the clerk said, again making eye contact with Bill.

"No," Bill answered truthfully, but almost cowering like a child caught with his hand in the cookie jar. "We don't own any weapons."

"Are you aware of anyone who might be a threat to our government or might oppose the laws and/or policies being enacted by our administration? If so, what are their names and addresses?" she continued.

This time, Bill only shook his head without speaking.

Suddenly, the clerk pushed herself out of her chair, and walked toward a table about twenty feet behind her, where a printer had suddenly come to life.

Jessica reached over Autumn's lap to grab her husband's coat sleeve and pull him toward her.

"What the hell is going on here, Bill?" she whispered, while keeping an eye on the clerk who stood, retrieving pages being spit out of the printer. "Whose business is it how we voted? If we own guns? Are they seriously asking us to rat out potential troublemakers?" she added.

"It's okay, Jessica," he said softly back to her. "They really aren't asking that much. I'm sure if I was buying a gun I'd have to provide the same information or more."

He suddenly leaned away from her and raised his eyes back to the front. Jessica looked left and, as she suspected from her husband's reaction, the clerk was returning with a sheet of paper in her hand.

She flopped back into her chair and rolled up to her desk. She turned the piece of paper around so that Bill could read the form. It was an official document written on government stationary.

The clerk pushed it toward Bill while reaching for a pen attached to her desk by a small chain.

"By signing this document, you agree that all information you've given today is true and accurate. You also pledge allegiance to President Barakat," the clerk said in a monotone voice. "You understand that providing false information or violating your promise of loyalty to the government could result in your arrest under the National Security Act."

Bill had already picked up the pen to sign, but the clerk's next sentence caused him to pause and look up from the form.

"You further agree by signing this document," the clerk continued, "that you pledge allegiance to President for Life Marcus Barakat and acknowledge the legitimacy of his office and his authority."

Bill looked at Jessica in shock, still holding the chain-anchored pen in disbelief.

The government worker sat silently, staring at Bill and waiting. After what seemed like forever but was only a few minutes, Bill slowly scrawled his name across a spot on the document beside an X mark and above his typed name.

He dropped the pen as if he had just committed a crime. The clerk tossed the form into a basket beside her desk and turned her attention to Jessica.

Like her husband, the same questions were directed at her. Jessica sat, arms folded, glaring at the clerk. She responded quickly and curtly to each question.

"I'm an Independent," Jessica said when asked, "and my husband already told you we don't own any guns, so why are you asking the same question of me?"

The clerk huffed and glared back at her. "I'm not speaking to your husband now, am I?" she said. "I'm asking *you* these questions."

Jessica bristled at the tone of the clerk's voice. When Jessica was asked if she knew of anyone who might be a threat to the government, her response was quick and cold.

"You are really asking me if I want to snitch on anyone who might be an enemy of the state, right?" Jessica spat out.

"What's your answer, yes or no?" the clerk responded, not backing down.

"My answer is no," Jessica replied, smirking.

The clerk deliberately punched a key on her computer, loud

enough for Jessica to hear, then stood up without a word and walked to the printer. She retrieved the same document and placed it on the desk before Jessica. Jessica realized this was the same document that had been presented to Bill just minutes before. When she laid the document down before Jessica and repeated the same dialogue about her pledging allegiance to the president, Jessica sat back in her chair, unfolded her arms and crossed her legs, placing her clasped hands over her knee.

"So what happens if I refuse to sign?" Jessica asked coldly.

A grimace came over the clerk's face and her shoulders slumped, but Jessica knew that she was reaching under her desk for an unseen button that would summon an NSF agent, exactly like what happened when the couple before them challenged the clerk.

"Don't worry about calling for help," Jessica blurted out cheerfully and reached out to sign the form with a flourish. "I was just asking."

The clerk studied her for a moment before sitting up in her chair and reaching into a large plastic storage bucket by her desk. She had grabbed a pink plastic bracelet. Jessica watched as the clerk plugged it into a device resembling a smart phone that was tethered to her computer by a long, curly cable. The clerk punched a few buttons on her computer keyboard, unhooked the bracelet, and turned back to them.

"Let me have your right hand, sweetie," the clerk said motioning toward Autumn's hand. Autumn obeyed hesitantly, letting the woman place the pink plastic piece around her arm. Jessica watched carefully, realizing that one end of the bracelet held a USB connection. With a snapping sound, the clerk released Autumn's hand and sat back in her chair as Autumn examined the data device she now wore.

"You have to wear this bracelet at all times," the clerk said, "I mean 24/7."

"What about bathing or swimming?" Jessica questioned loudly, as she pulled Autumn's wrist over to examine what the clerk had just placed on her.

The clerk turned to face Jessica, and replied coldly, "You wear them 24/7. They are waterproof, so you don't have to be concerned about getting them wet. What you need to be concerned with is being caught without a bracelet on your arm," the clerk said, with a tone of threat in her voice.

She turned, and repeated the same process on Bill, but Bill's bracelet was green. "If any government official or the police ask to see your bracelet, you are required to show it to them," the clerk stated. "If you're caught without your bracelet on, you can be arrested and charged with violating . . . "

Jessica loudly interrupted her sentence.

"Let me guess. Violating the National Security Act," Jessica said mockingly.

"You are absolutely correct," the clerk sneered at her.

The clerk went back to working with the small programming device. When she turned back to face Jessica, she held a bright yellow bracelet, and, without asking, simply motioned for Jessica to offer up her wrist.

Jessica obliged the clerk with no protest. After it was secured on her wrist, Jessica began hamming up her new hardware.

"Why look, Bill," she said, holding her hand toward him, her fingers pointing downward at the wrist. "Isn't it lovely? It goes with my eyes."

Bill sat quietly watching his wife as she hammed it up. Jessica suddenly stood and looked down at the clerk.

"Are we finished here . . . Jody," Jessica asked, turning her head to the side, so she could read the name on the woman's government-issued ID badge.

"We are for now," the clerk replied ominously.

Before Jessica could make another comment, Bill came up and began pushing her toward the door, as Autumn followed behind.

Not another word was said until they sat in the family minivan and were pulling out of the parking lot past the line of guards and military vehicles.

Bill was the first to speak, as he turned and looked grimly toward Jessica.

"What were you thinking, stirring up trouble back there, Jessica?" he asked, with a tone of anger in his voice. "Why can't you realize that the government is just trying to protect us from trouble and enemies during this time of emergency?"

Jessica slowly turned to glare at her husband before raising her right hand and shaking her yellow data bracelet in his face.

"Remind me, Professor Green Band, just who the government thinks the enemy is?" she shouted.

Chapter 10

Brigadier General William Thompson didn't like the man, and he sure as hell didn't like the situation. Being a career air force officer with over forty-five years in the military, the government still never ceased to amaze him with their stunts. Since the emergency was declared, Thompson had been busy enough commanding a nuclear airbase on high alert. Whiteman Air Force Base, home to the 509th Bomb Wing, was a sprawling facility sitting near the small country town of Knob Noster, Missouri. Whiteman, located just seventy miles east of Kansas City, sat smack in the middle of cow country.

At the height of the Cold War, Whiteman controlled enough nuclear intercontinental ballistic missiles and B-52 bombers to blow the Soviet Union into the Stone Age. The missiles were mostly gone now. The days of two air force officers sitting in a hardened silo underground waiting to turn the keys to begin World War III had been replaced by a more effective way of delivering the H-bomb. Now Whiteman was home to squadrons of B-2 Stealth bombers, the radar-invisible aircraft that could hit any target in the world, as had been proven over Serbia.

A few minutes earlier, General Thompson's aide, Captain Chris Monarch, an Air Force Academy graduate like himself, had come into his office obviously flustered.

"We have a visitor, General," the Captain said, nodding his head back over his left shoulder in the direction of his waiting area. "He's from high up and totally unexpected."

General Thompson had been staring at the computer screen of his laptop, a sober look on his face, his mind occupied in deep thought. General Thompson clicked a button on his keyboard and then shut the cover of his laptop. "No heads up at all, Captain?" he asked.

"Nothing, General. I'd ask if you want to see him at another time but he carries orders that don't give you that choice," the captain said, crossing his arms.

Thompson sat back in his chair and thought a moment. "What is Washington up to now?" he whispered to himself. "Show him in, Captain . . . but stay in the room. I want a witness to whatever boondoggle we're about to experience."

A few moments later, Captain Monarch pushed the door open and motioned behind him for the general's unannounced visitor.

General Thompson disliked the man the second he stepped through the door. After a career in the military, beginning with flying F-4 Phantoms on strike missions over North Vietnam in 1967, it only took Thompson a second to size up a man. One look at his pudgy body stuffed into a too-small, pinstriped suit, General Thompson knew the man squeezing past Captain Monarch had never seen a day of boot camp or walked a sentry post with a rifle.

The man stepped up to the general's desk and handed him a stack of folded papers without making an offer of a handshake. Thompson took the documents in one hand while staring with obvious displeasure at what little gray hair the man had pulled into a ponytail behind the rest of his bald head. With a huff, the man sat down uninvited and dropped his messenger bag on the floor beside him.

"General Thompson," the man said, folding his hands over his bulging stomach, "my name is Peter Anchors, and I am the new attaché between this military base and Washington. Until the president deems my services are needed elsewhere, I'm assigned here full-time."

General Thompson quickly made eye contact with Captain Monarch before looking back at Anchors.

"Since when does the Pentagon think we need an attaché, Mr. Anchors?" the general asked, staring directly at the pudgy man.

"It's not the Pentagon's decision, General," the man said, squirming deeper into his chair. "The president has decided that having an onsite person will keep him in the loop, so to say, on what's happening at his military installations."

General Thompson chuckled softly. "Since when did the president get the idea that military installations belong to him, Mr. Anchors? What's wrong with the system of chain-of-command we've been using for years?"

Anchors looked from the general to where Captain Monarch stood at parade rest with surprise on his face. He stumbled a moment for words before answering.

"President Barakat feels that, considering the emergency facing this country, he would like tighter control, just until things quiet down," Anchors said, straightening his bright red tie.

General Thompson pushed his chair forward and leaned across his desk to loom over his visitor. Peter Anchors, obviously intimidated by the general's posture, seemed to wish himself farther back into his seat.

"So tell me, Mr. Anchors, just when is this emergency going to end? We are still a little surprised how a cyber attack has the country shut down for this long. Please explain exactly what your role will be here at Whiteman Air Force Base."

Anchors sat up straighter in his chair to address the general. "From now on, General," he continued, "I'll be sitting in on all of your meetings, and you will run all orders by me first."

A wrinkle crossed over General Thompson's brow as he frowned at Anchors. "What military school did you graduate from?" General Thompson asked with sarcasm in his voice, as he reached into his pocket and withdrew a thick cigar.

"I don't have any formal military training, General Thompson," Peter Anchors replied, acting a little nervous. "My role isn't as a military advisor, sir. It's simply as a communication advisor for the president."

For several moments the two sat staring at each other in silence. General Thompson twirled his cigar between his fingers and then suddenly broke out in a huge grin as he stood up from his desk.

"Captain Monarch, get Lieutenant Branson in here. Have the lieutenant see to it that Mr. Anchors gets settled comfortably in one of our bachelor officer apartments."

General Thompson continued smiling as he came around the desk and extended his hand out to Anchors. The chubby man recoiled as if he was about to be slapped but then relaxed and took the general's hand firmly. General Thompson didn't release his grip but instead pulled Peter Anchors up to his feet.

"Glad to have you on board, Mr. Anchors," General Thompson said, turning him gently toward the door. "Captain Monarch is going to assign Lieutenant Branson as your personal aide to make sure all of your needs are met. First thing tomorrow, we'll get you a car and driver to help get you around while you're here. We don't have much going on right now other than maintaining our alert status, but we do have a staff meeting the day after tomorrow that I am sure you will want to attend."

Peter Anchors gave the general a slight smile as he began to follow Captain Monarch out of the office. "Thank you, General. The president and I both appreciate your cooperation."

"No problem, Mr. Anchors," General Thompson said, his hand on the knob of the door. "We're glad to help. Captain Monarch, if Mr. Anchors feels up to it, why don't you have Lieutenant Branson give him a quick tour of the base, then come back by and pick up my dirty laundry."

"Yes, sir, General," Captain Monarch said, his eyes holding contact with General Thompson for a few seconds before the general gave him a wink, unseen by Peter Anchors.

Captain Monarch nodded and walked out of the office. "Follow me please, Mr. Anchors, and let's get you settled in."

The General returned to his desk and opened his laptop again. He was busily studying the screen when Captain Monarch returned and stood rigidly inside the general's office in his impeccable uniform and buzzed hair cut.

"Have you seen this video, Chris?" the General asked, using his first name, without describing what he was even watching.

"I believe just about everyone has by now, General," Captain Monarch replied. "All the men have been talking about it."

General Thompson leaned back in his chair, his mind deep in thought, before closing his laptop with a snap and turning his attention back to his aide.

"Captain Monarch, you make sure that Lieutenant Branson sits on this spy and doesn't let him go wandering off by himself. Then I want a staff meeting called, and I want everyone, I mean everyone, to attend, even if you have to drag them here on their day off."

"Understood, sir," the captain replied.

"And, Captain Monarch . . . make sure this cheap spook the president just sent to report on us doesn't get wind of our meeting."

"Consider it done, General," Captain Monarch answered, turning on a heel toward the door. Just before he could leave, General Thompson stopped him.

"His arrival wasn't totally a surprise, Captain," the general said.

A few hours later, in a dark, windowless meeting room, several dozen air force officers, a mixed group of males and females, waited. Most were in uniform, a few still wore their civilian clothing.

"ATEN-HUT," Captain Monarch yelled, entering the room closely followed by General Thompson. The officers jumped out of their seats to stand at attention.

"At ease," the general said to the assembled officers, stepping up to stand in front of a large projection screen.

"Ladies and gentlemen, sorry to summon you here on short notice. This serious situation requires our immediate attention." The general stepped to the side and took a seat. "Start it, Captain," he said to his aide, who pointed a remote toward the screen and then took a seat himself.

The lights in the room dimmed as a video image appeared on the screen showing two yellow CAT backhoes busily lifting dirt in their shovels. The image was obviously shot from someone lying in a prone position. Brush fluttered by in front of the camera lens, impressing upon the viewer that the individual operating the camera was hiding.

Every officer in the room sat silently as the film rolled, first with the school buses coming into the scene and then the mass shooting. The gunfire echoed in the confined meeting room. There was a mixed response from the officers watching the killing. Some cursed, some moaned, and a few wept. Then Press Secretary Donna Koontz stood lecturing the survivors. The camera zoomed in on her bright red lips as she talked. It was obvious the cameraman was using professional equipment because, even from a distance, Koontz's voice could be clearly heard.

The video ended almost as it had begun, with the backhoes pushing dirt into the killing field ditch. The screen suddenly went blank, and the lights came back on.

General Thompson stood up and began to pace in front of the screen. He looked across the room, making sure that he made eye contact with everyone in the room. He then began tapping his index finger loudly on the table top, almost making the room jump.

"This is wrong, people," the general shouted, a grim look of seriousness upon his face. "I knew some of the people in this video who were murdered . . . you knew some of the people in this video who were murdered. I've served this country for a long time, but never, *never* in my wildest dreams did I ever think a day would come when we would be killing our own government leaders and imposing a police state on our own people."

Several officers murmured among themselves as the general began to circle the room. As he moved, the officers turned in their chairs to follow him.

"You've seen the video, now I want your comments and questions. We need to brainstorm on this, people. I want all of your thoughts. You guys know me. No matter what you say, you won't hurt my feelings."

The general's comments brought a laugh from his assembled officers, but seriousness quickly returned as the general's subordinates began to vocalize their thoughts. One asked if the video had been fabricated or Photoshopped in some manner. There was quickly a chorus of harsh responses.

"Knock it off," General Thompson shouted, "I said that I wanted everyone's thoughts on this."

After several minutes of discussion, the group unanimously agreed that the video was authentic. There were sidebars about who shot the video and how the government was responding.

A slim, dark-haired female officer stood and took the floor. "Washington isn't saying anything about the video," she said firmly, looking around the table. "The major news networks have been the only ones to make comments and they, like some here questioned, are claiming the video is fake. The foreign press, however, especially the Chinese, are all over this. They are calling it the overthrow of the United States."

She paused a moment and, with a sheepish look toward General Thompson, ended by saying, "My brother works in Hong Kong, and I've been getting information from him."

"Thank you, Major," the General said with a smile, as the woman sat back down. "Yesterday, the president sent an agent to *our* airbase to spy on us," the general said, raising his voice and putting an emphasis on "our." This is exactly how Soviet Russia was for over fifty years and Cuba, North Korea, and China are today. The difference here is that this spy isn't being called a political officer, but trust me people, his mission is the same. The president wants to make sure all of us are marching in lockstep with his agenda to the United States."

Reaching his position back at the head of the table, the general paused to gauge the expressions on the faces of his officers.

"I've been in touch with my contacts on the East Coast who tell me there are prison ships sitting in the harbor filled with U.S. citizens the government deems are a danger to the nation. *Habeas corpus* has been put in the shitter on this one. People are being arrested and imprisoned without charges, no opportunity to see a judge or even bond out. What are you going to do when this happens to you or to someone you care about? I remind you that our new base spy isn't here to be your friend. He's here to weed out anyone who shows any sign of dissent."

"What I'm going to ask of you is extreme, people. Some of you won't like it, and I respect that. However, we here at Whiteman hold all the aces, ladies and gentlemen. We here at Whiteman are able to stop what is going on and keep our own citizens from being murdered. This plan will only work if there is cooperation from everyone here. Captain Monarch is going to present my plan to all of you. When he's finished, you're either with us or you're not. If you are, I can assure you, we are going into harm's way. If you're not, like I said at the beginning of this meeting, I can respect that."

The general sat down in his chair as Captain Monarch pointed the remote control toward the screen where a PowerPoint presentation began. The first screen simply read "OPERATION RECOVERY."

Chapter 11

Maggie was thankful she had left her house earlier than usual for work. In the past few weeks she had learned the hard way that simply leaving for the office wasn't like it was in the past. Nowadays, she never knew how many security checkpoints might be set up between her apartment and her work at the Washington Post. Sometimes it was the city police or the army, but often it was the stern, no-nonsense National Security Force. These guys were the ones who frightened Maggie the most, especially after she had watched them beat a man into a coma at her subway entrance one morning. Once she was stopped at the checkpoint, God only knew when she would get waved on. Always the same questions, where are you coming from, where are you going, what's your business, and if they demanded her identification data bracelet to connect into their little mobile reading devices, she could be delayed an easy twenty minutes or more. As her thoughts wandered back to the present, Maggie looked down and found herself unconsciously twisting the black rubber data bracelet on her wrist.

The front of her office building remained surrounded by concrete barricades and armed troops, just like it had been since the night she watched her news colleague gunned down in the middle of a press conference.

As Maggie started to enter the building, she instinctively began to remove her data band. Then she heard a voice call to her. "That's all right, Ms. Kerr," the army corporal said, shouldering his rifle and waving her forward. "I know you belong here."

She gave him a nervous smile and slipped into the revolving door. She still couldn't get used to the huge portrait of President Barakat that had been hung in the lobby of the building. It always creeped her out because no matter where she was in the lobby, the eyes seemed to follow her. As she entered her cubicle, the first thing she spotted taped to her computer screen was a Post-it note from her editor, John

Stewart. "Maggie, come see me ASAP," the note said.

Shoving her purse into a desk drawer and setting her laptop case under her desk, Maggie strolled down the hall to John's office. She stuck her head in the open door and rapped on the frame with her fingers. John Stewart sat at his desk making notes, but when he saw Maggie he sat up with a smile and smoothed his lavender-colored tie. He called it his "Smurf" tie, even though it wasn't blue.

"Close the door, please, Maggie," Stewart said, half rising and looking past her, as if checking to see if she had been followed. She did as asked and then took a seat in front of his desk crossing her long legs.

"What's up, John?" Maggie asked, leaning forward in her chair.

John glanced at her, then looked past her toward the newsroom, his face a serious mask. "We've been summoned to a meeting," he said, finally pulling his attention back to her. "They're questioning everyone in the media about," he paused and lowered his voice, "the video that hit the Internet. I know you've seen it or heard about it."

Maggie nodded without responding. The grisly images flashed through her mind as she crossed her arms, hugging herself.

"So tell me, we're meeting with our government-appointed 'media editor?'" she said, meaning the official that had shown up on their doorstep the morning after the emergency had been declared. Ms. Lee, a short oriental woman, had taken up residence in an empty office. While a runt of a woman, Ms. Lee carried great authority and had explained to the entire staff on day one that no news story, editorial column, or obituary got published that wasn't reviewed by her first. Maggie and her colleagues learned quickly what Ms. Lee's exact role was, after something they had written was e-mailed back to them, completely edited and nothing like the original. Her edits were not for grammar or spelling; rather, they reoriented the articles to praise President Barakat's administration and give it credit for anything good that had happened. However, if the story shed negative light on the government, then the finger of blame was pointed at an external enemy, now regularly identified as right-wing extremists.

John Stewart rose from his chair and motioned Maggie to join him. He placed a hand on her shoulder as he reached for the doorknob and leaned in to whisper in her ear. "There are some serious people here today, Maggie, not just Ms. Lee. These guys are headhunters, and I would hate to be their prey."

Maggie nodded without speaking, as she and her boss walked across the newsroom floor and into the staff meeting room. The room was already full of the paper's staff when they arrived, but this meeting did not have the feeling of fun, as they did in the past. None of the men and women sitting in chairs facing the front wall of the room chatted with one another, shared jokes, or laughed. They all sat silently like children being sent to the principal's office for the first time.

Maggie and John took seats at the rear of the room. Only then did Maggie notice the man standing just inside the door.

"Is this everyone?" he asked flatly, looking at John Stewart. John replied that it was, and the dark suited man pushed the door shut and strode to the front of the room.

For a second he scanned the room looking from face to face. When his eyes made their way toward Maggie, she quickly looked downward, as if afraid he might steal her soul.

When the man spoke, his voice boomed, and several people in the room jumped in their seats. He stood, arms folded, and, unlike speakers Maggie had seen in the past, he didn't pace or motion with his hands or show a hint of a smile.

"I'm Mr. Wall, and I'm an investigator with the National Security Organization. Recently, it has come to our attention that fake video clips have been made and shown up all over the Internet. These fake video clips are very damaging to the government. I am sure you are aware of these video clips," Mr. Wall said, and again scanned the room with probing eyes. No one spoke or replied. Maggie thought she had never heard a room of people so silent.

The man continued. "We believe that our suspect has skill with video editing and the software necessary to fabricate such an atrocity and then try to blame it on the government."

Maggie glanced at Mr. Stewart, who continued to stare straight ahead.

"Suspect," Maggie thought to herself. For some reason, the word suspect, or maybe the way the man said it, made the hair stand up on the nape of her neck.

"We also think this criminal has connections with the media here in the Washington area," Mr. Wall continued, still standing, with his arms crossed. "So as loyal citizens, it is your duty to immediately report anyone you think is capable of committing this crime. We want names and we want them ASAP. You will call the hotline number and share your information with us."

"Who doesn't know the hotline number by now?" Maggie thought to herself. All over Washington, billboards had gone up urging the reader to report any suspect or activity resembling dissension. Then in huge letters, the phone number: "1-800-SAFE-USA." The same message followed every newscast. One of the local meteorologists that Maggie always enjoyed on the evening news, had for years always ended his segment by saying: "Watch your kids . . . around water." However, his final words had changed, along with the lighthearted way he had read his weather report. Now at the conclusion of his report, he looked seriously into the eye of the camera and said: "Report any suspicious or anti-government activity by calling 1-800-SAFE-USA."

"That concludes this meeting," Mr. Wall stated. "Everyone is dismissed, except for those who work in the photography or photo editing departments." Several people Maggie knew as staff photographers looked nervously at one another as she stood up and, along with her boss, joined the others filing out of the room.

Chapter 12

Captain Shade Ashman wasn't sure what to say as she stood in the small, dark mop and broom closet with officer Bob Sportsman. He leaned his tall, thin frame against the wall, holding a cardboard box full of his personal belongings. Shade had worked with the man for years and knew him as a tough-but-fair supervisor. Now he stood, shoulders hanging down in defeat, whispering to Shade.

"Why are they firing you, Bob? What explanation did they give you?" Shade asked. Sergeant Sportsman raised his head and shrugged his shoulders. "Guess I answered the questions incorrectly," he said, holding out his forearm toward Shade. She reached out, taking his hand and pulling it closer. Shaking her head back and forth, Shade studied the bright red data bracelet that he wore.

She knew what he was saying. Just a week before, she had been called into a meeting in an interrogation room with a field clerk from the National Security Force. The man asked her several questions before placing a band on her wrist. However, according to the clerk, because of her position within the police department, her bracelet was a different color from the others she had seen. Shade's bracelet was bright white. Sergeant Sportsman's bracelet was red and other civilians' bracelets were yellow, green, red, or black. The high-strung, long-haired clerk had also explained, in long-winded technical jargon, that her bracelet contained a GPS tracking device. When Shade asked why, the clerk's response was, "So you can be found if someone kidnaps you or if you get hurt somewhere."

"Why would I be kidnapped or hurt?" Shade asked him inquisitively, "I work at headquarters; I don't hump the streets anymore."

"Haven't you heard? There are many ultra-conservative crazies out there blowing up stuff and killing people," he said to her, like she had just emerged from a cave.

"So what now, Bob? Where are you going from here?" Shade

asked, concerned.

"Not sure. Maybe I can flip burgers at McDonald's. The NFS agent who just gave me my walking papers made it very clear that I was banned from any law enforcement or security position," Sergeant Sportsman said, flexing his jaw in anger.

Shade stepped closer and, reaching around his box of things, hugged him. "Good luck, Bob," she said.

He turned and walked down the hallway, then suddenly stopped and turned back. He shouted down the hall at Shade, and the twenty or so uniformed officers that were nearby also heard him loud and clear. "This is wrong, guys. It's wrong, and we all know it!" Sergeant Sportsman walked a little further and kept saying, "This is wrong." Shade watched him walk down the hallway and out a door with a large emergency exit sign over it.

The normal sound of activity in the emergency dispatch center had lowered around her, and Shade turned and realized all the officers were looking at her in silence.

Shade turned and squared off with the room. "Get to work, people," she snapped. "Unless you want to be carrying your own cardboard box to your car." Everyone immediately dropped their heads and returned their attention to their computer screens. The sound level began to rise as Shade walked toward her office.

Normally she left her door open in case one of her dispatch staff needed to quickly ask her a question; but not today. Pushing the door shut, she sat back in her office chair and turned to her computer. She Googled "white supremacy," which brought up a list of hate groups. Shade didn't give a crap about white supremacy, but she also knew the NSF agent assigned to her department could show up at any second. If he barged into her office uninvited and surprised her, Shade could tell him she was doing research on subversive groups the government attacked in the media every day. She just wanted to learn more about the enemy so she could properly train her team in the communications center. Yes, that would be a reply that would work, Shade thought.

Shade pulled her cell phone out and speed-dialed a number. As she listened to the ringing, she glanced out the glass pane beside the door to make sure no one was coming. The line clicked, and she heard her brother's voice answer.

"What's up, Shade?" her brother asked automatically.

"Hey, big brother. I need to get with you tonight. You still have my wine bottle opener. You never gave it back. I'm not going to lend you anything again if you don't have enough manners to return it. Next time buy your own bottle opener and get your own corks out." Shade scolded him.

Charlie Ashman hesitated a moment before answering. It took him a minute to realize Shade was using their special code, the one developed for speaking over a phone that could possibly be bugged. She would call him with some feeble request to get together in a place far away from where either lived. The week before, she wanted him to look at her tires to see if he thought the tread was coming off. They had met in the parking lot of a Firestone tire store, where she had slipped him information about a pending neighborhood lock-down and search the NFS was about to conduct. Charlie had been uploading clandestine video footage to the Internet since the crackdown across the nation had began. It was Shade who had alerted Charlie late one night that the senators and members of congress were going to be rounded up the next morning. Even then, Shade didn't know the particulars until her shaking brother showed up on her doorstep later that day.

Fortunately, due to her position as a command officer in the communications division, Shade was privy to operations being conducted in conjunction with her police force and the NSF. Shade was also very aware that she had to use extreme caution. She and Charlie had developed specific security measures to hopefully keep both of them from being arrested and marched in front of a firing squad.

"Stop busting my balls, Shade," Charlie responded. "Meet me at Pizza Hut by the old skating rink after work, and I'll return your stupid bottle opener. I will even buy you dinner to make up for keeping it."

Shade stood up from her desk and walked over to open the door of her office. "Sounds great, Bro. See you then," she replied. Shade snapped her phone closed and walked out into the communications area to see what additional information she might gain before her meeting with Charlie.

Chapter 13

Moshe Kravitz sat at the large, oak meeting table, engrossed in taking notes. A paper folder sat beside him full of documents and photographs. The word "CLASSIFIED" was stamped across the top of it in bright red letters. As leader of Israel's famous Institute for Intelligence and Special Operations, more popularly known as the Mossad, his job was to keep its leaders notified of events both harmful or beneficial to the nation of Israel. More often, he found himself meeting daily with the prime minister as events unfolded in the United States, Israel's biggest ally.

Despite a crackdown on every form of communication by the United States, news still poured out. Moshe had been awakened by one of his staff at four o'clock in the morning to tell him of the emergency and crippling attack upon the United States. Moshe had risen and gone immediately to his office, where he watched the U.S. broadcast report.

The same stories were being repeated on American news stations, such as CNN and ABC, as well as the foreign news stations, like the BBC and even Al Jazeera. According to media reports, a cyber attack of unequaled proportions had struck America. A new, unknown press secretary, Donna Koontz, had appeared leading an official White House televised address. She was comparing the attack to the same terrorist strike of 9/11 and added that martial law had been ordered by President Barakat for the safety of the nation. When Koontz said the White House suspected Chinese involvement in a conspiracy with members of its own government, Moshe had sat forward, concentrating on every word coming from Koontz's bright red lips. It didn't take an intelligence expert to notice that there were no murmuring voices coming from her unseen audience. Nor were there the constant questions from the news staff, even after Koontz had added "home grown, right wing terrorists" to the list of suspects.

Something about the timing of the event and the imposition of martial law made Moshe skeptical when he saw the first broadcast.

The appearance of a new press secretary also raised his senses. He made a mental note to find out first thing in the morning what had happened to the old press officer.

His suspicions were rewarded hours later when he spoke with the Israeli ambassador to the United States in the Washington consulate. During the conversation with the ambassador, which was scrambled for privacy and security, he was told that employees, including the ambassador himself, had observed U.S. troops moving into the city long before the phones went dead, power clicked off in some areas, and the Internet went offline. Shortly after, a secret message was relayed to the ambassador from a mole within the U.S. government, that something was happening.

The opening of the door caught his attention and Moshe rose to shake hands with the prime minister. In tow behind him were a staff of aides and military officers.

"How are you, Major?" Prime Minister Ben-David asked, taking Moshe's hand firmly in his. Ben-David still used Moshe's rank to address him from years before when they had first served together in the Israeli Defense Force. Prime Minister Ben-David had commanded an armored unit, and Moshe was an officer with the Israeli paratroopers.

As Ben-David released his iron-like grip on Moshe's hand, both men sat beside one another as the staff took seats across the table from them. Moshe knew that everyone was listening quietly, but he kept his eyes on the prime minister and spoke directly to him.

"Our intelligence reports tell us that President Barakat is clamping down on the American people with an iron fist. There are stories being released daily that U.S. citizens are being held in specially created prison ships, docked in every major harbor. Detention camps are being built everywhere the government feels there might be trouble or opposition. One of our agents confirmed prison trains being used nationwide." As he ended his sentence, Moshe opened the packet of documents beside him and slid some photographs toward the prime minister. Ben-David studied each one individually, before handing them back to Moshe.

Moshe cleared his throat and continued. "The mass killing video of the members of congress and senators has, for all intent and purposes, been substantiated, Mr. Prime Minister," Moshe said, pausing for the words to sink in.

"How do we know this video isn't a fake? That is what the American government is suggesting," the prime minister said. "Computers can do some amazing stuff, good and bad, in the right hands."

Moshe was prepared to be questioned about the authenticity of the video. He handed the prime minister another piece of paper. "These are the names of every congressman and senator who has gone missing. President Barakat has replaced these people with hand-picked individuals of his own choosing. These people listed here have vanished off the face of the planet, and either their families have vanished with them or the ones still in their homes are not talking. Nobody seems to know where the families have gone, and all their houses have a blacked-out van sitting on the street."

"They are being watched, I assume?" said the prime minister, raising an eyebrow.

"Yes, sir."

The prime minister rubbed his chin and studied the list a minute before addressing Moshe again. "While it seems that President Barakat is operating out of the Joseph Stalin playbook, this is all an internal matter. How does any of this concern Israel?"

"First, Mr. Ben-David," Moshe said, "the U.S. is pulling troops out of Iraq and Afghanistan as quickly as they can and moving those troops into military police duties in its own cities. The US presence at every military base abroad, including Germany, Turkey, and South Korea is also being lowered to a minimum."

The prime minister raised a hand, interrupting him. "Again, Major, how does this affect the security of Israel?"

Moshe stood and walked to a corkboard wall at the head of the table. He quickly stabbed pushpins right and left until four pictures hung for all to see.

Pulling a red marker out of his pocket, Moshe began using it to point and circle on the photographs. The photos were obviously shot with a long-range camera lens, however, they showed several American transport aircraft. USAF stood out clearly on the side fuselage of each plane.

"These pictures are of the United States Air Force's Air Mobility Command cargo and trooper transport planes," Moshe said. Moshe was addressing everyone in the room, not just the prime minister, for the first time. "Our agents report C-5 Galaxy aircraft and other smaller transports loading troops and equipment. All of this activity, including the takeoff and landings, have occurred in the dead of night."

"Major Kravitz, I hate to ask again," the prime minister said, looking up at him, "what concern should Israel have that the United States is schlepping its troops around in the middle of the night or at anytime of day for that matter?"

Moshe raised his voice loudly and stabbed at the photographs with the marker in his hand.

"Because, Mr. Prime Minister, these photographs weren't taken at an American facility, and they aren't loading up U.S. troops. These photographs were taken at the El Jazeba airbase near Tehran. The U.S. is loading up *Iranian* troops, mostly members of the Iranian Revolutionary Guards, and flying them to the United States. We've been following them, and the first wave just met their midair refueling aircraft over the Pacific Ocean. They will be in the states late tomorrow."

For a moment, there was complete silence in the room. Prime Minister Ben-David's face paled.

"Are you absolutely sure of this, Major?" Ben-David asked, swiftly rising from his chair.

Moshe looked at him with a sad expression. "I'm afraid I am, Mr. Prime Minister. It appears the American President has made a deal with Iran to help him with his takeover of the United States. My fear, Mr. Prime Minister, is what President Barakat has promised the Iranian government in return."

The prime minister turned to his aide, an attractive, slim dark-haired woman, who had been sitting across the table from him, scribbling notes. "Ms. Cohen, I want to call an emergency meeting of the Knesset." He then turned to an army general who snapped to attention. "Have our troops put on alert, and be prepared to activate our reserve forces on a moment's notice." The general saluted, and, turning on his heel, marched out of the room with an aide following him. Prime Minister Ben-David turned to Moshe. "Keep up your work, Major. We must know what President Barakat and Iran have planned."

Chapter 14

Captain Roscoe "Rocky" Tyson was barking orders at his flight crew as they began to safely maneuver their C-5 Galaxy transport plane away from the refueling aircraft that had just topped off their tanks. High over the Pacific Ocean, Rocky held the yoke of the powerful aircraft in his gloved hands, while his copilot, First Lieutenant Janet Drace, communicated with the pilot of the refueling plane. She was coordinating a safe separation between the aircraft because everyone knew of the dangers involved.

The huge C-5, the largest transport aircraft in the United States Air Force, shuddered as the long refueling hose detached from their aircraft and then began to pull up, banking to the left and out of sight.

Rocky was sure the pilot of the tanker was veering off to feed another of the thirty transport planes in his formation. The captain did a quick systems check with Lieutenant Drace and his electronics officers and told his copilot to keep the plane on course while he stretched his legs. They had been up in the air for about ten hours already and Rocky's muscles were tightening up, but he also wanted to take another look in the cargo hold of the ship and assure himself he hadn't lost his mind.

Unhooking his seat harness, Rocky began making his way toward the rear of the cockpit. He put out his hands to steady himself as he squeezed by the three other seated crew members as the four-engine giant rocked sideways. Turning the handle of the door separating the cockpit from the top deck of the fuselage, he was immediately met by the unsmiling faces of his three loadmasters, including the crew chief, Master Sergeant Huppman. Rocky could feel their eyes burning a hole through him as he approached. They had apparently been having a heated conversation just before he came through the hatch.

"A moment of your time, Master Sergeant Huppman, if I may," Rocky yelled over the roar of the aircraft. "How about you two find something to do," Rocky said to the two other loadmasters, as they looked at him blankly.

"When you say something to do, I guess you mean babysitting those assholes in our aircraft," the taller of the two said, with venom in his voice.

Rocky turned on him in anger.

"As you were, Airman Rodriquez," Rocky yelled, reminding him of who was in charge.

Silently, Rodriquez and the second airman began to shuffle away. Rocky motioned for Master Sergeant Huppman to follow him, and led the way to a cramped area. It contained three bunks but offered the two men a little quiet and a degree of privacy.

Huppman, a career air force man, crossed his arms over his massive chest as he twirled one end of his non-regulation, handlebar mustache and eyed Rocky.

"You know, Cap'n, we've been together a long time, and the men are just asking the same thing we're all thinking. Permission to speak candidly, sir," Huppman asked.

Captain Tyson pulled his blue cloth hat off. He already knew what was coming.

"Go ahead, Master Sergeant Huppman, say what's on your mind." Rocky replied.

"Well, excuse me, Cap'n," Huppman said, jerking a thumb back over his shoulder. "Do I have security clearance to know why there are 300 armed Iranian Guard troops sitting in the rear of my aircraft?"

Captain Tyson glanced over his shoulder to where dozens of camouflaged troops armed with AK-47 assault rifles sat crowded in like sardines. He turned back to Huppman.

"Huppman, you don't have a high enough security status to even know that we were in Iranian airspace, let alone wheels down on the ground," Rocky told him soberly. "I can't say anything further. Just tell the men to follow orders, and don't ask any other questions, all right?"

Huppman stared at him silently, his body swaying with the motion of the aircraft, his hand around a web strap hanging from the ceiling. "Orders will be followed, Cap'n, just not sure why we're doing what we're doing," he said, snapping a salute toward Tyson and heading in the direction of where his other loadmasters had gone.

Rocky watched him walk away, and thought to himself that Huppman was speaking the truth. Rocky was following orders, but he was as much in the dark as his crew chief. The original orders were to fly back to Afghanistan, something they had done frequently, especially since the president had ordered all troops out of the Middle East. They had made the same trip so many times it was becoming routine. However, now things looked suspiciously different. It began when Rocky and the other transport pilots were called into a secure briefing in a nearby hanger. A ranking air force officer accompanied by a civilian who reeked of CIA laid out their mission orders. The pilots would be crossing into Iranian airspace, following a flight plan the unidentified civilian handed out to all the pilots.

There had been a chorus of murmurs around the room, and several hands had shot into the air. The civilian immediately waved them down.

"Unless your question has to do with the technical aspects of your flight plan, don't ask it," he ordered, looking around the room. "Fly your aircraft to point A. Pick up your cargo, then fly to point B. It's that simple. This is a 'need to know' only operation, so keep a short leash on your crews." With that, the air force colonel had resumed the briefing, warning the pilots not to be concerned when Iranian fighter aircraft intercepted them as they crossed into their country's airspace. The Iranian fighter aircraft would simply be escorting them, the Colonel said.

A few hours later, Rocky had found himself taxing the massive C-5 toward a set of hangers, away from the main complex and control tower of the airport. At least four trucks with 50-caliber machine guns mounted on the roofs and a squad of armed troops in the back had followed along beside his aircraft as he rolled to a stop on the tarmac. A soldier pointed his rifle at Rocky the entire time.

Rocky had ordered Lieutenant Drace to assemble the crew in the rear loading area of the plane as he shut down the four powerful jet engines. As his crew circled around him, Rocky kept it simple.

"Just do your jobs, people. Don't ask any questions, and don't speak to anyone coming aboard," he had ordered them.

A minute later, his crew had lowered the rear loading ramp and began the routine inspections they performed every time upon landing.

Fuel trucks pulled up beside the aircraft, and men jumped down and began stretching long black hoses toward the constellation.

The captain stood at the bottom of the ramp, arms crossed, as a thin man dressed in camouflage, limped toward the hanger. Reaching the rear of the aircraft, the man didn't salute or show any sign of emotion.

"I am Commander Farbod Hamidi," he said to Captain Tyson in broken English. "You will communicate only with me. Are you ready to begin?"

Rocky stared at the man a moment, noticing the nasty scar that ran across his face. Rocky didn't offer a verbal reply to the man but simply turned sideways and motioned toward the huge interior of the aircraft, as if he was a waiter showing someone their table.

The Iranian commander had turned, and raising a whistle from around his neck, blew it shrilly. Immediately, four columns of camouflaged soldiers, AK-47 rifles held close to their chest at port arms, had come double-timing from the rear of the hanger. They crossed the short space between the building and the C-5. Hamidi gave an order Rocky couldn't understand, and the troops began walking onto his aircraft.

Each crew member, including Master Sergeant Huppman, looked on silently as the lines of men boarded the aircraft. Some of the troops had flashed them angry looks but none had spoken.

Before re-boarding the aircraft, Rocky had pulled a stunned Huppman aside.

"Have your crew go around and make sure these Mexican bandits get squared away properly. We're taking off in fifteen minutes."

A voice brought him out of his thoughts. It was one of his flight engineers.

"You're needed up front, Captain," the younger man said. "Priority flash message coming in for you."

Rocky nodded and followed the airman back to the control center of the plane. He squeezed himself back into his seat and placed his headset over his ears.

"This is Captain Tyson," he said into his microphone.

Copilot Janet Drace, like the other crew members in the cockpit, wasn't privy to the conversation the captain was having on a private, secure channel, and she tried not to eavesdrop on what Rocky was saying. What she did hear was mostly "Yes, sir" and "No, sir" anyway. However, Drace had served with Captain Tyson for nearly two years, and she had learned that the furrowed brow he was displaying was a sign something was wrong.

She turned her attention back to piloting the huge C-5 Galaxy. She had confidence in Captain Tyson, but she didn't have confidence in whatever plan had sent them into Iran. As she looked out the windscreen of the C-5, she thought to herself that the entire operation stank.

Chapter 15

"Allahu Akbar, God be praised," Commander Farbod Hamidi thought to himself, as he sat in the uncomfortable web seat deep in the rear of the American aircraft. He had been reading the Koran, which he kept in the pocket of his shirt. Finally, God was opening up the path to victory over the infidels, he said to himself.

Hamidi had begun his journey into extremism as a teenager. Born near the capital city of Tehran, he was the eldest of six children. His father had taught at the university during the frightening reign of the shah, when the secret police arrested men and women without cause, other than suspicion that they opposed the government. These people were then subject to cruel torture in dark, cold interrogation cells: whippings, electric shock, and fingernails being pulled out. Most were executed. The lucky ones were just shot, without the pain and suffering that lead up to a bullet in the head.

His father knew better than to openly oppose the shah, but his opinions were well known within the family. Hamidi hung on every word his father said at the nightly dinners. Then the day came when Hamidi returned from running errands to be met by his tearful mother and the news that his father had been arrested at the university and hauled away by agents of the infamous SAVAK secret police. Hamidi and his brother had run to the police station, seeking answers, but no one knew anything. There was no record of his father being arrested anywhere.

Hamidi and his family would never see their father again or know the details of his fate. Ten days after he vanished, an envelope showed up on their front door step. It contained his father's wallet, glasses, and rings. Hamidi, as well as the rest of his family, knew the package brought the announcement that their father was dead.

While his family mourned, Hamidi grew angry. He began to join growing crowds of protesters who called for the downfall of the shah. The protests grew larger and more violent. One day, government troops, tanks, and aircraft fired into the crowds, killing over 4,000 people. Finally, claiming he was seeking treatment for cancer, the shah fled Iran with his family to the United States. Hamidi had prayed the cure for cancer would work and that the shah would return to Iran to face charges for the terror he had doled out on his own people. It was not to be. Instead, the people filled the streets led by the rhetoric of the recently returned religious leader Ayatollah Khomeini, and Hamidi was in the front ranks.

When protestors overran the US embassy in 1979, Hamidi was there helping to loot the buildings and capture the American staff inside. As the violent revolution spread and the shah's armories were emptied out, Hamidi joined the other armed militants, taking orders now from the ayatollah. He took part in revolutionary courts in which anyone associated with the shah or his regime were tried. The list was huge, including friends, family and army officers. The hearings and death sentences took less then two minutes. The ayatollah had ordered that death was the only verdict, and Hamidi was more than willing to follow the great religious leader's wishes.

Hamidi had been the member of many firing squads that shot down begging, crying prisoners. He graduated to leading the same execution squads. His blood ran cold even after the ayatollah had sealed his power on the country and decreed Islamic law upon the nation.

Through all the death and killing, Hamidi felt that he was avenging his father's death and serving Allah. He blindly followed the orders of the ayatollah, even forcing his mother and sisters to throw away their western clothing and return to wearing the long black body covering dress and hijab, or head covering.

When war broke out between Iran and Iraq, Hamidi was serving in the army. It was a bloody conflict with Iraq. Iran nearly lost the conflict, due to the fact the ayatollah had executed all the trained generals and other commanding officers. What Hamidi and his fellow troops lacked in military training they made up for in revolutionary zeal. Hamidi was so incompetent that he led thousands of young men like himself to death in mass attacks on the Iraqi military positions. Iraq was backed by the support of the United States. The Iraqi had good officers who knew how to lead, and lots of military equipment, including its deadly artillery. Hamidi found out the hard way early one morning when he and his troops were attacked in the swamps in southern Iran. The screaming elite Iranian Guard troops that Hamidi had been leading quickly bogged down in the wet mud and mire of the swamplands. Hamidi had slung his rifle over his back and was waving the red flag of the revolution over his head when he heard the whine of artillery coming in. The scene around Hamidi quickly became a nightmare of explosions, screaming, and death. He was fortunate to be one of the few to survive, but he did not come out of the conflict unscathed. Hamidi did not see or hear the high explosive round that hit fifty feet from him. The warhead had buried itself deep in the bottom of the swamp before exploding in a blinding eruption of mud and shrapnel. Hamidi had been blown through the air and landed like a rag doll in the cold water and mud.

When he awoke the next day, lying among hundreds of other wounded and dying in a fly infested field hospital, he learned the true extent of his injuries. Blood-soaked bandages covered the left side of his face where a razor-sharp piece of the bomb had carved a jagged, inch-wide laceration that ran from the top of his ear to the corner of his mouth. The violence of the explosion had also shattered his left leg, leaving him with a permanent limp.

Despite his injuries, Hamidi's revolutionary devotion never waned. He moved up to a position of leadership within the elite Revolutionary Guard. When the opportunity rose, he traveled to Lebanon, Syria, and Iraq to help fight the infidels and do Allah's work.

Now it seemed he could reap the rewards of his devotion to the Islamic cause. Hamidi wasn't a politician or a leader of his country, but, just weeks before, he had been invited to a secretive meeting in Tehran. There, it was laid out that Hamidi and other zealots like himself would travel to the "Great Satan," the United States, on request of President Marcus Barakat.

Barakat had requested the cooperation of the Iranian military to help him secure the iron grip he was attempting to establish upon his own people. Information gained by Iranian intelligence reported that perhaps Barakat had bitten off more than he could chew. His prisons were overflowing, thousands had suddenly gone missing on his orders, and now resistance groups were striking back across the country.

Emissaries had met in the strictest of secrecy, and President

Barakat had forwarded his proposal. If Iran would provide troops to help him police some areas outside the major cities, he could use his own military to pacify the major population areas. That offer alone, the opportunity to travel to the land of his enemies and subjugate the people he hated, would have been reward enough from Allah. When he had shared this news with his troops deep in the Iranian desert, his men had gone wild, chanting "ALLAHU AKBAR" and firing their weapons into the air.

Hamidi was delighted to see his men so happy as they danced or knelt in the sand to pray. It also made him sad that he couldn't share the greatest secret of all. In exchange for Iran's role, President Barakat pledged the support of the American military to assist Iran in capturing all of the Middle East. President Barakat was willing to provide everything from military aircraft, cruise missiles, tanks and ammo. He also promised the U.S. would turn a blind eye to Iran's aggressive actions when the time came.

Yes, once Iran held up its end of the bargain in the U.S., the U.S. would assist Iran in defeating and capturing all the Middle East, reestablishing the glory of the Persian Empire, and imposing Islamic law as Allah wished it to be.

Most important to Hamidi was that the road to victory would begin with Iran destroying the evil of all evils . . . the nation of Israel.

Chapter 16

The odor of blood, sweat, and fear filled the prison train car as the people inside swayed side-to-side, traveling down the tracks, an hour west of Denver. Until four days ago, Art Peter had been a patrol officer with the Sturgis police force in South Dakota. That was until a van caravan of NSF agents appeared early one morning and took over the station house. Every cop, dispatcher, and clerk were called in or hauled in against their will and questioned about recent attacks on government forces near Sturgis. Art, like the others in the station house knew about the attacks because news traveled fast, especially in the small, rural area of South Dakota. Strangely enough, Art's agency had received little official information about the attacks from the state or county law enforcement agencies other than to be on the watch for subversive activity.

The NSF agent in charge announced that the entire Sturgis Police Department was to be decommissioned and unarmed. Most of the officers, including Art, had protested loudly. They soon found themselves being disarmed and handcuffed at gunpoint. As Art sat in shock on the curb with the other officers, the chief of police argued with the leader of the NSF team. Without any notice, the NSF agent pulled his side arm out and shot the chief through the heart, dropping him on the sidewalk into a rapidly spreading pool of blood.

Art and the others had been roughly loaded onto school buses soon after and transported to the closest railroad tracks, where three large, odd-looking train cars sat behind a loudly idling engine. Ten black-clad NSF agents met them and led them into the rear car. Art glanced around where a dozen disheveled men and women sat, each with one arm handcuffed to a ring in the wall. Art and the other officers soon found themselves shackled with the group as the train began to move.

Three NSF agents were sitting on a bench near the only door into the prison car, talking and laughing among themselves. All three of the agents had their sleeves rolled up to their elbows. Art studied their tattoo-covered arms and hands. The only white male agent in the group had the word "FUCK" tattooed across the knuckles of one hand, which Art immediately identified as a jailhouse tattoo. "Where did they scrounge up these losers?" Art thought to himself.

Just like the other prisoners, Art had no idea what time it was because he, like the others, had been stripped of all belongings, including his watch, but he did know the sun was down. The NSF agents had even snatched the eyeglasses off their prisoners, leaving them unable to see. There was no food or water offered to any of the prisoners. When one of the chained officers demanded something to drink, a Mexican-looking NSF agent walked up and kicked the man in the face, leaving his nose broken and bloody.

"Shut the fuck up," the agent said coldly, before returning to stand with the other two agents.

There did happen to be a stainless steel toilet in a corner of the train car, but its use was refused to all the prisoners. "Hold it or shit yourself," snapped a female NSF agent with short-cropped hair.

Sitting on the hard floor, his right hand cuffed to a ring on the wall, Art's shoulders and arms begin to ache and burn. He tried to sit up straighter and closer to the wall to take the stress off his muscles when suddenly the train car was rocked into the air and a loud explosion came from just outside the prison car. The three NSF agents sitting on the bench were roughly thrown across the floor as some of the prisoners, chained to the walls, let out frightened screams.

The three agents quickly scrambled to their feet and headed to the only exit on the train. The Mexican one reached the door first, sliding it open and jumping down into the dark. The other two followed right behind him. Suddenly the sound of automatic gunfire roared just outside the train car. Bullets began to hit against the steel sides of the prison car. Everything suddenly went eerily quiet. Some of the prisoners jerked at the handcuffs, trying to get free.

There was a scuffling of feet as a camouflaged, masked figure entered the car, a pump action shotgun held against his shoulder. He turned swiftly to the right, staring down the barrel of his weapon as he pointed it all around. Lowering it safely toward the floor, he turned his head and whistled. Almost immediately three more masked figures leapt into the train car, weapons slung over their shoulders. One held a video camera and began filming Art and the other prisoners, while another produced a handcuff key and began opening up everyone's handcuffs.

"Come with us and do what we say. You're safe now," the first figure said, addressing the prisoners. Art and the others were helped down the stairs of the prison car and into the cool night's air. Glancing left, Art saw the engine of the train on fire, sitting on its side. As his eyes adjusted to the dark, he counted the figures of at least five NSF agents lying crumpled, dead on the ground. Two others knelt in the center of a ring of camouflaged figures with their hands held over their heads in surrender.

Art and his fellow officers were separated from the other prisoners.

"Step to my left side when I read your name," said a masked woman clad in camouflage. She called roll from a list in her hands, and Art obeyed when his name was yelled out, joining his fellow officers on her left side.

"Everyone's here," she said to another member of her group, who was gently herding about seventy rescued prisoners toward trucks towing long stock trailers, that had been sitting, hidden behind a thicket of trees.

"Ladies and gentlemen," the masked, armed woman said firmly to Art's group, "please load up in the center trailer, and take a seat. Please don't look outside. We're taking you to a safe house so you can get some food and medical care, if you need it. I know you have many questions, and they will be answered soon. For right now, you will just have to trust us."

Art began to move with the others and, as he was nearing the trailer, he heard the rattle of an automatic weapon. Turning in the direction of the gunfire, Art saw the circle of camouflaged men moving away. The bodies of the NSF agents who had surrendered lay crumpled on the ground.

"Too fucking bad, assholes," Art thought to himself, stepping into the central trailer and taking a seat on a pile of soft straw beside his fellow officers. A minute later the trailer drove off into the darkness. Other than spent bullet casings, the only evidence left at the scene was the Ace of Spades playing card tossed on the ground.

Chapter 17

Charlie Ashman sat at a small table near the back of the noisy, smoke-filled bar. He had purposefully taken a seat with his back to the wall so he could watch anyone new coming in the front door. There were double doors leading to an emergency exit that sat to his right in case he needed to make a hasty exit. He had already scoped out the other patrons of the bar. All looked innocent enough, mostly just tables of the "just got out of work" crowd. A week before, someone had shared a trick with him to glance at a person's data bracelet. Anyone in the NSF or military had a unique wristband which had two colors, unlike the solid ones worn by the rest of the population. Charlie looked at the patron's wristbands as he stepped through the front of the tavern. Charlie observed many black bracelets and at least a couple of yellow ones but none that put him on edge.

Charlie could go to many places that offered WiFi, like Starbucks and other coffee shops, but he heard that agents of the NSF were watching these places and monitoring Internet activity by its patrons. So Charlie moved from one place to another making it more difficult to be tracked down.

Opening his laptop, Charlie realized he wasn't the only one taking a deadly gamble in the efforts to expose the government and its atrocities. Stories, photographs, and videos came across the Internet every day. Most of it was quickly deleted off the websites by persons unknown, but Charlie suspected that government agents were closely monitoring every social media site. Facebook, being the largest, had made it nearly impossible to upload a video to its site, and people posting anti-government comments were finding their accounts suspended as punishment.

Charlie checked his e-mail, an address he had created with as much fake information as he could, to stay hidden from prying government eyes. There was the normal spam that Charlie quickly deleted with a few clicks of his keyboard. However, there were a handful of messages that contained relevant information to his mission. An e-mail from someone named Nascar Bob told him that the army and NSF agents had been seizing all the rifle and pistol ammunition from Walmart in the Springfield, Illinois area. Another anonymous writer talked about a shoot-out between NSF agents and some armed citizens in Little Rock, Arkansas. Gunfire erupted, leaving one agent dead after they tried to evict an old woman who had refused to register herself with the government. Another email told two stories of family members being taken from their homes in the middle of the night.

Through his continued postings on various forums, Charlie had become a clearinghouse for abuses by the government, mostly the now-notorious National Security Force. Some of the postings on the forums were just messages of something seen or heard. There were pictures and, now more often, video clips of people being dragged down the street by soldiers or NSF agents. One video showed a family standing next to their car, with even the children holding their hands up, as if surrendering, while their car was torn apart during a random stop and search.

As Charlie continued to surf the Internet, he was surprised to see anything new. That was until he opened the video clip from someone identified simply as "woodCharlie." The filming had been done at night and the scene opened with a bright light coming toward the person holding the camera. The thundering sounds of a train engine could be heard, and it was immediately obvious that the locomotive was the focal point of the film. Charlie watched as the train neared and then the image went completely white and a thunderous boom was heard. The individual operating the camera, while rocked by the blast, had quickly focused the camera back on the train. Charlie watched, stunned, as the engine rocked to one side, caught fire, and then skidded off the tracks and furrowed a path through the brush near the railroad tracks, surrounded by a cloud of dust and smoke.

The car directly behind the burning engine had jumped the tracks. It bounced several times, veering off in the opposite direction of the flaming locomotive and coming to rest at an angle. The other two cars had followed along behind it but remained on the railroad tracks. Charlie continued to watch and saw that within thirty-seconds, the doors on the first and second car opened and black-clad individuals began to pour out, cursing and yelling. One of the individuals had the words NSF printed across the back of his jacket in large white letters. He began to scream orders and point. Charlie could see figures moving around in the burning light of the train engine. The leading agent continued shouting orders as he reached into his pocket and was trying to pull out a phone or radio. At that moment, a barrage of rifle fire erupted out of the brush near the train. Charlie counted at least nine firing positions by the muzzle flashes in the video. The leader went down first, as did two other black-clad figures that had exited the train car behind him. Three others figures from the second car froze at the doorway. The agent closest to the door had just begun to draw his weapon out of its holster when his body shook and fell, riddled with bullets. The two NSF agents behind him suddenly surrendered and threw their arms up in the air. The video then swung left to where more gunfire had erupted. The new scene showed two more agents lying on the ground outside the third car. Charlie could just make out the legs of a third, lying in the stairwell.

A moment later, a dozen men dressed in dark camouflaged uniforms began to carefully approach the train cars. All held their weapons at the ready, scanning them right and left. It reminded Charlie of when he went through combat training in the U.S. Army. Half of the men stayed fixed in place guarding while the others split up into twos and entered the train cars. A moment later a figure near the rear car stepped out, whistled and motioned. The video recording stopped. When it started again, Charlie was seeing the point of view of the camera operator as he began entering the train car. He quickly panned right and left showing at least thirty people, men and women, young and old, sitting on the floor, right hands cuffed to steel rings welded onto the walls. He zoomed in on some of the people, showing their gaunt, scared faces and their cuffed hands, wrists red and raw from the rubbing of the manacles. Just before the video ended, a hand moved in front of the lens holding a playing card, the Ace of Spades.

Charlie shook his head in disbelief and then quickly uploaded the video clip onto all his websites. He also added the video to a group e-mail. He knew the government would find and delete this video once they discovered it. However, Charlie knew they couldn't do anything once it showed up in the foreign press. All that would happen is that the press secretary, Donna Koontz, would show up at another press briefing and explain how the video was a fake. It had become the government's most common response to everything.

Waving his arm, Charlie called over a young waiter. He ordered a beer and some buffalo wings as he closed down his computer, pleased with the work he had just completed.

One block down from the bar sat a black van, with no windows in the back of the vehicle. Several antennas reached out from its roof. Inside the van, a man sat hunched over a glowing, green computer screen. He wore a black headset. The man suddenly sat up straight and lifted one of the earpieces away from his head.

"I got him," he shouted to the other two men in the van.

Chapter 18

Twenty-five thousand feet in the air, the flight of thirty American transport planes neared the West coast of California. Five of them suddenly dropped altitude and banked, heading in another direction from the formation. One headed toward San Diego, two toward Los Angeles, and the remaining two toward San Francisco.

Captain Tyson stared out the windshield, his hands holding the yoke while Lieutenant Drace studied a clipboard in her lap. She paused after scribbling a moment and, without speaking, handed a folded piece of paper over to the aircraft commander. Rocky glanced at her and then unfolded the note and read it.

"Captain Tyson, should we be arranging for another refueling tanker to meet us? We can't figure out our range without a destination. I realize this mission is beyond classified, but this is information needed for us to do our jobs . . . SIR."

Rocky crumbled up the piece of paper and tossed it at his copilot, giving her a look of surrender. He pushed a button and the headsets of his entire crew crackled to life.

"Listen up, people. I'm going to share some information with you. This is highly classified so after I tell you, I'll have to kill you."

Several laughs from his crew members came over the radio. Captain Tyson locked eyes with his copilot before continuing.

"Lieutenant Drace has volunteered to be my first victim."

More laughs.

"People, in a few hours we will be coming across Kansas and making our approach into Whiteman Air Force base east of Kansas City. Our ETA is approximately 0730. I need all of you to be on your feet and ready to go to work. That is all."

Rocky turned toward his copilot. "Take the wheel, Lieutenant," he said, unhooking his harness and rising out of his seat.

"Staff Sergeant Huffman, meet me forward," he said into his mic before walking out of the cockpit.

Chapter 19

His fingers dancing across the keyboard of his computer and his mind buried in his work, Charlie Ashman failed to see the figure quietly enter the bar. Most of the tables were full of customers, some laughing and talking, others speaking quietly. A skinny drunk man wearing a blue work shirt with his name, "Hank" over the pocket, a cigarette dangling from his lips, was trying unsuccessfully to strike up a conversation with an attractive brunette. The woman sitting two stools from him was much more interested in texting on her phone and ignored him.

The tall and stocky man stopped just inside the doorway. He wore black trousers and a waist length pilot's jacket with his hands in the pockets. His hair was cut into a short flat-top, and he swiveled his head scanning the room until he spotted Charlie at the rear, bent over his laptop.

A waitress walked up and pulled a menu from a stack sitting by the cash register. "Just one tonight?" she asked smiling. "Would you like a table or do you want to sit at the bar?"

The man pushed by, ignoring her. He elbowed his way past two men who were standing watching a basketball game on a flat screen TV. He walked toward where Charlie sat, his eyes glued on him like an animal stalking its prey.

So involved in his task, Charlie failed to detect the man until it was too late. Maneuvering himself behind Charlie's chair, the man reached out his right hand and roughly grabbed Charlie's shoulder, causing him to jump in his seat. Charlie jerked his head up, looking up at the man as a bolt of fear surged through his body. Every muscle tensed.

"Get up now," the man ordered sternly, almost lifting Charlie to his feet.

Charlie jerked, pulling his shoulder from the man's grasp and squaring off with him.

"So, what am I under arrest for?" he asked trying to build his courage.

The man glanced toward the doorway, and Charlie turned his head in the same direction in time to see three black-clad men rush through the front door, their eyes darting right and left.

"Look, Charlie," the man said, knowing his name, "come with me and do what I say or you are going to get arrested." The man took Charlie's upper arm in a vice-like grip and pushed him toward the exit door, just a few feet away. Charlie grabbed his messenger bag and laptop and allowed himself to be led toward the door that said, "Emergency Exit Only."

The three men began to move into the center of the restaurant, a large black NSF agent in the lead. "Check the shitters," he ordered the last man in the trio, who quickly ran toward an arrow sign that read "Bathrooms."

The commanding NSF agent spotted Charlie and the other man standing at the rear of the restaurant and began to move in their direction. Most of the restaurant patrons ignored them, but some looked up with concern on their faces.

Suddenly a fat man wearing grease-stained overalls and a ball cap with the Denver Broncos football team logo on the front stumbled in front of them. The NSF leader stopped suddenly, causing the NSF agent behind him to lurch to a halt.

The drunk gave a toothless grin and began to jabber, stumbling close enough that the lead agent stepped back as the man invaded his personal space.

"I don't give a shit if she wants to leave. I've had enough of her crap," the man slurred, waving a mug of beer in the air over his head. "Go stay at your sister's. You two bitches deserve one another."

The lead agent stepped back away from the man's beer-smelling breath. "Get out of my way," he ordered stepping to the left, but the drunk swayed back in front of him.

In the restaurant, an alarm began to sound causing the lead agent to stretch his head right and left, trying to see around the man who had planted himself in front of him. Several of the customers turned their heads searching for the cause of the shrill sound.

"I'm the bread winner, and she just sits on her ass all day," the drunk yelled, spittle flying onto the stubble of beard on his chin. He motioned at himself with his glass of beer, spilling most of it on the floor between himself and the agent.

His face flushed red, the NSF agent struck out angrily. "I said get the fuck out of my way, asshole," the agent screamed, roughly slamming both hands into the drunk's chest, shoving him backward and causing him to lose balance. The man fell onto his ass with a thud, his beer mug shattering on the floor.

The drunk began to curse as the two NSF agents hurdled into the air over him. The bartender, who had been watching the confrontation, rushed out from behind the bar and bent down to help the drunk, angry man to his feet.

The two agents raced to the back of the bar, their eyes searching right and left. The leader ran to the exit door and, stepping through it, looked right and left. A couple of employee cars and a big, green trash dumpster were all that could be seen.

Moments before, Charlie and the man had run out of the restaurant as the alarm sounded behind them. A big red, extended cab Dodge pickup truck sat running beside the building.

Without looking back, the man ran toward the open driver's door of the truck. He made a circular motion with his hand.

"Get in the truck, Charlie," he yelled, jumping behind the wheel.

Charlie hesitated for only a second, glancing toward the exit, expecting to see the three NSF agents burst through behind them. He didn't see anyone following them. He ran around the back bed of the truck and climbed into the passenger seat, even as the driver shoved the truck into gear and tore out of the parking lot. The man drove around the back of the building and turned left onto the street.

Half a block down the road he began to slow the vehicle.

"I have a quick stop to make, Charlie," he said, pulling the wrong way across the street and stopping. Charlie watched in confusion as a man wearing overalls over a flannel shirt suddenly darted from between two parked cars, opened the door behind the driver, and jumped into the back seat.

"Let's go, Skipper," the man said, slapping the rear of the driver's headrest and glancing quickly over his right shoulder and out the back window.

The driver guided the truck into the proper lane and began to head down the street. He didn't say anything for nearly four blocks but kept staring into the rear view mirror as if he thought someone was following them.

"Are we clear, Virgil? What's the situation?" he asked, looking into the mirror at the man in the rear seat.

Charlie turned in his seat until he could see the passenger behind him. The overall-clad man turned and looked out the rear window for a moment, straining to look up into the sky before turning back and relaxing his posture.

"All clear, Skipper. No tails that I can see and no choppers," the man said as he pulled a cigarette out of his pocket and began to light it.

The driver raised his right hand and loudly snapped his fingers. "No smoking in the truck. How many times do I have to say it?" The other man rolled his eyes and shoved the cigarette back into the front pocket of his overalls.

"Charlie Ashman," the driver said sticking a hand out toward Charlie. "I'm Russ Kerr, and that ugly guy in the back is Virgil."

Charlie reached out and took the man's hand, but then shook his head in confusion.

"Do I know you, Mr. Kerr? I'm confused," Charlie said, looking toward him as the truck sped down the road. "Who are you guys?"

The man in the back spoke first. "We just saved your ass, sonny. The marines have landed," he said, laughing.

"I'm Maggie's father, Charlie. We've just never met," Russ said, keeping his eyes on the road. "The NSF is tracking people like you, Charlie. It just so happens that Virgil and I were out looking for you. Maggie said we might find you here. Turns out the NSF had tracked you too. We saw their van sitting down the street with dudes getting out. Virgil and I knew they were preparing to make a move, and we figured you were inside. We made a quick plan to have Virgil distract them while I went in after you. We made it just in time, too, or you'd be on the way to some serious physical and mental interrogation."

Charlie fell back into his seat like a deflated balloon.

"Looks like I owe you guys a big debt of gratitude," Charlie said, realizing he still clutched his bag and laptop to his chest.

"Once we get you to a safe place we'll talk in more detail, Charlie," Russ said, aiming the truck down the dark roadway.

Chapter 20

Shade stood in the communications department with a dozen of her staff, all looking up at a television screen. It was the Monday morning White House pressroom broadcast. Shade knew their television wasn't the only one tuned in because every American citizen was now required to watch the broadcast. They watched Donna Koontz do her usual routine, her red lips making her look like a freakish marionette with her arms waving like they were attached to invisible strings coming from the ceiling.

"Jesus Christ, the last time I saw a mouth that big, there was a hook in it," Shade thought to herself in disgust.

Today, Koontz was on a rant blaming domestic terrorists for the reason the country was under siege. "These murderers are killing our own citizens, our police officers, *and* even our National Security forces," Koontz's voiced boomed, as she smacked the top of the podium with the flat of her hand. "We need your help, people," Koontz pleaded. "Help bring these terrorists to justice."

With that, Koontz picked up a few sheets of paper and stepped off stage. Immediately, the president, dressed in a dark blue suit and red tie, came into the camera's view and took Koontz's place on stage. The president looked toward the camera, his eyes dark and serious as he began to speak.

"After several months of intense investigation by the FBI and the NSF, it has been determined that domestic terrorists are behind the disappearance of a large number of our beloved senators and members of congress," the president said with little emotion. "A very phony video was posted on the Internet by the terrorists in which they attempted to mislead viewers, saying that our government was behind these kidnappings. I can assure you, this is not true. Experts have proven that this video was filmed by this terrorist group using highly technical movie-editing software. Do not believe all that you see or hear," he warned. "Our nation is under attack by a group of killers bent on its destruction."

The president paused for a moment to let his words sink in and then lifted up a sheet of paper and held it in front of the cameras. The government seal could clearly be seen at the top, but the small lettering below it was ineligible.

Shade, her arms crossed, stepped closer to the television screen, trying to see what was on the sheet the president held. She could only detect with certainty three or four typed paragraphs.

"Early this morning, I received alarming news," the president said, turning the sheet of paper around and appearing to read from it. "Through the determined efforts and professionalism of our intelligence organizations, it has been ascertained that agents of the Israeli government, in collaboration with domestic terrorists, were responsible for the crippling cyber attack upon the United States just a few short months ago."

There was a flurry of voices in the room as the president ended his sentence. Shade looked around at the shocked faces of her staff. She wanted to yell at them, make them see the truth. "Pay attention, people. This is bullshit. Why would Israel want to attack us?" Shade thought to herself, but didn't say a word. She had to keep her beliefs to herself and not raise any suspicions.

The president continued.

"Therefore, I have ordered the staff of every Israeli consulate in the U.S. expelled immediately. We will put a stop to the attacks upon our country and eliminate those who wish to harm it."

Again, the president paused for his words to sink in. The president made an effort to slump his shoulders, letting his head hang down, as if in disbelief. Finally, he stood with his back straight up. "I am shocked and saddened that Israel, a nation the United States has supported since its founding, has chosen to turn on us. This is a dark day for relations between our two countries. Are there any questions?" the president asked, looking toward the camera.

"Yes, Mr. President," an unseen voice asked, "can you tell us who these domestic terrorists are?"

"We believe there are numerous ultraconservative groups working in coalition with one another, but all have been receiving direction from the nation of Israel."

"Is there a name for this group of rebels?" the voice asked.

"Ace of Spades." The President said sternly, seconds before the broadcast ended.

Reaching for the remote control, Shade turned the television off. "Back to work, people," she said. "Be sure to get the word out about the Israeli agents in the country. Maybe someone knows something."

A shiver ran through Shade as she made this statement. She had several Jewish friends and felt as if she were now betraying them. "Keep up the image, Shade," she said to herself.

Shade slipped into her office and called Charlie. It immediately went to voice mail. Shade chattered a minute, leaving a benign message about catching a movie. Unbeknownst to Shade, her call, like every call made to Charlie's cell phone since he slipped through the fingers of the security agents, was being logged and flagged.

Fifty-eight hundred miles away in Israel, telephones began to ring at the prime minister's office, and the embassy teletype machines began chattering with urgent messages from the United States.

Less then an hour after the president's speech, the first firebomb struck a synagogue in Chicago, Illinois.

Chapter 21

Peter Anchors was excited but angry as he sat in the passenger seat of the air force Humvee. He wasn't used to waking up early, and the morning had started off badly when Lieutenant Branson had pounded on his door at seven o'clock in the morning. However, once the reason for the early call was explained – that they were needed on the flight line – Peter Anchors brightened up. "This is finally happening," he thought to himself.

"You have thirty minutes to shit, shower and shave, sir," the young lieutenant had said, smiling. "Well, that's what we call it here in the Air Force," Lieutenant Branson said, jokingly.

In the short time allotted to him, Anchors took a quick bird bath, threw on the same suit he had worn the day before, and, after digging through a small red bag, snorted a line of coke off the dresser. He double-checked the mirror and wiped under his nose to eliminate any trace of the white substance. He then quickly stepped into the hallway to where the lieutenant patiently waited.

Now, Lieutenant Branson sped down the streets of the air force base, his eyes hidden behind dark aviator sunglasses. At one point, Anchors noticed about seventy-five airmen preparing to board white buses. USAF was painted on their sides.

"What are they doing?" Anchors asked Branson, watching as the buses disappeared. "Those are just troops going on leave, Mr. Anchors. We give our troops a lift to some of the bigger towns on the weekend," Branson answered.

Turning his attention back ahead, Anchors realized they were crossing the tarmac. They raced past two long, wide landing strips toward an assembly of parked military vehicles.

"Have you ever seen a plane that big before, Mr. Anchors?" the lieutenant asked, pointing his finger toward the passenger window. Anchors twisted his head, his mouth dropping, as his eyes settled on the C-5 Galaxy parked at the far end of the runway. Even at that distance, the aircraft looked like a mountain. A smile came to his face. Anchors couldn't believe he had missed spotting the immense, four-engine monster.

Anchors had the door open and was stepping out before the Humvee could come to a complete stop. General Thompson and Captain Monarch stood beside a cluster of airmen, including a woman that Anchors didn't recognize. A circle of heavily armed air force security police officers surrounded them. Anchors counted four Humvees with airmen in their turrets operating 50-caliber machine guns.

Like a school kid at his first circus, Anchors pointed toward the C-5 sitting a half-mile away and trotted over to where General Thompson stood, his arms folded, puffing on a cigar.

"Is that them, General?" Anchors asked, still pointing.

General Thompson nodded his head and blew out a puff of blue cigar smoke.

Stepping face-to-face with the general, Anchors puffed out his chest and put his hands on his hips, obviously agitated. He pointed toward the C-5 and began to chastise the General, talking down to him.

"Those people on that plane are our guests, General," Anchors yelled, spittle forming at the corners of his mouth. "Why is their plane sitting way out there?" he said, thrusting his finger towards the aircraft, and then turned and angrily strode away in the direction of the parked airplane. General Thompson continued to puff on his cigar, and Captain Monarch just watched as Anchors turned to face them, his voice deep and threatening. "General, get those people off that aircraft. Feed and house them until they are reassigned. You have your orders."

General Thompson leaned back against the Humvee, took a long draw off his ten-dollar cigar and then, unfolding his arms, began to march menacingly toward the short man. Captain Monarch fell into lockstep right beside him.

Commander Hamidi stood at the top of the open rear cargo ramp of the C-5 Galaxy. He had just finally shared the details of their secret mission with the 300 men of his command.

"Today, Allah has led us into the heart of the Great Satan, the land of the infidels," Hamidi shouted to his men pacing in front of them. He raised his hands upward. "We come as conquerors. America's own president has called out to us for help. Today, for the first time in history, the army of Islam marches into the country of our enemy. "

Hamidi was shouted down by the screams and cheers from his men. The noise echoed inside the cargo bay of the aircraft. A chorus of "Allahu Akbar" began to chime.

Motioning downward with his hands, Hamidi quieted his men.

"By aiding President Barakat and enforcing order on the pigs of his country, Allah will reward us by destroying the Jews."

Every one of Hamidi's 300 men jumped to their feet, hugging one another and screaming. One soldier came close to Hamidi and bending over, kissed his hand.

"Come, it is time to pray, my brothers," Hamidi shouted over the voices of his men, and motioned them to follow him into the sunlight and onto the tarmac beside the aircraft.

His men quickly formed into lines, making a square, and once reaching the tarmac, they all knelt down on the ground facing east, their heads lowered to the ground as they began to pray.

Hamidi and his lieutenants knelt in a line in front of them and lowered their heads as well. When they rose for the first time into a kneeling position, Hamidi paused, noticing that the seven-member air crew of the plane, including the whore woman, were nowhere to be seen.

As Hamidi's troops bowed again, the commander sat up and looked into the distance to where a group of vehicles sat.

General Thompson crossed the short distance to Peter Anchors as quickly as a run away truck. The small man stumbled backward, afraid the general was going to run him over, but Thompson pulled himself up short. Tossing his cigar onto the ground, General Thompson grabbed the back peddling Anchors by the front of his shirt and pulled him onto his toes, his nose just inches from the smaller man's face.

"I recognized your name the first time we met," the general snarled into Anchor's quickly paling face. "You're the old buddy of President Barakat, the one who belonged to the Weathermen back in the day. I remember your group. You set off bombs and you killed people. You had this grandiose plan of overthrowing the government and establishing a Marxist State," the general said through seething teeth.

Anchors tried to mumble a response, but General Thompson gave him a rough jerk, shutting him up immediately.

The general released his hold on Anchors, who pushed away from him and stood looking scared and angry, his face flushing red.

"So, the president is herding up weasels like you to spy on us, to give us orders, to enforce the rules," General Thompson sneered, before pointing at the C-5 aircraft parked near the end of the runway. "Well, Mr. Anchors, your guests are sitting down there waiting for you. What now?"

Peter Anchors glared at the general as he straightened his shirt and tie. His voice seethed with anger when he finally spoke. "General, I order you to take care of those people immediately, and by the way, I will be reporting your actions today to the president."

General Thompson turned to Captain Monarch and both men let out a chuckle.

"Captain Monarch, you have your orders, take care of our guests," the general said, shrugging his shoulders and then turning back to Anchors.

"By the way, Mr. Anchors," the General said, jabbing a thumb towards Captain Monarch who was speaking into a walkie-talkie. "Be sure to put this in your report, too."

The men beside the plane continued sitting up and then bowing in prayer, but Commander Hamidi was on his feet. Something wasn't right. He began to turn, scanning all around him. Then, Hamidi spotted the small silver shapes of two aircraft coming in low from directly behind them.

Before he could scream a warning, the two planes had the group in their gun sights.

At only 500-feet altitude, the pilots of the two A-10 Warthogs had a clear view of their target ahead, the square of kneeling men, and the C-5 Galaxy that dwarfed them.

"Engaging now," the lead pilot said into his microphone, as his finger began to squeeze the trigger of his aircraft's weapon.

To an observer on the ground, the sound of the M61 Vulcan cannon mimicked someone revving up a chain saw, as puffs of smoke flashed from the nose of the A-10 ground attack aircraft.

Hamidi was the only man in his group who saw death approaching.

The others were still bent over, heads to the ground, as 20-caliber cannon rounds began to tear through their formation. Bodies exploded into pieces as the deadly projectiles pierced flesh and the asphalt around them.

The pilots of the two aircraft maneuvered their A-10s, crisscrossing their target with a cannonade of death.

Hamidi, who had escaped the initial rain of bullets around him, turned to run. He made it less then four feet when the pilots of the two aircraft released their 500-pound bombs and then roared past the parked C-5 and began to make a tight circle back toward their target.

A second strike wasn't necessary.

As close as the Iranian troops were to the C-5, it was inevitable that cannon rounds from the attacking A-10s would hit it, and several did. It began to smoke as pieces of the fuselage were blasted away from the aircraft, some slicing through the packed Iranian Guard soldiers, adding to the carnage.

The detonation of the two bombs in quick succession killed any who had escaped the deadly cannon fire. With a tremendous boom, the fuel bladders in the C-5 exploded, destroying the aircraft on the ground. A wave of burning jet fuel engulfed the bodies of Hamidi and his men.

The first Islamic army to set foot on the soil of the United States also gained the distinction of being the first to die in the land of their enemies.

The fireball from the burning C-5 rushed into the air up to 500 feet, forming a mushroom cloud of black smoke that could be seen six miles away. People in nearby Knob Noster and those driving down Interstate 50 gasped in shock, fearing that a nuclear weapon had gone off.

Peter Anchors was mentally planning his message to the president in his mind. He would see to it that General Thompson was arrested and replaced. Unfortunately, his train of thought was interrupted by the heat and shock wave that knocked him on his ass. It took just a second for the noise of the explosion to catch up and be heard.

Anchors sat stunned on the ground watching the fireball begin to rise into the sky. He looked to his left in time to see General Thompson rise from behind one of the armored vehicles, where he and his troops had taken cover. The general began to walk toward him, smoking a fresh cigar. As he approached, the general squatted down next to the shaking, terrified spy for the president.

"Now, listen up you pathetic skid mark, we're taking you to some buses that are loaded with a few troops who don't want to stay with us. Your little weasel body will be delivered to a safe place. If you're not aware of it, Mr. Anchors," General Thompson said, pointing at him with his cigar, "I've got nuclear weapons here and aircraft to deliver them, so be sure to tell that to your butthole buddy, Barakat, when you see him. By the way," he added pointing at the large, dark stain on Anchor's crotch, "I think you wet yourself."

General Thompson stood, turned, and walked away from the trembling Anchors as two air force security officers walked past, rifles slung. Each grabbed an elbow and jerked Peter Anchors to his feet, before walking him roughly toward a Jeep.

General Thompson stood next to Captain Tyson. They both stared silently at the fire and smoke bellowing at the end of the runway.

"Sorry about your aircraft, Captain Tyson," the general said. "You still know how to fly fighters don't you?"

Chapter 22

Charlie Ashman sat at a long oak dining room table nursing a cup of hot, black coffee. He had awakened just after dawn, listened to a rooster crow for a few minutes, and then quietly dressed and tiptoed downstairs. He thought he was the only one awake until he entered the kitchen where Russ was already scrambling eggs in a bowl.

He was greeted warmly by Russ, who offered the world's best eggs, but Charlie waved off the offer, settling on coffee instead to clear his head. After his near-capture by the NSF and a winding trip into the Virginia countryside in the dark, Charlie still felt rattled.

Charlie glanced out the window and was rewarded with a scene of picturesque farmland beauty. An old red-brick silo rose up from a field of wheat. Dozens of sparrows held court on a wooden picket fence, and a big man in blue overalls stared back at him from the porch outside.

He jerked, startled for a moment, until he recognized Virgil from the night before. Charlie thought Virgil should get an Emmy Award for his performance of a pissed-off drunk the night before. His antics had given Charlie and Russ the time they needed to make a getaway.

When Russ spotted Virgil, he waved him in. "Morning, gents," Virgil said, grinning at Charlie like nothing had happened. He sat down at the table. Russ brought him a cup of coffee and then sat down as well.

"Did you get any rest last night, Charlie?" Russ asked, before drinking from a mug with a US Navy logo on it.

Charlie shook his head. "I slept with one eye open all night. I have a feeling I may be doing that for a while."

"Charlie, you obviously need to be filled in on what's going on. Since the emergency went into effect, you have been funneling videos, pictures, and eye witness statements onto the Internet. What you've shared has gotten much attention. There are individuals, like myself, and governments all over the world who are visiting your websites.

Fortunately for you, but also unknown to you, we've been following you from the shadows for quite a while."

"Who is 'we?'" Charlie asked, staring directly at Russ.

"Well, let's just say people like Virgil and me," Russ said, motioning toward Virgil who was busy emptying a pink Sweet'N Low packet into his coffee. "Citizens are mortified at what's happening to our government, Charlie, our *country*. Virgil and I, along with the concerned citizens, have joined to put up a resistance."

Charlie turned and looked at Virgil, who gave him a gummy grin.

"Look, no offense guys," Charlie said apologetically, "but you guys don't strike me as trained mercenaries. I'm thinking I'd stand a better chance on my own."

Charlie could sense an immediate change in the atmosphere and instantly regretted what he had said.

Russ leaned across the table, a stern look on his face. "Let me share something with you, Charlie. Virgil and I served in 'Nam together years before you were walking. We took missions that would make you wet your pants. If you think we're not the caliber of people you are looking for, then let me remind you that we knew the NSF was tracking you and saved your skinny ass when you didn't even know they were on your tail. So tell me, Charlie. Still want to try it on your own?"

"I'm sorry, Mr. Kerr," Charlie said. "I appreciate your help. I'm still a little shell-shocked after last night."

"This is the situation, Charlie," Russ continued. "The government has been tracking your websites and your computer. It's only going to take them a couple of days to figure out who you are, and then they'll be hot on your trail."

"Fucking A," Virgil chimed in. "Like a coon on a rabbit."

"Once the NSF puts a positive ID on you they're going to begin trying to find and question friends and family. People like my daughter, Maggie, and your sister, Shade. I'm sure they won't be nice and polite about it either."

Charlie shook his head in agreement. "I've seen close up how the new government is managing the non-believers."

"The information you are sharing on the Internet is getting viewed by millions of people. Some good, and some bad," Russ continued, folding his hands and looking across the table at him. "The government has been using some very high tech equipment to track what people are saying and doing. You came onto the government's radar, Charlie. I'm a little surprised they didn't find you earlier," Russ said, as Virgil lit up a cigarette.

Charlie smelled the burning match and pointed at Virgil. "Those things will give you cancer, Virgil," Charlie warned him.

"Too late, Sonny," he replied, blowing a cloud of smoke into the air.

"I want to show you something Charlie," Russ motioned for Charlie to follow him out of the kitchen and onto the front porch. Sticking his two little fingers between his lips he gave out a piercing whistle. Immediately, Charlie spotted a dozen armed and camouflaged figures appear from concealed positions around the farmhouse. At least four came out of hiding near the house and another stuck his head out of the top window of the barn. To Charlie's amazement, a man holding a sniper rifle gave him the thumbs up from the top of the old silo he had been looking at earlier.

"We are members of the anti-government militia, Charlie. There are a hundred organized groups just like ours getting ready to fight. My job is to keep the movement organized, and, so far, I have been successful."

Russ gave a wave, and the armed figures quickly disappeared back into their hiding places. Virgil walked up next to Charlie and laid his huge arm around his shoulders. He extended his other hand in front of Charlie palm side up.

"I'm afraid I need your cell phone, Sonny. We don't wanna give the government an easy way to track you now, do we?"

Charlie reluctantly handed over his cell phone.

"Hey, can you hear me now?" Virgil asked mockingly, dropping Charlie's phone onto the porch and then crushing it into pieces under his cowboy boot.

Charlie stood looking stunned at Virgil, who was calmly stuffing a wad of chewing tobacco into his mouth. Suddenly, Charlie turned to Russ as a thought raced into his mind.

"*Maggie*. If they're looking for me, then she's in danger," Charlie yelled.

Russ held up a hand at Charlie and smiled. "Maggie's safe, Charlie. Our people picked her up last night, and they are bringing her here." Russ's eyes dropped for a moment before looking back at Charlie.

"We couldn't get to your sister, I'm afraid. Her building is guarded like a fortress. But we have eyes on her. If we get the chance, we'll snatch her in a second," Russ said, putting a hand on Charlie's shoulder.

Charlie gave him an iffy look, raising his eyebrows. "You're going to snatch my sister? Tell your guys good luck with that. You don't know Shade very well."

For over an hour, Russ explained the Ace of Spades resistance organization to Charlie. They talked about its formation, goals, and operations. Russ told Charlie that the first group of resistance fighters to strike was a militia unit deep in the Mojave Desert west of Phoenix. While President Barakat used the military to clamp down on the large cities, groups of resistance fighters rushed to prepare. They quickly sprouted up nationally in places like Arkansas, Oregon, and Maine. Every state had citizens fighting back and Russ was the leader of the entire movement. Russ had the organizational skills to make this assortment of resistance groups succeed. Russ explained, "a single group acting on its own might be a bee sting on an elephant, but a thousand groups could make a huge impact." Russ' experience and training in black operations made him the perfect leader.

Russ went on to explain that there were individuals inside the government, military, and law enforcement departments leaking information to the resistance, including Charlie's sister, Shade.

"You mean to tell me that since this all started Shade has been giving you intelligence behind my back?"

"Sorry, Charlie," Russ said, with a wink. "We have to keep our sources secret. Even from big brothers."

"For security reasons, I can't give you many details," Russ said. "I can tell you our sources relay intelligence to our command group. The National Security Force is an open target, but we try to avoid casualties to the military and police when we can. The NSF agent slime bags are hand-picked henchmen of Barakat. Some of these agents were taken straight out of our wonderful prison system."

"I've seen them at work. They are as cold as ice," Charlie replied, nodding. "So is the resistance group making progress?"

"We're making strides in the big cities but just enough to keep Barakat's security forces and the military tied up guarding power plants, government buildings, and such," Russ answered. "I am sure we have convinced the NSF that it is not safe to travel freely in the country."

Russ waved a hand toward Virgil, who was busy eating a glazed doughnut. Reaching inside his overalls, he pulled out a folded map and tossed it through the air to Russ. Russ spread out the map of the United States on the table between him and Charlie. There were several red circles drawn on the map.

"We know most of what Barakat is up to, but we still don't have a handle on all of it," Russ said, directing Charlie's attention to the map.

"Our scouts have reported that foreign troops – Arab soldiers, Charlie – were landed at each of these locations. We suspect that Barakat has plans to use the Arab soldiers to supplement his military in some manner. We're just not sure how yet."

An alarm suddenly rang in the house, causing both Russ and Virgil to jump to their feet and head out of the kitchen. Pausing in the kitchen on his way out, Virgil swung open a cupboard door to retrieve two M16 rifles. Virgil thrust one toward Russ who snatched it away. Heading toward the porch door, both men pulled back the charging handles of their weapons in unison. With a loud metallic sound, they slammed a round into the chamber.

Charlie suddenly felt naked, wishing he had a weapon of his own. He watched Russ and Virgil take up positions on either side of the porch door, peering out.

The tension suddenly vanished as Charlie saw both men relax their postures and lower their weapons.

Russ turned and gave Charlie a smile as he opened the door to the porch. "Maggie's here."

Charlie followed the men onto the porch. A blue Volkswagen bug was bouncing down the rough driveway, a cloud of dust billowing behind it.

The VW pulled into the circular parking area out front under the cover of a hundred-year-old oak tree, and both doors opened. Maggie bounced out and met her father in a bear hug they both held for a few seconds before walking toward the house together. A middle-aged woman in jeans and work boots also exited the car. She wore a red flannel shirt and long pigtailed hair. A handgun on her hip and the way she carried herself announced that she must be part of the resistance group.

Charlie felt a twinge of excitement and relief upon seeing Maggie. She carried the brown cloth "bug out" bag he had bought for her. They had packed it together just in case something like this happened and Maggie had to leave in a hurry. The knee-length dress and high heels that Maggie was wearing told Charlie that the people sent to rescue Maggie must have picked her up as she was leaving work.

Maggie's green eyes twinkled and her smile brightened, showing her dimples, when she saw Charlie. Reaching the top of the steps, Maggie walked toward Charlie, who turned to greet her. Suddenly the imposing figure of Virgil stepped between them.

"Wait your turn, Sonny," Virgil said with a grin and opened his arms wide to Maggie. For a second she stopped and then, still smiling, Maggie grabbed the straps of Virgil's overalls. Pulling herself up on her tiptoes, she planted a big kiss on his cheek.

"When are you going to run off with me?" Virgil asked, tilting his head, waiting for an answer.

"How about we revisit that question when you are a single man, like after your wife runs away with another man."

"What? That old heifer's never gonna leave me."

"I'm going to tell her you called her an old heifer," Maggie said, pointing an accusing finger at Virgil, who bent down to lovingly kiss the tip of her finger.

Stepping around Virgil, Maggie rushed into Charlie's waiting arms. For a long moment they just hugged, Maggie's face resting in the crook of Charlie's neck. Maggie straightened and gave him a soft, wet kiss.

"I've been worried about you."

"Well, I've been worried about you so now we can both relax."

Dinner bordered on festive, yet with a touch of solemnity. Virgil's wife, Ann, had been cooking all day. Older and plump, her gray hair in a bun, she bounced around the kitchen like a culinary expert. A dishrag across one shoulder, she had chicken frying on the stove top while mashed potatoes and fried okra cooked. A loaf of fresh bread sat on the kitchen counter.

Charlie walked to the refrigerator to get ice when he suddenly found himself cornered by Ann. She planted one hand on the fridge door beside Charlie, and stuck the end of her bread knife to his Adam's apple with the other.

"Little Maggie is like a daughter to us, Charlie," she said, threateningly. "Don't do anything to hurt her, or you will see my dark side."

"This isn't your dark side?" Charlie replied sarcastically, his back against the fridge.

Ann lowered the knife and gave Charlie a grin as she patted his cheek. She glanced out of the kitchen toward Maggie and back at Charlie as she leaned in close.

"Maggie loves you, Charlie, and in these dark times, everyone needs somebody."

Charlie nodded. Ann went back to her cooking.

"Go tell everyone we're eating in twenty minutes."

Charlie went into the dining room and sat at the table with the others. The woman who brought Maggie to safety sat next to Russ. Charlie had been briefly introduced to her. All he knew was that her name was Robin Shipman. What she did and where she did it was classified information, Russ had advised him.

"I'm not going to bullshit you, Charlie," Robin said, looking directly into his eyes. "Your sister, Shade, is missing, and we think the NSF has her. We sent a team to the police station to try to reach her, but she was gone. What we know is that one minute she was at work and the next minute she was gone. Our source inside the police department said there was a large presence of NSF agents hanging around right before she vanished. An hour later some government-assigned drone appeared and told everyone he was running the communications center. I'm sorry, Charlie, but we're still trying to find her. There is always a chance we can arrange a snatch-and-grab if we can find where she is." Charlie listened intently, taking in what Robin had said.

Later in the evening, lying in bed and unable to sleep, Charlie stared at the ceiling with a thousand thoughts running through his mind. Where was Shade? Was she hurt? What was happening to her? Charlie knew it couldn't be good. He wanted to drive back to Washington and find her, but he realized that he was being hunted at the moment and needed to stay right where he was.

The last phone message he had received was from his building manager, a sweet widowed woman. It had been a quick cell phone call to let him know that the NSF was all over his apartment tearing it apart and carrying out box loads of stuff.

Charlie was trying to figure out his next step. Russ had requested his presence at a meeting in the morning with other members of Russ's cell of resistance fighters.

An alarm sounded in Charlie's head as he heard something outside his bedroom door. He had been trained as an Army Ranger to always be alert and ready to do battle at any given moment. He sprang to a sitting position, unmoving, listening. He could hear the shuffle of feet outside in the hallway, so he silently slipped into a kneeling position on the opposite side of the bed so he could see the doorway. As he did so, Charlie snatched a .40-caliber automatic Russ had given him off the nightstand. Bracing his hands together he took aim on the doorway. Through the crack at the bottom of the door he could see a shadow of movement. As the doorknob began to slowly turn, Charlie snapped the safety off his automatic and began to add slight pressure on the trigger. He squared his sight picture on the center of the door and made a quick mental note of the rounds in his weapon. Losing count of your bullets in the heat of a firefight could mean death.

Inch by inch the door began to open, stopping after a foot. A figure silently began to squeeze through the opening. Charlie took aim on the figure's center mass. He took and held a deep breath. There was no chance he would miss at this range, but Charlie didn't know how many others waited in the hallway.

Charlie let out a long breath and relaxed his posture as he recognized Maggie's long bare legs. She silently pushed the door shut behind her.

"You almost got shot," Charlie said, lowering his weapon as he stood.

"Shush," Maggie said, crossing the room to Charlie and putting her hand over his mouth. "Be quiet! Do you want my father to kill you?"

"Kill me? You're the one sneaking into my room."

"Trust me, if my father caught us, you'd be the guilty one. Death without trial," she whispered into his ear, pulling Charlie close.

He stepped away to sit his gun back on the nightstand. Maggie, wearing a shear knee-length nightgown, slipped under the covers of Charlie's bed.

"Are you sure that was death without trial?" Charlie asked jokingly, sliding under the covers beside her.

"Definitely. No trial," she purred into his ear, throwing one leg over Charlie's thighs. She rose, straddling Charlie's hips. Leaning forward she put her mouth over his, their tongues finding one another. Charlie slid his hands up to cup Maggie's pert breasts, feeling her erect nipples through the thin fabric of her gown.

"Remember, death without trial," Maggie said softly into Charlie's mouth. Rising up, her back straight, Maggie tossed her long red hair over her shoulders and lowered herself onto Charlie's hard erection.

Chapter 23

President Barakat sat at the head of the conference table, with his arms folded, and a scowl on his face. He simply stared at Peter Anchors across from him. Anchors had stopped making eye contact with the president five minutes into his report. Now, he just let his eyes dance from the tabletop to midway up the president's red tie. Having related the events at Whiteman Air Force Base and General Thompson's warning, Anchors waited for a response.

The silence felt like torture.

"Mr. King, I think our visitor is finished here. Can you arrange a new assignment for him?" the president asked, never breaking his stare from the defeated shell of a man.

Max King strode over and jerked the wheeled office chair backward three feet from the table, taking Peter Anchors on a ride. Anchors quickly gathered his paperwork and cell phone, rising to his feet. He headed toward the door but then paused while reaching for the handle.

"I'm very, very sorry, Mr. President. I didn't realize . . ."

"*Get out!*" the President snapped, turning his attention back to a folder on his desk.

Spinning around to leave, Anchors realized that Max King was holding the door open for him. A thug of a man in black waited just outside the door.

"Assign Mr. Anchors to Project T," Max King said to the man, who simply nodded and reached out to take Peter Anchor's skinny bicep in a vice-like grip.

"What's Project T?" Anchors stammered as he was led down the hallway and out of sight. By the end of the day, Peter Anchors would discover that his new assignment was lying dead, a bullet behind his ear, in a long trench far outside of Washington. He never did get to find out that Project T stood for Project Termination.

Max King closed the door and took his seat next to the president, while Donna Koontz sat as usual, smiling her fake nervous smile.

Without warning, Barakat slammed both fists down on the tabletop causing Koontz to jump and lose her mannequin smile for a minute. Max King simply crossed his arms and gave his boss a dispassionate look.

"Can someone tell me what the *fuck* is going on here?" the president screamed, looking from Koontz to King. "Can either of you explain to me why my plans are falling apart? I want information, and I want it now."

Max King glanced at some notes on a yellow legal pad before speaking.

"Here is the Reader's Digest condensed version, Mr. President. A commanding general at Whiteman Air Force Base in the middle of Bumfucked, Missouri staged a mutiny and about 93% of the base chose to go with him. When a C-5 transport plane landed, the general toasted it and about 300 of your new pals from the Iranian Guard. Now he's hunkered down, waiting to see what we are going to do."

"He can't launch any missiles without my authority!" Barakat spat, pointing toward an adjoining room where an air force officer sat with the "football," a briefcase containing the launch codes necessary to begin World War III.

"He can't launch any missiles because he doesn't have any, Mr. President. All missiles were removed years ago and the silos that held them were buried. However, the general does have some of the most sophisticated aircraft sitting in bomb-proof hangers ready to launch, and they carry as much punch or more than the old ICBMs."

"Aren't there supposed to be safeguards to prevent this type of thing, Mr. King?"

"Under normal conditions the general couldn't launch aircraft without your orders. These orders have to be confirmed by the next-in-command, and so on. General Thompson wouldn't be able to just order a pilot to fire up his Stealth Bomber and fly off. These nuke-loaded B-2s are ringed by security troops, you know, the grunts with all the rifles, and these guys won't let anyone, and I mean anyone, get near them without all the pieces of the puzzle put in place."

Barakat continued to listen, his body language swelling with anger.

"A little fly got in the ointment when the general, his wing commanders, the pilots, the security personnel, hell, even the cooks and drivers, crossed to the other side. Your security measures vanished like a fart in the wind when everyone at Whiteman joined the mutiny. Every swinging dick that is still there is in on the plan. If the general says launch the ready aircraft on the A line, they are going to launch, Mr. President. The only question left for us to figure out is what their target is going to be."

President Barakat jumped up and began pacing. He suddenly stopped and thrust a finger at Max King.

"Don't we have an army base somewhere around there?"

"Yes, Fort Leonard Wood, a few hours away."

"Then let's get them mobilized and up there. I want this base captured, and I want an example made of that general. I want his head on a pole."

Max King flipped a page over in the notebook in front of him.

"The good news, Mr. President, is that a large number of infantry, combat engineers, and armor are already at Knob Noster in Missouri. The bad news is that these men are also the mutinous troops who abandoned their positions at Fort Leonard Wood, grabbed all the gear they could haul, and hightailed it to Knob Noster. Now the troops from Ft. Leonard Wood have joined the men there and reinforced this rogue air base."

Barakat stared at him with coal-black eyes. For a moment, he didn't move.

"Nuke em . . . *nuke* the base," Barakat hissed. "I'll show them how we deal with traitors."

Donna Koontz, who had sat silently for the past several minutes, raised her hand like a child in school, until the president turned to face her.

"You have something to add, Ms. Koontz?"

"Let's get this correct, Mr. President. You want to drop a nuclear bomb on American soil? I'm obligated to remind you that our administration is square in the gun sights of the remaining free world. Destroying a US city isn't something we're going to be able to hide or lie our way out of."

"You also forget," Max King interrupted, "Whiteman is a nuke base, Mr. President. It's designed to defend itself. It has the best radar and early warning system money can buy. General Thompson has the means and material to keep strike aircraft in the air twenty-four hours a day so don't even think about firing a missile, dropping a bomb, or trying to take them out with a ground assault. Whiteman has strike aircraft like the A-10 Warthogs just waiting to make mincemeat out of any troops or tanks you send their way. This is a very serious problem."

"I hate to add to the problems Mr. King just stated," said Donna Koontz, "but things seem to be going sour very quickly, Mr. President. There is desertion in the military in such numbers that we are having to cut down on checkpoints and the number of targets we can protect. We even have navy ships sailing into friendly foreign ports seeking asylum. Yesterday, the United Nations voted in more embargoes on the United States for human rights violations. Our former British, French, and other European Union allies are promising to take aggressive actions against us. Russia is grumbling and China is sending war ships to block Cuba because word leaked out you were asking for Cuba's help."

"I need to add a few more things, Mr. President," Max began. "Iran is flexing its muscle and bragging about the upcoming death of Israel. They have even begun amassing troops, tanks, and artillery along the Syrian border. The Jews have addressed the UN with photographs and other intelligence and have asked why U.S. transport planes are ferrying troops between Iran and the United States. Israel has mobilized their armed forces. They don't intend on being caught by surprise."

"Mr. President," Koontz said, leaning across the table. "We need to do something. We've spun as many stories and lies as we can, and filling up more mass graves isn't the solution."

President Barakat walked to a map of the world hanging on the wall. He silently studied it for a moment, rubbing his chin. "Are you sure Syria is on board with letting the Iranian military cross its borders to get to Israel?"

Max King was opening his mouth to answer when a thunderous explosion rocked the room, throwing everyone to the floor like rag dolls. Pieces of the ceiling showered down and the room was thrown into darkness.

Outside, air raid sirens began to howl and anti-aircraft guns around the Capitol began to fire wildly into the sky.

Chapter 24

Captain Shade Ashman was reviewing daily dispatch logs in her office. Things were getting worse every day. More police officers were going AWOL. It was just months earlier when the police officers were ordered to stop protecting the citizens and start acting like goons terrorizing the citizens.

Shade rubbed a hand over her eyes as she read the dispatch logs. Officers sent to search a house for guns based on an anonymous tip. Officers dispatched to a local park to disperse a group of mothers chatting while their kids were playing. The government didn't want more than three people together in public at one time. Detectives were sent to question a woman at a senior center because she was criticizing the government during bingo.

The list went on.

At first the cops in the street felt they were simply doing their jobs during a national emergency, Shade thought to herself. That was before the National Security Forces began showing up armed with the authority to order both the police and the military around. Police officers who questioned or refused orders from the NSF faced discipline or even arrest.

"Yes," Shade thought to herself, "it was all spiraling down the shitter."

Shade glanced at the clock on her computer screen. She had a meeting at 8:10 a.m. with her major and saw she had about two minutes to spare.

Tossing the reports on her desk, Shade headed out. She stuck her head into the communications center long enough to inform the crew she would be out for a few. She took the elevator to the sixth floor. The door chimed as it opened, and Shade began to step out. A large thug of a man, an NSF supervisor who oversaw the day-to-day operations of the station, stood like a statue in front of her. Shade stepped to the side to let him enter the elevator past her. She counted two other NSF agents behind him and sensed the danger a second too late. Shade saw a flash of movement but didn't feel or remember the huge fist that smashed into her face. Shade's body went limp and tumbled backward into the elevator.

As Shade began to wake up, a bright light was the first thing she saw. She was woozy and felt detached from herself. Her head pounded and her face ached. She could taste blood in her mouth.

Shade lost track of time. She passed out and regained consciousness until finally her mind began to clear and her eyes focused. The room was freezing and Shade realized that someone had stripped her naked. Her arms were drawn painfully behind her, and she could feel cold handcuffs locked around her wrists. She tried to rise up but found she was bound firmly to the frame of her chair.

One glance around told her she was in one of several interrogation rooms the NSF had set up deep in the basement of the police station. A bare, single light bulb hung from the ceiling. An iron table and two folding chairs sat against one wall.

The sound of a door opening captured Shade's attention. She recognized the same NSF agent that had sucker-punched her in the elevator as he stepped into the room. The man was huge. Shade figured him at six feet four, easy. He had muscular, close-cropped blonde hair and Aryan features. She thought the man would make the perfect poster child for a 1940s Nazi recruiting poster. His shirt displayed black lieutenant's bars on his collar and a white embroidered name tag over his right pocket that read "Salzman."

Following close behind Salzman was a Hispanic female NSF agent that Shade had never seen before. She was short but stocky and leaned against a wall with a look of mild interest. Salzman stepped in front of Shade and towered over her with his arms crossed. "How long have you been leaking information to your brother?" Shade raised her head to stare at him. "I don't know what you're talking about." The punch came immediately, unexpected. Salzman connected with the left side of Shade's face, knocking her with a crash onto the floor. Shade lay, still cuffed to the chair on the cold floor, stunned and hurting. Salzman roughly pulled her and the chair upright. Pain raced through Shade's cheek.

Anger filled her body. "How long have you been leaking

information to your brother?" Salzman repeated. "FUCK OFF!" Shade snapped. Salzman hesitated just a second this time before driving his fist into Shade's face again.

Shade felt her nose shatter and blood flow as she toppled over, this time straight onto her back with a bone-jarring thud. She began to cough and spit blood. She turned her head so she would aspirate.

Salzman straddled her, hands on his hips. "We can keep this up all day if that's how you want to play it," he growled. The other NSF agent stood, arms crossed, smirking down at her.

Chapter 25

Israel was in a state of alert. Every military unit was preparing for battle as thousands of reserve troops began pouring in. Armored columns raced to pre-determined defensive positions. Navel ships steamed off shore and state-of-the-art fighter aircraft soared in the skies above. The Jewish nation had no intention of being caught by surprise.

In the Gaza Strip, Palestinians filled the streets screaming "Death to Israel," and firing guns into the air. Spurred by the announcement that the United States would no longer honor defense treaties with the Jewish State, and with the American naval forces sailing out of the region, the border had become a powder keg. PLO terrorists began firing Qassam and Fajr-5 rockets across the border at Israel who responded back with deadly helicopter attacks.

Three days after the first salvo of Palestinian rockets had streaked into the sky, an Israeli spy satellite flashed a message to the Israeli Ministry of Defense. Iranian war ships were sailing through the Red Sea toward Israel.

Chapter 26

Evading radar, the B-2 Stealth aircraft roared back toward Missouri and the safety of the airbase there. Behind it, smoke and flame rose from the White House. On the ground, panic rose. Sirens and car alarms screeched as people on the street ran for cover across glass-littered streets.

A dozen bodyguards and NSF agents poured into the meeting room where Barakat, King, and Koontz still lay on the floor, the air thick with dust. Grabbing Barakat, they practically carried him into the hallway and began running with him.

"What just happened?" Barakat yelled, his own ears buzzing from the explosion.

One of his bodyguards pressed a finger against his earpiece, squinting to hear.

"An unidentified aircraft dropped a bomb on the White House but it went off prematurely in the air. No reports of any real injuries or damage."

"Any radar signature on the attacking aircraft?" Max King asked flatly, as he caught up with the group who were just stepping into an elevator.

The agent spoke into a lapel mic and waited for a reply. He turned to Max shaking his head negative.

"It was a B-2 Stealth Bomber, probably from Whiteman," King said, stepping to stand beside President Barakat.

"Sounds as if your base commander isn't that talented," the president said to King with a mocking voice and a nervous grin. "Their bomb didn't even hit us. All that sophisticated hardware and they couldn't hit a target the size of the White House."

Max King stared at the president for a moment as if the commander in chief was crazy. He turned his head back and forth, uttering "idiot" under his voice.

"This was a warning, Mr. President. The bomb didn't miss the

White House because of pilot error or an equipment malfunction. Its proximity fuse was set to detonate in the air on purpose. The aircraft didn't drop its entire payload, only one single bomb. We would all be dead if that is what they wanted. General Thompson just sent you a message saying he can hit you whenever he wants."

Chapter 27

Beaumont, California: A woman with two little children in tow stood at a teller window at a bank. She had been crying, her nose and eyes puffy and red. Across the counter the teller and her supervisor stood glumly. The mother's bank account had been suspended by the government because her husband had once worked for a conservative organization and he was now missing. Until her husband was found or turned himself in, the young mother was restricted to withdrawing less than $100 a week. Neither her tears nor the helpless women at the bank could change that.

Panama City, Florida: Two NSF agents stood by idly smoking near a U.S. Army checkpoint. Every so often one of them would whistle at the soldiers and wave a hand, signaling the soldiers to perform a weapons pat-down on vehicle occupants. Every time they made the signal, the occupant of the car was an attractive woman or someone elderly. For the elderly, the NSF agents would laugh mockingly. After several hours of the game, a sergeant in charge of the squad walked up to where the black-clad agents stood. A decorated veteran of the Iraq and Afghanistan wars, the sergeant calmly raised his rifle and fired a burst into the chest of one agent. Before his stunned partner could react to his comrade crumpling to the ground, the sergeant turned and emptied his clip into him.

Yuma, Arizona: A little before sunrise, a pickup truck drove down a dusty road into the Mojave Desert. It rolled to a stop near the collapsed rock wall of an old horse barn. The driver and passenger, their faces concealed by ball caps and bandanas, remained seated in their idling vehicle. For several minutes they sat silently in the ninety-plus-degree heat. The driver finally walked toward the broken rock wall. He scanned the ground until he found what he was looking for. Moving a rock, he picked up a package of papers protected inside a heavy plastic bag. The militia member took the packet of intelligence information and his team's next mission orders. He knew nothing about the other cells he worked with, and they knew nothing about him. If the NSF captured any team member, there was no information to give up on the other militia cells, even under torture. It was a safety measure closely adhered to by all the militia groups. Returning to the truck, the driver began to drive back toward the highway and into Yuma. Three nights later, a string of electrical power poles were blown to the ground, blacking out half of Yuma.

Springfield, Illinois: The church-minister-turned-activist had worked up the crowd into a frenzy. For an hour he had been preaching about the accomplishments of President for Life Barakat since the emergency had gone into place. Sometime after thirty minutes, his oratory began to change. Pointing and waving his arms, he began blaming the suffering of the listening crowds on those who owned the stores and ran the factories. He missed the important fact that these same people provided the jobs for this listening crowd. Soon after, small angry mobs began hunting their perceived enemies. Two men were dragged out of their car at a nearby intersection and stabbed to death. Another man walked into a neighborhood grocery store and shot the Asian owner in front of his wife. The crowd outside cheered him on while others set fire to the building.

Honolulu, Hawaii: Two U.S. Navy ships sat anchored near one another. Much like the pirates of 300 years ago, the captains and crews had put a question to democratic vote. The decision to be made was to stay loyal to the government, or sail their vessel to a friendly port and sit out the conflict. The tally counted, the crewmen shook hands, gave words of support, then changed ships depending on their choices. One ship, a missile frigate, sailed toward the Philippines and the former port of Subic Bay. The other, a destroyer, headed to the navel port in Honolulu. Once there, the entire crew was arrested by NSF agents and shore police. Despite pledging their allegiance to the government, all were publicly executed on the ship's pier. A no-nonsense government official charged the crew with collaborating with the enemy by allowing the traitor ship to sail away without engagement, as it was an act of treason.

Los Angeles, California: A crowd of television and Hollywood celebrities were gathered on an outdoor stage. The event had been kicked off by a speech from a well-known liberal documentary producer. The overweight, sloppy-looking man had worked the crowd into a state of excitement. Every time he praised the government, he had to pause until the cheers and shouts from the crowd died down. Several of the members in the audience wore white T-shirts showing a smiling image of President Barakat. The words, "I'm a Believer," were printed below the president's image. When the fat man finished his spiel, one by one, movie, television, and recording stars stepped up to the microphone. Each repeated the same message, that the changes made by the government were wonderful and awesome changes. They reiterated that every citizen needed to show support for President Barakat and his administration. The celebrity speaking would be drowned out by the loud response of the crowd. Finally, an actress, well known for her liberal and controversial movies, took the stage. The crowd became silent as she held the microphone and wept about the innocent people the domestic terrorists were murdering. As she was urging the crowd to report anyone suspicious to the authorities, four pounds of military explosives detonated directly under the stage where she stood. The explosion destroyed the stage, sent the crowd screaming in horror, and blew the actress's body more than 300 feet away.

Atlanta, Georgia: The man was a coward. However, due to the state of emergency, and the constant heed to call and turn in enemies of the state, he had been given a false sense of power. His first victim to turn in as a traitor was a prior employer who had fired him for sexual harassment after a string of complaints from female workers. His next call to the 800 number was to rat out a neighbor who had gotten him evicted from his apartment building after catching him peeping into her bedroom window. Next was a woman he had been stalking at a local coffee shop. He had been arrested and the woman held a protective order entered against him. He wished he could remember the name of the police officer who had called him a sexual predator. He would have put him on his revenge list. Yup, he had a long list of people he was paying back, thanks to the government. The coward was sitting in his dingy kitchen, cell phone in hand, ready to fake up charges against a store owner who had kicked him out for stealing. A knock at his door caught him just as his phone was dialing. He rose and walked to the door. Holding the phone to his ear, he opened the door. A very neat, nicely dressed couple stood outside smiling. Both wore black pants and white dress shirts and carried black messenger bags. Still smiling, the man held out a pamphlet. "Do you know the Lord?" he asked. The coward glanced at what he had been given. He saw the image of the Ace of Spades printed on the front of the pamphlet and the words "Death to Traitors." The coward raised his head, confused. The woman was pointing a silenced pistol at the man's face. "Jesus saves," she said, shooting him between the eyes.

Chapter 28

Feelings of anger and frustration were felt throughout the platoon of National Guard troops as they loaded gear into desert-camouflaged Humvees and trucks. The soldiers kept looking at the formation of foreign troops just one hundred feet away. The troops mumbled and cursed.

"Who are these bastards?"

"Arabs. Somebody said Iranian."

"You gotta be shitting me."

"Nope, a transport guy hauled a bunch of them up to Baton Rouge to guard some oil factories yesterday."

"You gotta be shitting me."

"Nope."

"Where are we headed?"

"To go point our rifles at U.S. citizens somewhere else."

"A dude in intelligence says some British jets smoked a shit load of Cuban ships headed toward Miami."

"KNOCK IT OFF AND MOUNT UP," a lieutenant snapped.

The troops climbed into the trucks and a minute later the convoy began to pull away. The soldiers glared at the Iranian troops as they drove past. One flipped them off.

"Go home, assholes!"

Chapter 29

The president and his staff sat in a secret bunker deep underground. A sense of fear and dread hung over the room. Arial photos hung from the walls with pushpins, and every member of his staff was busy working on his or her notepad, computer, cell phone or was scribbling in a notebook.

An army general, a member of the Joint Chiefs of Staff who wore battle fatigues and was surrounded by junior officers, commanded the attention of everyone.

"At approximately 0935 this morning, an unidentified aircraft dropped what we estimate to be a 500-pound bomb over the White House. There was no warning of the aircraft and no radar signature. It was definitely not a foreign aircraft. We believe from eyewitness reports and the lack of early radar detection that the aircraft was a B-2 Stealth Bomber, most probably launched from Whiteman Air Force Base in Knob Noster, Missouri. While there is some physical damage around the White House from the blast wave, injuries to civilians is minimal and most of the injuries are from flying glass. At this point, we have all available troops on high alert and intercept aircraft are on station over the city."

President Barakat held his hands as if praying, his chin resting on his fingertips as he listened.

"What do you mean when you say available troops, General?"

The general dropped his eyes for a second before standing straight and answering.

"Our desertion rate is increasing. A large number of our troops are joining the resistance. We are finding our units understaffed for the missions they are being given."

"Deserters are to be shot, General, do you understand that?"

"We have been conducting executions of deserters according to your orders, Mr. President, but the troops are becoming reluctant to shoot their own men."

"Then execute those who refuse to obey orders, General. You do know how to follow my orders, don't you?" the president said, with menace in his voice.

"YES, SIR," the General responded, snapping to attention.

"Now tell me about the incident off of Florida," said the president. The general relaxed, slightly.

"Cuban President Raul Castro agreed to your request for troops. However, France and Britain warned they would enforce sanctions handed down by the United Nations, strictly forbidding any foreign troops on American soil. Yesterday, despite warnings, Cuba sent five troop ships and escorts toward the port of Miami. While still in international waters they were attacked by Harrier Jump Jets launched by the British. Three troop transports and two escort ships were sunk. The survivors turned tail and headed back toward Cuba."

"Why didn't our navy or aircraft protect the Cuban fleet?"

"The navy commander reports they were out of position to help and the air force says the incident took place in international waters."

President Barakat sat in his chair stewing for a moment. He gave an angry look toward Max King.

"See to it the commanders of the navy and the air force are arrested and brought to me today, Mr. King."

King nodded without answering.

"General, is there anything else that you need to share with me today?" the president asked, turning his attention back to the group of officers.

The general cleared his throat. "The Iranian troops now on American soil are coming under attack. They are being hit by units of the Death Card resistance movement, and in the past two days there have been three incidents where U.S. troops have turned their weapons on Iranian soldiers resulting in fatalities. We are classifying them as incidents of friendly fire."

"Friendly fire, my ass," the president spat.

"So let me get this straight, General," the president said, crossing his arms. "Stealth Bombers are flying unchallenged over Washington. The heads of my navy and air force can't seem to control their forces, and now you're telling me your soldiers are shooting at our guests, the Iranians? Does that sum it up, General?"

The general paused a moment before answering. "Each incident is being investigated, Mr. President. I assure you we have a handle on it."

Barakat turned, ignoring the group of officers.

"Mr. King, will you follow up with the general on these incidents and guarantee they're being managed properly?"

Max King again nodded silently.

The group of army officers stood quietly for several moments. Finally, the president looked up at them as if annoyed. He made a shushing motion with his hand as if waving off a pet.

"You're dismissed, General."

The general snapped to attention, saluted the president, and then walked out the door, his officers following. Alone in the hallway and well clear of the bunker door the general turned to his staff of officers.

"Execute Operation Falcon," the general said with authority. Each officer nodded his or her understanding.

Chapter 30

Three NSF agents sat on the squirming figure under them. One held a canvas bag tightly around the prisoner's struggling head. A second straddled the chest and a third poured a large orange bucket of water over the prisoner's covered face, letting it soak into the material.

Bare legs kicking and thrashing, Shade coughed and gagged. She felt bile rising in her throat and fought for breath.

"Tell us where to find your brother or you're taking another ride on the submarine," Agent Salzman growled, pausing the waterboarding, waiting for a response he doubted would come. After three days of interrogation, Shade had refused to make so much as a whimper.

The sound of someone clearing their throat turned the heads of the three NSF agents.

"Wouldn't y'all think after all this playing in the water we'd have some answers?" Donna Koontz asked sarcastically, sitting in a steel chair filing her bright red nails.

"Agent Salzman, I'm here because the president wants answers. You are going to get me answers . . . correct?"

"I'll get you answers, Ms. Koontz. It just takes a little time."

"Time is what we don't have."

Koontz stood up and walked to stand beside the agents. She motioned for them to remove the bag over the prisoner's head.

The second the canvas bag was jerked away Shade glared at Koontz, water glistening on her short-cropped hair. Her face was black and bruised. One eye was swollen shut and the other half closed. Blood was caked under her nose and on her puffy lips. A three-inch open cut adorned Shade's left cheek.

"Howdy," Koontz said comically, staring down at Shade. "Ya know we're gonna find your brother with or without your help. So why don't ya save us all a heap of time and you a whole bunch of hurt. Just tell us where he is and this can all come to a stop."

A grin slowly came to Shade's battered face. She raised her head off the concrete floor and suddenly spit a mouth full of blood-tinged saliva onto Koontz's white pants leg.

Immediately, Salzman swung his right fist into Shade's already swollen cheek, knocking her unconscious. Her body went limp on the wet floor.

Donna Koontz jumped back and stared at the stained material. When she looked up, her eyes fumed.

"Officer Salzman, tomorrow we're gonna use an old, tried-and-true technique that my great-great-granddad used with good results."

Chapter 31

When Maggie came down to breakfast, she found Charlie and her father already sitting at the table drinking coffee. She had tiptoed out of Charlie's room in the early morning and sneaked back to her own bed.

Her father greeted her with a warm hello, but Charlie could only come up with a goofy smile and a guilty look in his eye.

"Your father just told me about Virgil's lung cancer," Charlie said to Maggie. "I hate to hear about that and wish his prognosis was better."

"Virgil's a sweetheart. I've known him my entire life," Maggie said, pouring a cup of black coffee. "There are tons of Vietnam veterans who were exposed to Agent Orange who are having serious health issues now."

Charlie turned to give Russ a somber look. "How long are the docs at Veterans Hospital giving him?"

"Maybe six months," Russ replied, staring into his coffee cup. "He's a fighter." There was an awkward moment of silence before Maggie joined them at the table. "So what now, Dad? We know Charlie and I are being hunted so our movement is limited. We are both apparently unemployed and on the run." Russ pulled a white index card out of his pocket and studied it for a moment before speaking.

"This is the daily report. Virgil delivered it early today. Two states report that army or marine troops have engaged in gun battles with the Iranians that Barakat flew into the country. Military units are leaving their posts or returning to their bases. The BBC reported last night that Iranian infantry and armored units are crossing into Syria and toward Israel. The UN is up in arms, Israel is on high alert and President Barakat's ambassador to the UN is blaming all the trouble on Israel."

"Holy shit, Russ," Charlie said. "Israel isn't going to just sit back and wait for a UN resolution condemning Iran. The IDF will open up a can of whoop ass first."

Russ nodded in agreement. He took the index card, held a lighter to its bottom edge until it was afire and dropped the burning piece of paper into an ashtray on the table.

"That isn't all. Here is the big news," Russ said, looking from Maggie to Charlie. "Yesterday morning a bomb burst in the air over the White House. There was minor damage and one hell of an explosion. Intel says it was sent from an air force base in Missouri, and it shook the hell out of Washington, physically and psychologically. Barakat's press secretary, Donna Koontz, came on TV long enough to say that agents of the Israeli government tried to set off a bomb near the White House. She even showed some video footage of dead bodies they claim were the attackers and praised the efforts of the National Security Force, which she says, thwarted the attempt."

"So what's the plan now, Russ?"

"You sit tight here at the farm. Just hope that the powder keg in the Middle East doesn't go off and the next plane that hits Washington doesn't drop a nuke."

Chapter 32

Sirens began to sound over Tel Aviv. People on the streets scanned the skies as children were herded into their school bomb shelters. Tel Aviv, like every Israeli city, bustled with military activity. Armed soldiers and vehicles guarded every intersection. On the northern border with Lebanon, Syria, and Jordan, Israeli armored units, operating the most advanced Abrams battle tanks, dug in and waited. Miles behind, artillery and rockets waited to receive fire missions. Miles above, fighter aircraft circled the skies waiting for targets.

Commander Amreen Yekta stood on the bridge of the Iranian destroyer Damavand as it bobbed through the waves. His sister ships, the Babr and Palang, sailed beside him. Also making up the convoy were the frigates Avland and Moje and several supply vessels trailed behind. Yekta was sailing toward ports on the Palestinian West Bank. His orders were to first deliver arms, ammunition, and rockets to the PLO fighters and then, when directed, support them with offshore artillery fire when they attacked Israel.

Yekta was fuming that the Arab nations in the region had been reluctant to come to the aide of their Muslim brothers. "Wait until we have the Jews running in defeat, and all of them will want to join in and claim victory," he thought.

A hurried shout from his radar operator, quickly followed by those of crewmen on the deck, brought Yekta away from his thoughts.

"Radar contact northeast, Captain, but it's moving too slow to be a jet aircraft," the operator said, glancing up from his radar display.

Captain Yekta ran from the wheelhouse and trained his binoculars to where sailors were already pointing into the clouds. It just took a second for him to spot and identify the object as an unmanned drone. He watched it vanish behind some puffy clouds. Yekta smiled to himself and then, lowering his binoculars, crowed loudly to his crew.

"The Jews are watching us. They are like pigs staring at the farmer who is coming to slaughter them."

Cheers and laughs echoed from his sailors. Yekta turned to enter the bridge when his radar man began screaming again. This time the man turned to look at Yekta, panicked, his face pale, eyes full of fear.

Less than four miles away, Colonel Avi Schramm and his flight of four Israeli F-15 Silent Eagle fighters skimmed a mere one hundred feet over the waves, racing toward the Iranian task force. Guided by the IAI drone shadowing the enemy, they had hugged the sea and used the radar-absorbing material of their aircraft to remain hidden until it was too late for the Iranian ships to respond. Colonel Schramm gave the order to his fellow pilots, and two Tomahawk missiles ignited and raced from below each of the aircraft's wings. They quickly gobbled up the short distance between them and the Iranian ships.

Commander Yekta had just begun screaming orders to his crew when the first missile tore through the steel side of the Damavand, seventy-five feet behind its superstructure. A microsecond later, it detonated deep below the water line. Yekta and the bridge crew were slammed off their feet as if hit by a runaway truck. A huge fireball engulfed the ship just as a second missile exploded in the engine room. The Damavand was already breaking apart and sinking as the four Israeli jets roared overhead, their engines thundering as they swept past. Fireballs rose from two more ships, and Klaxons rang as those not hit began a zigzag maneuver to evade their attackers. Their efforts were in vain as another flight of F-15's tailing just behind Colonel Schramm added their Tomahawk missiles to the carnage. Colonel Schramm and his flight made a tight bank, the G-force pressing them into their seats. They set their sights on the unarmed supply ships. Their canons spit fire as they began blasting thousands of holes into the thin steel of the heavily loaded cargo ships. Crewmen began jumping into the cold waters of the Red Sea as the Israeli fighters blasted anything still floating. The frigate Moje was making a sharp turn to starboard when a rocket found its ammo magazine deep below deck. In a blinding flash it exploded into thousands of pieces, which rained down on the sea around it as if a giant had suddenly thrown a handful of pebbles into the ocean.

Within three minutes the attack was over. Colonel Schramm eyed the targets below, but all he saw was flaming debris floating in the sea and a ship's bow slipping below the waves. He and his attacking squadron turned and headed back to Israel. The Iranian sea threat was gone. The ammunition and rockets promised to the terrorist fighters on the West Bank settled quietly upon the ocean floor.

Chapter 33

Max King and President Barakat stood silently in the shattered Oval Office, surveying the damage. The President stood, arms folded, and shook his head in disbelief. Books, furniture, and pictures littered the floor along with pieces of the ceiling. King leaned against a wall, his hands calmly folded behind his back.

"How did this happen, Mr. King? One minute everything is running smoothly and the next our own warplanes are bombing the White House. My officers in the military are broadly interpreting my orders, and our friends in Iran are beginning to doubt me."

Max King crossed his arms and began to circle the president.

"When you revealed this plan to me to vastly reshape the government, I warned you it came with great risk. You can't suddenly take freedom away from a nation that has enjoyed it for over 200 years and expect everyone to jump on board. America isn't a third-world nation that has been under some form of dictatorship for its entire existence."

"Lenin said that 'a man with one gun can control one hundred without one,' so what's the problem?" replied the president. "I'm beginning to think we're being too lenient."

King stopped his circling and stood facing the president. He purposely stepped into Barakat's personal space, forcing the president to shuffle backward.

"You're correct. Lenin did say that, and look what happened. The Soviet Union eventually murdered more than twenty-million of its own citizens. Are you willing to be that ruthless? Russia invested the majority of its income enslaving their people, and they still failed. You are going down a very dangerous path, Mr. President, I tried to warn you of that. Now you're repeating mistakes . . . serious mistakes. You're ordering the arrest and execution of your military officers. Stalin tried the same trick. So did Hitler. You're losing control, Mr. President. Now your military is abandoning their posts in the cities and returning to their bases. The majority of your navy has sailed away and what you have left couldn't defend the Great Lakes. Our nuclear force isn't answering their phones and your military chiefs of staff have all vanished because they saw what was going to happen. You think they're going to stick around and wait for a bullet behind the ear? What loyal troops you still have couldn't repel an invasion by the Mexican army. You have General Thompson sitting at a nuke base and he is not going to back down from you. Look around this room. Thompson could have easily killed you. He could have leveled the White House, at the very least. There were over twenty-five assassination attempts on Hitler during WWII by his own people, and I assure you, Mr. President, the same is being plotted for you, even as we speak. All you have left are the National Security Force and a few thousand Iranian troops who are getting picked off daily by the Death Card resistance. The truth, Mr. President, is that you – *we* – are in a bad situation. Now, how do you propose we fix it?"

King stopped speaking at the sound of his cell phone ringing. He reached into his pocket and answered it, without taking his eyes off the president.

"Where? Are you sure? Put the team together and meet me in thirty minutes."

He shoved the phone back into his pocket.

"We found Ashman, plus others," he said to the president.

"How?"

Max King raised his arm to expose the plastic ID data band on his wrist.

"We tracked him with this," King said turning and heading for the door.

Chapter 34

Shade Ashman stood on her very tiptoes, her arms stretched toward the ceiling pulling every muscle in her arms taut. Rough brown rope bound her wrists together, blood speckling where the harsh hemp had scraped against her flesh. The rope ran to a steel ring in the ceiling. A dirty piece of duct tape covered her mouth and added to the grotesque appearance of her beaten face. A loud clap filled the small interrogation room, and Shade's body shook from the blow of the long, leather strap across the naked flesh of her back. NSF agent Salzman brought the whip back, preparing to land another blow. Shade's back, buttocks, and legs were covered with viscous red whelps from the lash.

The Hispanic NSF agent stood near the door while Donna Koontz stood in front of Shade, busily smacking on a piece of bubble gum. She stuck a finger under Shade's lowered chin and raised her head up to look into her blood-caked and bruised face.

"I warned you yesterday, darlin', that I had some tricks up my sleeve my great-great-grandfather used to keep his slaves in line down in Alabama. The kiss of a whip worked back then, and, by God, it isn't worth passing up on today," Koontz growled, her nose a few inches from Shade's.

Koontz stepped back and nodded at Salzman, who landed three blows across Shade's bare flesh in rapid succession.

Shade's body jerked with each blow, her knees buckling. Koontz stood watching without expression, her red lips still smacking her gum. She finally held up a hand motioning for Salzman to pause the beating.

"Ready to tell us where your brother, Charlie, is hiding?" Koontz asked dryly, figuring Shade Ashman was near her breaking point.

When Shade didn't respond, Koontz looked at the officer and said, "Salzman, let's re-visit this little whipping scenario later. For now, what say we take a little break. Cut her down."

Koontz looked into Shade's battered face that held an expression of terror. A trickle of a tear ran from Shade's one, undamaged eye. Agent Salzman jerked a long, pointed blade knife from a sheath on his web belt. He swiped easily through the ropes around Shade's wrist and she fell to the floor with a thud. She began rocking in a fetal position, her hands wrapped around her knees pulling herself into a ball. Her body began to quiver as her crying filled the room.

Koontz nodded at Salzman and the other NSF agent who grabbed Shade, jerking her off the floor and held her in a standing position in front of Donna Koontz. The press secretary stared coldly at the trembling, sobbing figure. "Begin, Officer Salzman."

Shade suddenly found herself thrown face down over a table near the center of the room. The steel tabletop felt ice cold against her bare flesh. She felt Salzman move close behind her, pushing his pelvis against her buttocks. Shade began whimpering. The sound of a zipper being undone behind her sounded like a rifle crack.

Donna Koontz kneeled down so she was face-to-face with Shade.

"You know, girlie. My great-great-grand dad knew how to deal with uppity niggers back in the 1800s, and, by God, I can sure handle a traitorous, goddamn nigger like you today."

Shade could feel Salzman's strong hands on her hips and his hard penis as he began pressing against her.

There were a few things that Shade Ashman enjoyed in her free time and knitting, crafts, and scrapbooking weren't any of them. Shade was a physical person, joining cop buddies for a game of basketball after work, running early in the morning, lifting weights, and working out. But mostly, Shade lost herself in practicing one of three forms of martial arts she had excelled at for years.

Shade Ashman was the person you wanted on your side during a brawl. Shade had also been a fairly accomplished actress in high school, a talent she had relied on when she became the crying, whimpering victim lying on the floor a few minutes before.

Salzman kicked her legs roughly apart and began thrusting himself against her as Shade weakly glanced at Koontz, who kept smacking her gum like a cow chewing its cud, while the other female NSF agent stood looking bored.

Shade Ashman had lured them into a false sense of security and control.

With the speed of a cobra, Shade struck. Drawing every ounce of energy in her battered body, she suddenly thrust herself backward off the table, the back of her head smashing into Salzman's face, shattering his chin and fracturing his wind pipe. For a second, Salzman stumbled almost comically, his black uniform pants around his ankles and his erection bobbing bizarrely as he clutched at his shattered throat, gasping for air. The female NSF agent reacted quickly, snapping open a telescoping police baton as she took a two-handed swing at Shade, like a ball player preparing to rocket one into center field. As the baton came at Shade's head, she suddenly ducked down, letting it cut through the air inches above her. She popped up a second later, planting her right foot behind the agent as she reached around her neck, swept her off her feet and then smashed the back of her head down into the edge of the table with a bone shattering crash. As her body collapsed, Shade jerked the agent's knife from her gun belt.

The attack happened so quickly that Donna Koontz didn't have time to react. She turned toward the cell door to scream, but Shade Ashman had already hurdled the table and was on her. She clamped her left hand over Koontz's mouth, pulled her backward and stabbed the knife into the soft spot behind her ear lobe, sinking the long, edged blade to the hilt into Koontz's skull. Shade felt Koontz go stiff. She wiggled the blade around scrambling Donna Koontz's dying brain and then dropped her dead body onto the floor of the cell.

Shade paused, letting her breathing return to normal. She waited, expecting guards to come streaming into the room but the door remained closed. Shade stripped the female agent out of her uniform. The clothes hung on her thin, emaciated frame and the boots were a little large but they would do. She snapped on the dead agent's gun belt and hat, then went over to where the body of Donna Koontz lay. Shade ignored her wide-open lifeless stare and dug into her pocket until she found what she was looking for. Opening the package, she popped a piece of bubble gum into her mouth and stood listening at the cell door. Music coming from a purse Koontz had left on the floor caught Shade's attention. She peeked inside and removed a cell phone. Shade read the text message from someone named Max King.

"We found Ashman. Kill his sister and get over to the White House."

Shade stuck the phone in her pocket. She then removed the cash from Koontz's purse and slowly opened the cell door. The hallway outside was empty. Shade calmly walked to an exit door at the far end. Pulling her hat down over her eyes, she opened the door, walked into the sunlight and vanished.

Chapter 35

Moving through the brush, undetected by the forty-eight NSF agents slowly encircling the farm house, the team leader, using hand signals, directed his troops until they had formed a ring around the home. From behind trees, sheds, and other cover, the black-clad figures aimed their weapons. All wore Kevlar helmets and knit masks that left only their eyes exposed, and their eyes hidden behind tinted goggles.

Pressing a switch on his headset, the team leader reported that they were in position and waiting for orders.

A mile away, two large, 16,000-pound armored SWAT vehicles known as BearCats sat on a dirt road beside an irrigation canal. Three NSF agents stood around the open rear doors of one. They watched as Max King, wearing a $300 suit, an oddly opposite look from the troops around him, bent over a laptop computer busily punching its keys. On the screen an aerial view appeared. From the altitude of the satellite, details of the ground showed a jumbled mix of forest, roads, and fields. Small dots were spread out on the display. Some white, some yellow and a few others red. King wheeled his finger over the mouse pad and the image enlarged showing more detail of the land. A few clicks on the keyboard and the white dots vanished.

"There you are, fuckers," Max said, with a smirk. King's fingers sped over the keyboard again and the satellite image zeroed in on an area showing an L-shaped home with three cars parked out front. Barns, outbuildings, and a round grain silo were clearly visible. King tapped a key and the image became even larger. Around the main building was an uneven ring of white dots but in the center of the house was an almost red blotch.

"Move out," King ordered, jumping into the passenger seat of a BearCat. The three other troopers quickly followed. They left the dirt path and turned right onto a gravel road, a cloud of dust behind them. Normally, in an operation like this, there would be choppers overhead providing air support, but Max King didn't want to spook off his prey. He was keeping the element of surprise.

Russ came up from the basement with two stuffed, olive-green duffel bags. He plopped them down on the living room floor where Maggie and Charlie sat in overstuffed chairs in front of a crackling fire.

"I've put together a bug-out bag for each of you. Tonight you're both getting picked up by friendlies and being moved into the Midwest. We're in control now that Barakat has been pulling his NSF troopers and Iranian scum back into the major cities."

"Any word on Shade, Mr. Kerr?" Charlie asked, leaning forward in his chair.

"Nothing, Charlie. Sorry. Things are really heating up in and around Washington. Word has it that D.C. has become an armed camp. Barakat is consolidating his troops since the military took its ball and went home."

Maggie came over to give Charlie a sympathetic hug and sat on the arm of the chair beside him.

A sudden, loud alarm went off causing Maggie to jump to a standing position. The pigtailed girl who had brought her out of the city suddenly appeared.

"Code red," she yelled pulling the automatic out of her holster and crouching down, scooted toward the front picture window. Russ threw open a closet and jerked out two rifles. He tossed one through the air toward Charlie who was now on his feet.

"Still remember how to operate one of these?"

Charlie snatched the rifle out of midair, knelt down, and, as if he'd practiced the maneuver a thousand times, checked the magazine of the AR-15 and pulled the steel slide back, jerking a round into the chamber.

He turned to Maggie and pointed. "Stay on the floor," he said roughly. Charlie began to move away, then quickly ran back to kiss Maggie on the lips and give her a smile.

"I wish Virgil was here," the pigtailed girl said, barely peeking through an opening in the curtain of the window.

"Virgil's on a mission," Russ said, crawling up to look out the window beside her. "Grab a 12-gauge out of that closet, and go watch the stairway. If they come in through the back on either floor, they'll have to get by you."

The woman nodded and slid across the floor to the open closet door. She pulled a Mossberg pump-action police shotgun out and jacked a round into the chamber with a loud, metallic click before heading out of the room.

Charlie and Russ scanned outside the farmhouse. A moment later a cloud of dust began to rise, signaling a vehicle nearing the house. Both men watched as two armored, black SWAT vehicles came into view.

"Wish I had a LAW rocket right about now," Charlie whispered to Russ. "Which reminds me, where is your private defense force I saw yesterday?"

"I gave them the day off."

Both of the vehicles pulled up fifty feet short of the porch facing in. The doors opened and the three crewmen jumped out and stood safely behind the thick, steel doors of the vehicles.

A moment later, a figure in a suit marched, unconcerned, from the rear of one vehicle. He held a bullhorn in his left hand and was leading someone with him, obviously a woman, from the dress she was wearing. A black cloth bag covered her head. She stumbled along, as the figure in the suit roughly clutched her left forearm. Her hands were flex-cuffed in front of her.

Max King dragged his prisoner in front of the two parked BearCats where he pushed her down on her knees in the gravel.

"Throw down your weapons and come out," King ordered, his voice booming through the bullhorn. "You're surrounded and have nowhere to run."

Charlie and Russ crouched with their backs to the wall. Russ slowly eased himself up, taking a quick peek through the curtains. He turned to face Charlie and turning his right hand, pointed at his eyes with his first and second fingers in a V pattern, signaling that he saw something. He then held up four fingers to signal how many enemies he could see. Charlie nodded his understanding back.

King raised the bullhorn again. "We know who you are and how many of you there are. Come out now before someone gets hurt." He lowered the bullhorn to his side and listened. Besides the rumble of the two BearCats' engines, all he could hear was the sound of birds and crickets around the farmhouse.

"All right, have it your way. But I don't know why you would want to hurt such a nice neighbor lady like Mrs. Reed."

Charlie watched as Russ shook his head sadly and let his chin fall onto his chest. Maggie looked up from the living room floor and began to sob.

"Who?" Charlie asked confused. "Mrs. Reed?"

Russ looked toward him, his face red.

"Virgil's wife. They have Ann," Russ hissed angrily.

Charlie remembered Ann from the night before when she had threatened him with a bread knife. He clutched his AR-15 closer.

Outside, Ann still knelt on the ground. King reached down and tore the black mask off her head. She blinked her eyes, adjusting to the sunshine and then glared up at him.

"Tell them to come out, and I'll let you live. Hell, I'll even let that cancer-ridden husband of yours spend his last days in a jail cell."

King smirked coldly, letting Ann know he knew more information about them than they realized.

Ann, still staring at Max King, struggled to her feet. She turned and began to shout toward the house.

"Don't come out, and don't give up. Keep up the . . . ."

The rest of Ann Reed's sentence was interrupted by a gun blast as Max King calmly drew a 9 mm pistol out of a shoulder holster and fired into the side of her head. Ann's head snapped sideways, and she crumpled to the ground, a pool of bright red blood forming in the gravel where she lay.

Maggie, who had sneaked into a kneeling position near a living room window suddenly let out a scream and began to rise. Charlie sprang from his position and tackled her around the waist. The two fell to the floor just as bullets began to blast through the house. Wood splinters and glass showered down. There was a crashing noise and an explosion from the rear of the house.

"STUN GRENADES!" Russ screamed, belly crawling from the shattered front window toward where the pigtail girl lay, her shotgun aimed toward the end of the hallway. Pictures and decorations on the walls of the room began to explode from the impact of bullets. Russ grabbed a wooden lamp table near the couch and tossed it on its side, sending books and remote controls skating across the floor. Suddenly a side door leading into a rear bedroom at the end of the hall opened. A small black object bounced into the hallway.

"COVER!" Russ screamed, throwing himself behind the end table. Charlie lay over Maggie, covering her with his own body. There was a moment of silence before the stun grenade went off with a blinding flash and a booming roar. Pigtail girl lay stunned for just a second, her arms covering her head as a black-clad figure stepped into the hallway, his short-barrel H&K MP5 pointed in front of him. Pigtail girl quickly raised her shotgun and fired the same moment that the gunman sent a volley of bullets tearing through her torso and splintering up the wood floor around her. Her head dropped lifeless. However, her round caught her killer in his right groin, the shotgun slugs taking his leg out from under him and severing his femoral artery. As he hit the floor, he grabbed at the spurting blood coming from his leg.

Just feet away, Russ raised his AR-15 as a second gunman appeared in the hallway, stepping over his fallen partner. Russ knew they would be wearing heavily armored bulletproof vests. He deliberately targeted a spot below the man's Adam's apple and fired a controlled burst that climbed up the assailant's throat and ended at his forehead. As the man collapsed backward, Russ took aim on the helmet of the other moaning NSF trooper and fired a string of bullets through his neck and the side of his helmet, silencing him.

Max King held a walkie-talkie to his mouth as he stood beside the passenger door of a BearCat.

"ALL UNITS MOVE IN . . . MOVE IN!" King ordered. An NSF agent stood up in the turret of a BearCat and raised a multi-chambered grenade launcher. He began to walk high-explosive rounds through the front two story windows and walls of the house, their detonations blasting glass and wood out onto the yard in a shower of debris. Somewhere in the rear, a second grenadier followed suit. The lethal assault continued unabated for a full minute. There was a lull as the shower of grenades ended. Quickly moving in over watch, one trooper moving forward, covered by the others, then a second and a third, as the assault teams closed in on the house. Glass crackling under his boots, the first NSF agent inched his way through the front door, his gun darting right and left. The rest of his squad followed close behind him.

In his earpiece Max King began to hear his teams report in.

"Top floor secure."

"Bedrooms secure."

"Front secure."

"Body count?" Max King asked calmly.

"One female."

King jerked his head up, a puzzled expression on his face. He began to walk rapidly toward the shattered front door. A mantra he had heard a thousand times in the army sounded in his head.

"Walk swiftly and with purpose. DON'T RUN!"

King stepped into the shambled living room. A dozen troopers stood guard, their guns pointed at the floor. One towered over the bloodied body of pigtail girl. King spotted the body of two NSF agents in a heap at the end of the hallway.

"They escaped, sir," a black-clad squad leader said to King, who turned on him angrily.

"There's no *fucking* way they escaped. Now tear this place apart."

It took less than two minutes into the search to find the hidden hatch in the living room floor under the debris-littered, southwestern print rug. King ordered it opened. Every assault team member in the room trained their weapons on it as another carefully hooked his fingers in a ring depressed in the wooden lid and lifted. He stepped backward jerking it open and an object attached to the bottom of the hatchway raised up with it. Several assault team members recoiled, but what some expected to be a booby trap didn't materialize.

King stood and stared into the tunnel beneath the floorboards of the house. A ring of over a dozen red, government issued data bracelets hung from a piece of wire duct-taped to the bottom of the door.

"Get some people down there to follow this tunnel!"

A squad leader snapped an order and two troopers immediately lowered themselves into the dark tunnel.

"Watch for booby traps," King said calmly, turning and walking out the front door. As he did, he stepped over the shattered picture of a much younger Russ as a Navy SEAL. In it, Russ stood beside a small river patrol boat with several other armed men.

Max King was sitting in the passenger seat of a BearCat when a team leader came up and reported the tunnel had ended several hundred feet from the house under a cattle water tank. There was no sign of anyone.

King let out a frustrated huff. "Let's get some choppers in the air and see if we can spot them. I want them flying all night using heat thermal cameras in case our targets plan on just hunkering down in the dark."

"Yes, sir," the trooper responded.

"Mount up. Let's get out of here."

The man vanished toward the rear of the BearCat as the driver took his spot, put the vehicle into gear, and eased past the dead body of Ann Reed. The inside of the vehicles were crammed with NSF troopers and their gear. A half-dozen stood at the open rear doors holding onto specially equipped handles as the two BearCats began to bounce down the rutted driveway.

Max King began composing a message on his phone to the president. He had tried to contact Donna Koontz but the bitch was apparently ignoring his calls. They were nearing the end of the driveway where the main road began as King completed his message. Holding his cell phone on his thigh King was about to press the send key when something caught his eye. The trooper behind the wheel was wearing a pair of muddy cowboy boots.

King turned to stare at the driver just as he brought the BearCat to a stop. Lifting the Kevlar helmet off of his head he sat it on the dash and pulled the knit mask below his chin. He held out an item toward Max King who glanced quickly at it. Dropping the Ace of Spades playing card, he reached into his jacket and began to draw his automatic.

"FIRE IN THE HOLE!" Virgil Reed yelled with a toothless smile as he detonated the heavily laden suicide vest under his stolen NSF uniform.

In a microsecond the lead BearCat exploded in an earth-shattering explosion, killing everyone within five feet. The vehicle split open like a soda can that had burst from within. The doors and hood sailed through the air as an immense fireball engulfed its skeleton. A rear door propelled by the energy of the blast sliced through the driver's compartment of the second BearCat, decapitating the driver and passenger. Its fuel tank, ruptured by the blast wave from the lead vehicle incinerated everyone inside. A few troops standing at the rear were blown through the air and away from the burning wreckage. The scorched figures landed in the dusty road, dazed and shattered.

A dozen armed, camouflaged figures concealed in holes near the driveway suddenly appeared and made quick work of the wounded survivors.

Chapter 36

Andrew Dean was a small, unassertive man. This was a quality that made him Donna Koontz's favorite aide and whipping boy. He had trailed behind her for five years.

"Get me coffee, Andrew. Get so-and-so on the line, Andrew. Have my car washed, Andrew."

She had patted him on the top of the head once and referred to him as her perfect slave.

Now Andrew had been selected to deliver the daily report to the president, something everyone else seemed terrified to do. In a room filled with NSF security agents and a dwindling support staff, Andrew read from a prepared list. Sitting like a scolded child in the principal's office, Andrew never made direct eye contact with the president. He felt it best to begin with the least damaging news.

In the Middle East, a navel force sent toward Palestine had been destroyed by the Israeli Air Force, which held control of the skies. The Iranian army was stuck in Syria. Syria's own government, not a fan of Iran's support of rebel fighters in Syria's own civil war, was expressing dissatisfaction with Iranian armor and troops on its own turf. Now, Iran was reluctant to invade the small Jewish nation of Israel and was accusing the president of reneging on his offer of U.S. military planes and ships to aide in the attack. Iran didn't have the capability of providing the air power to counter the well-trained, experienced, and equipped Israeli Air Force. There was also no help coming from Iran's Arab allies, Egypt and Jordan, who were sitting this skirmish out except for their fiery rhetoric about the death of Israel. Jordan and Egypt, unlike Iran, had learned a painful lesson in previous battles with the Jews.

The entire nation of Israel was on high alert. It wasn't going to be a surprise attack like the Arab armies had tried in 1974. This time, every unit of the Israeli military down to the reserve forces were locked and loaded. If Iran attacked Israel, not only would they be fighting one of the best armies in the world, there would also be an armed Jewish citizen hiding behind every olive tree ready to send an Iranian soldier to Allah.

Just one day earlier, an undetected Israeli fighter had suddenly appeared over Tehran. As sirens blared and fighters scrambled to get airborne, the Israeli aircraft filled the sky with thousands of bright yellow leaflets. Written upon them was simply Albert Einstein's famous equation, $E=mc2$, a subtle reminder that Israel was a nuclear power and had no intention of becoming victims to an invading Arab army.

Tehran was now in a furor demanding the return of the Revolutionary Guard troops that had been sent to America on President Barakat's request. What the Iranian government did not know was that the soldiers, or what remained of them throughout the country, were now surrounded by armed militia fighters and defected U.S. military troops.

The United Nations was raising charges against President Barakat and his administration for crimes against humanity. His top hit man and leader of the National Security Force, Max King, was dead, along with some of his top lieutenants in a bloody ambush in Upstate New York. With the head of the NSF chopped off, the tail didn't know what to do or who to take orders from. The president's own press secretary, Donna Koontz, had been found with the six-inch blade of a knife buried in her brain and a highly valued prisoner was missing.

The most damaging news came when Andrew Dean informed the president that members of Congress and Senate were pleading privately with the UN and other free-world governments for help. Many who had gleefully sided in the beginning with President Barakat's takeover were now making their own deals of clemency or seeking asylum in other countries. Most of the president's staff had disappeared, but those who chose to stay were hard-core supporters who would stand beside him even as the flames licked at their heels.

During the fall of Berlin at the end of World War II, Adolph Hitler spent his finals hours hidden in a bunker giving deranged orders to military units that no longer existed and issuing commands that were impossible to follow. Now, like the crazed dictator of sixty years before, President Barakat began giving unrealistic orders to the men and women gathered around him. He demanded the military return to the streets to put down the insurrection. The US Army, Navy, Air Force, and Marines all refused. A week earlier, he commanded his National Security Force to move into several military installations, to arrest the officers and take command of the troops within. Following these orders with a fanatical enthusiasm, the NSF had marched against large military bases like Fort Benning and Camp Pendleton. The soldiers and U.S. Marines had made mincemeat out of the NSF thugs, who were used to taking on and executing unarmed civilians. Going nose-to-nose with well-trained, disciplined military troops was a slaughter for Barakat's private army.

The president had raised the idea of dropping his own nuke on a major U.S. city to warn the population and any other opposition that he meant business and would regain control. However, his advisers reported that he could no longer order nuclear weapon strikes. Those with the power, such as NORAD, would not launch against American citizens. In essence, the air force officer carrying the "football," a briefcase containing the nuclear missile launch codes, was a paper tiger. General Thompson still held the nuclear card over the White House from his base deep in Missouri. At the conclusion of his report, Andrew Dean, his hand shaking as if he had just drunk twenty cups of coffee and ten power drinks, handed the president an envelope. Barakat took the single sheet of paper out, unfolded it and read silently to himself. "How long is this offer good?" He asked, looking across his desk at Andrew Dean. "Forty-eight hours, sir."

Chapter 37

Israeli Prime Minister Ben-David was awakened shortly after five o'clock in the morning with an important phone call. It was his head of MOSSAD, Moshe Kravitz. He sat up in bed and pulled on his reading glasses. Holding the phone to his ear, he listened silently.

"Are you positive, Moshe? Make sure it's not a trick, and don't change our posture until you hear from me. Thank you, Moshe. I'm happy, too."

Israeli intelligence had reported the Iranian troops in Syria were withdrawing back towards their own border.

Chapter 38

Maggie was bent over at the waist, her long red hair hanging downward, shaking dirt out of her hair. Charlie and her father, Russ were more occupied with cleaning their weapons. Both sat on the ground, their M14 rifles already field-stripped in front of them. As Maggie tried to dust herself off, the two men were busy with rags and cleaning solution scouring their weapons inside and out. Back at the farmhouse, Russ had spotted the NSF trooper raising his grenade launcher. Just seconds before the grenade rounds began exploding inside the house, Russ had herded them all into the hidden tunnel below the house. On hands and knees, they had crawled in the darkness of the cool, earthy-smelling tunnel for what seemed like hours. Maggie had been born and raised in the home. Her father and late mother had owned it longer than Maggie had been alive, and Maggie had never been told or ever suspected an escape tunnel ran below the family room. It didn't surprise her knowing her father and his "always be prepared" thought pattern. She would get the tunnel details from him later but right now she was just glad to be alive.

Once they had slid into the tunnel, Maggie felt as if World War III was erupting over them. The explosions were deafening and dirt fell from the roof of the tunnel with every blast. Maggie had forced herself to fight off the fear of the tunnel collapsing and kept crawling as quickly as she could. With her father in front and Charlie behind her, Maggie felt protected. As the sounds of the explosions began to slacken to soft thuds behind them, Maggie began to calm down. Finally, they had come to a stop. Her father, rifle in one hand, slowly raised himself upwards. He worked to shove something out of his way and sunlight suddenly filled the tunnel. Maggie had to shield her eyes, because they had just grown adjusted to the darkness. Russ raised his head up, exposing his eyes. Slowly, he looked right to left before climbing out into the light and motioning for Maggie and Charlie to follow. The end of the tunnel had been carefully concealed behind an empty cattle water tank, which sat beside an ancient windmill. Its rusted blades turned slowly in the wind, making a creaking sound.

Crouching low, Russ had led them to a large clump of bushes near the water tank. With Charlie's help, they had removed a large square camouflaged net revealing a pair of green four-wheel ATV's underneath. With her father riding one, she had leapt on the other, holding tightly to Charlie's waist. For over an hour, they had traveled through the woods steering between trees and rocks. They were passing by a crystal-clear stream when a loud explosion echoed in the distance. Maggie's father suddenly stopped his ATV and stared for a moment in the direction of the blast before twisting the handle of his ATV and climbing the opposite bank.

Overhead, the sun was bearing down, and at one point, Maggie's father signaled them to jump off their machines and hide under a clump of tall oak trees. Russ and Charlie stood with their backs against the tree trunk and Maggie followed suit. After a moment, a flight of black helicopters with white NSF initials on their tail sections raced overhead. The choppers didn't notice the three, seeming hell bent on getting somewhere else.

"We wait here for now," Russ said, removing the bungee cords that held a duffel bag on the rear of his ATV. He leaned his back against a tree and slid into a sitting position, his rifle across his thighs. Opening the bag he tossed a water at Charlie and then gently handed one to Maggie.

Maggie began drinking her water when she suddenly looked up, startled, her eyes tearing up.

"They murdered Ann," she blurted. "What did they do to Virgil?" Maggie suddenly began to replay the shooting of her friend in her mind. She looked toward her father, seeking answers.

"Ann went into town early today but never came back," Russ said, looking sadly at Maggie. "That was the warning we were waiting for. We've been expecting the NSF to show up and have had a plan in effect. We figured they would strike in the dark of the night, not the middle of the day. That's why there weren't any sentries posted. We wanted them to think they had surprised us."

Maggie scooted across the ground in front of her father. "Where is Virgil, Daddy?" she asked, staring into his eyes but fearing the answer.

There was a pause as Russ finished his plastic bottle of water. "If the plan Virgil came up with worked, he's not here anymore, Maggie, but I promise you he took the bad guys with him. He was going to sneak home and try to rescue Ann if he could. I don't know what happened there. Probably never will."

Russ set his rifle beside him and opened his arms up, taking Maggie in a long bear hug. "You know Virgil was sick and didn't have long to last. He wanted to do something before he died. As for Ann, well, Ann just became another victim of the NSF."

Maggie pulled away from her father and began to wipe the tears from her eyes when there was a sudden snapping of a twig in the woods. It sounded like a shot. Charlie quickly threw himself into a prone position, his rifle pointed toward the sound of footsteps. Russ pushed Maggie down and was lifting his rifle when a voice called out.

"Tropic."

Russ lowered his rifle.

"Thunder," he replied.

A second later six camouflaged men carrying rifles appeared out of the brush. The leader shook hands with Russ while the others formed a defensive circle around the group looking outward.

"What happened to Virgil?" Russ asked the man quietly.

"Sorry, skipper, but he's gone. Took over forty NSF agents out with him plus their head guy, Max King. We took care of the rest."

Russ thought for a moment before answering.

"With King gone that should rattle Barakat's cage."

"More news, Skipper," the man said, motioning toward Charlie. "Seems your friend's sister killed two NSF agents with her bare hands, and then stabbed Barakat's lipstick-wearing press secretary to death in an interrogation cell."

"Where is Shade now?" Charlie almost yelled.

The squad leader motioned for Charlie to lower his voice. "We don't know, sir, except she slipped out of the building wearing an NSF uniform that she took off one of her victims. I'd say she's either holed up somewhere or she's headed here."

"All right, listen up," Russ said to the group. "Once the sun goes down, we leave the tree line and head across that field." Russ raised an arm and pointed to a meadow ahead of them. "See that tree line on the other side? That's the river and right in front of it is where we are headed to the safe house."

Charlie looked toward where Russ pointed. The squad leader handed Charlie a pair of binoculars and he raised them to his eyes and scanned off in the distance. The blue sparkle of water showed Charlie where the trees ended and the river sat. Just before the trees sat an old building, its roof and sides made out of weathered sheet metal. There were old gas pumps out front and several disheveled and run-down single-wide mobile homes and fifth-wheel campers around it. Discarded farm equipment and trash dotted the tall grass around it. To Charlie it looked like junk that a junkyard wouldn't take. He handed the binoculars back to the squad leader.

"All right. Everybody settle in until dark and then be ready to move out." Russ ordered.

As the squad leader and Russ spoke quietly to one another, Maggie curled up next to Charlie resting her head on his shoulder.

Chapter 39

Shade was shuffling down the sidewalk wearing a pair of dark sweat pants and a Washington Redskins hoodie. She had left the NSF uniform outside a local thrift store and pilfered a pile of clothes left sitting beside a donation receptacle to create the outfit she now wore. During the beatings and interrogations Shade had lost track of time. She didn't know if her ordeal had lasted for one day or one week. But Shade knew things had changed. She could feel it in her bones, and it wasn't for the better. A light mist had been coming down and Shade walked with the hoodie drawn around her bruised and swollen face. Every bone in Shade's body throbbed with pain and bloody rings surrounded her wrists where she had been tightly handcuffed for hours. The gun she had taken from the NSF agent was shoved into the pocket of her jacket.

Every business Shade walked by appeared closed, except for some seedy looking bars. The sounds of automatic gunfire and explosions echoed around the city. Sirens seemed to be coming from everywhere, and the thump of helicopter rotors could be heard in the distance.

Shade had found a Chinese restaurant open and ate a quick meal in a corner booth, courtesy of Donna Koontz's money while keeping an eye on the front door. A woman who Shade took to be the wife of the man who waited on her at the counter kept running to the front door and looking up in the sky. She wore a bright pink jogging suit with matching shoes and kept screaming and waving her arms at the man. Shade was just finishing up when she saw the man approach.

"Very sorry," the man said, bowing with a grim look on his face, "must close now. Very bad. Very bad," he repeated, pointing out toward the street.

Shade nodded, shoved an egg roll into her pocket and walked back into the dusk. Up ahead a shouting mob was smashing out the front window of an appliance store and then scrambling inside like a swarm of ants. Shade felt it wiser to avoid the scene and turned right at the next street. She had walked about a block when she sensed that she was being watched. She turned her head ever so slightly to look over her left shoulder. She saw the DC Metropolitan Police cruiser slowly tailing her less then thirty feet away. Shade turned her head back to the front and fingered the automatic in her pocket.

She shuffled down the sidewalk, head lowered, when she heard the sounds of a car door slamming.

"Excuse me," the voice said. Shade kept moving, trying to decide to run or fight. Either way, Shade felt she would lose. Despite her hand-to-hand fighting skills, she was too weak to put up much resistance, and her tortured, shaking hands wouldn't be of any use when she had to sight-in on her target, especially against a pair of healthy, prepared police officers.

"Excuse me! Stop!" Shade could hear footsteps on the sidewalk behind her. She obeyed, letting her shoulders slump. The thought of pulling the automatic and sticking it to her own head crossed Shade's mind. "Better than being tortured to death," she figured. A pair of hands reached out and took hold of Shade's biceps and she felt a head lean in close to her hooded face.

"It's all right, Captain Ashman," the voice whispered. "Just act drunk and come with us. We'll take you somewhere safe."

Shade suddenly felt weak and let the two policemen guide her back towards their car. One held the door and the other helped her into the back seat. Closing her door, they slid into the front and pulled away from the curb. A muscular black cop in the passenger seat turned and slid open a window in the middle of the wire prisoner's cage. Shade recognized him. Stan was his name. He had ridden with her when she was his field training officer years before when he was a fresh, naive rookie right out of the academy. He gave Shade a big smile.

"Relax, Captain. It's all good. We're going to take you somewhere safe and hand you over to members of the resistance. You know, the guys making the noise all over town. Word has it, they'll probably capture Washington in the next two days."

Shade sat back in her seat, relieved. She reached into her pocket and retrieved another item she had taken from Donna Koontz's purse. She hummed a little tune to herself as she applied a layer of bright red lipstick onto her smiling, sore lips.

Chapter 40

Just as the sun was setting Maggie, Charlie, and Russ were escorted by the militiamen across the field to the steel building near the river. Several times, the team leader suddenly stopped, dropped to one knee, and held his right hand raised in a fist. The other men, including her father and Charlie, immediately did the same. Maggie learned quickly to follow their actions. The leader would carefully scan ahead of them before rising and motioning them to resume their march. They had picked their way around abandoned hulks of cars and discarded refrigerators until finally reaching the structure. Once there, another squad of camouflaged men appeared out of the shadows. When they finally reached the building, two of the men slid aside a large steel door allowing Maggie and her group to enter. Maggie's first impression was that the inside of the large garage matched the outside. Old steel lockers lined one wall, along with fading red toolboxes. Something hung from every rafter in the building: extension cords, ropes, and even an old toilet seat cover. Flickering Coleman lanterns gave off the only light in the garage. A deer head mounted on a far wall only added to the atmosphere of chewing tobacco and Coors beer.

Inside the old tractor barn sat a room built into one corner. Light illuminated from inside it, and Maggie could see several figures moving around. As they neared, a tall thin woman walked towards them, came to attention and snapped a salute to Russ who returned it before shaking hands. Maggie's father then turned and introduced her to Charlie and Maggie.

"This is Major Ginny Mueller, the Operations Commander for the Washington district," Russ said to them. "She's been a busy woman, and we're here to help."

Turning, they walked toward the room. Maggie and Charlie stood looking at one another until Russ motioned for them to follow.

The room was larger than it appeared from the outside. On the walls were several maps and satellite photographs of Washington and the surrounding area. Several red circles and arrows marked them. One man was talking into a huge walkie-talkie and writing on a yellow note pad.

Russ and the woman sat at a steel table overflowing with Styrofoam coffee cups and office supplies. Major Mueller pulled a cigar out of her jacket pocket and lit it with a powerful cigar lighter. Russ motioned to Charlie and Maggie to join them.

"We have work to do and a ton of it. We could really use your help," Russ said to both of them. "The government is collapsing. Our militia armies across the United States have captured every city except a few, like San Francisco, Miami, and Washington, but the fighting in these cities is intense. President Barakat's private NSF forces are shedding their uniforms and deserting in droves. The rumor is that Barakat's cronies he put into power in Congress are seeking private amnesty deals with the World Court."

Russ paused for a moment and pointed towards a corner of the room where a computer center had been set up. "In about two hours, we will have control of the communications center, and we'll be able to start sending out information to the citizens, letting them know what's happening. Charlie, I need you and Maggie to make that happen. Start creating some video clips assuring the people that the government has fallen and Barakat's reign of terror is over. Be ready to get them onto the Internet, pronto. We would like for you to keep broadcasting to the citizens that an emergency government is being put into place with the help of the United Nations. Urge the police and other EMS personnel to return to work. We have to regain order, Charlie and Maggie, because right now things are a mess. Tell the citizens not to panic if they see the National Guard in the streets. These troops are coming out to help under orders from the interim government and not from the direction of Barakat or anyone affiliated with him."

Russ sat back in his chair and looked from Maggie to Charlie.

"Any questions?"

Charlie and Maggie flashed one another a smile, hopped out of their seats, and raced over to their waiting computer equipment.

Chapter 41

Air Force One sat on the tarmac of Andrews Air Force Base. Hundreds of black uniformed NSF agents mingled with camouflaged military troops and ringed the aircraft. Armored vehicles had made a wide cordon facing out. Men stood in the circular gun turrets arming 50-caliber machine guns. In the distance, rifle and machine-gun fire crackled. A line of black SUVs and private cars were parked outside of the defensive ring. Individuals and groups of civilians ran from the vehicles, suitcases in hand. Many carried children and several women were crying. Even the men's faces were a mix of fear and panic. A wall of armed NSF troops blocked their way. Several were shouting, waving sheets of paper, and pointing at Air Force One.

"I'm on the list!" screamed one short, fat man wearing white golf shorts, a pink Polo shirt, and deck shoes. "I'm on the list!" he screamed again at an NSF agent, who ignored him behind a pair of mirrored sunglasses.

Inside Air Force One, President Barakat slowly sipped on a glass of whisky and soda. He stared at a plasma screen on the wall. The words "News Special Report" had been sitting stationary on the television station for over an hour. Suddenly, it faded and the scene became that of the CNN newsroom. An older man with graying hair in a dark suit appeared. He introduced himself as Alex Booth and began speaking directly to the camera.

"Fighting is currently raging across the United States as members of the National Security Force battle to hold ground against forces of the Death Card militia and bands of armed civilians."

As Alex Booth spoke, his image was replaced with video of camouflaged men with rifles racing across streets and firing from behind cars and walls.

The president pointed a remote control at the screen and the channel changed, showing another news report. This time a female and male news team were discussing the surrender of the Iranian

Revolutionary Guard troops. Video showed several dozen disheveled Arab men in uniform, leaning on their knees, their hands behind their heads. Another quick clip showed similar men surrendering and walking out of a building. They all had a look of fear on their faces. Armed militia members and gun toting civilians encircled them. The reporter on the scene was explaining how very few of the Iranian troops were fighting back. The screen flashed to the scene of two bloodied bodies lying beside a bullet-riddled FedEx truck.

By the third channel, the president was visibly enraged. He slammed his glass on the table beside him as a reporter with a strong British accent was being interviewed on a foreign talk show. Below his image, the words "Live from London" was displayed.

"It's being reported that American President Marcus Barakat has been promised asylum in an unnamed Middle Eastern country if he orders his private security force to lay down their weapons. The second demand is that United Nations' peacekeepers from Britain and France be allowed into the country to direct a peaceful transition of power and assist in re-establishing law and order."

Wiping a hand across his face, the president clicked the television off. He looked across the table where two plainclothes NSF agents sat silently.

"Have you confirmed the deaths of King and Koontz?" the president asked.

"Yes, sir," one answered. "Donna Koontz was killed by a prisoner along with two other agents. Mr. King and his assault group were killed in a roadside ambush, possibly an IED. Troops went to the scene but there were no survivors and no sign of the attackers."

President Barakat pondered the news for a moment and then picked up a phone.

"Send in Andy Chaet."

Opening a drawer, the president grabbed a sheet of paper and began writing on it as the two NSF agents silently watched.

"In the 1700s, pirate captains often gave their crews a letter of marque so if they were captured, the sailors could claim they were forced by the captain to act in an illegal manner. I am hoping this letter will aide in your defense if you are brought up on charges."

The president slid the sheet of paper across the table. Both U.S.

agents looked at it with a sense of confusion.

"Two hours after we are in the air, order all of our troops to lay down their weapons. I would urge them to run and hide. Now you have your orders. Leave Air Force One, and let those with approval board the plane. Tell the captain I want to be wheels up in forty-five minutes."

Both NSF agents rose, looking as if they had just been fired from a job. As they headed toward the door, it opened and another man entered. He stood aside as the two agents left, then closed the door and took a seat opposite of the president. He looked distressed, wearing khaki pants and a wrinkled denim shirt.

"So, what's the plan, Mr. Chaet?" the president asked, finishing off his whisky and soda, the ice cubes clinking as he set the glass down.

"Our destination is Tehran. The British have agreed to meet us for an in-flight refuel, and no government has said anything about forcing us down to be detained."

"Why are we so lucky?"

"Because the World Court hasn't drawn up the legal charges yet and some of the Arab nations are causing enough interference to delay a warrant until we reach Iran. However, Mr. President, charges will be filed. That is a given. The Iranian government is pissed about the loss of their Revolutionary Guard troops in the U.S. and our failure to hold up our end of the bargain to support their invasion of Israel. Your saving grace is that Iran won't honor an extradition treaty and hand you over. The downside is that none of us can ever leave the borders of Iran again unless we want to end up in prison."

"Where will I be staying, Mr. Chaet?"

"The Iranians have promised you'll receive a comfortable home, but don't think you are going to have servants or living at the Ritz. The rest of us get to join the Iranian working class or stay here in the U.S. and take our chances."

Staring into his empty glass, the president pondered what the man had explained to him. He picked up the phone.

"Have the steward bring me another drink and tell the captain to get us in the air."

Chapter 42

A smiling Charlie Ashman looked towards the camera lens on his computer. He held some printed copy that Maggie had written for him.

"Hello everyone, this is Charlie Ashman with an update on our current situation. The good news is that the police and other EMS personnel are back on the job, and most of the NSF have gone into hiding. There have been reports of citizens capturing and dishing out their own retribution on these guys and other Americans who collaborated with them. Please don't join in this type of assaults. Let our law enforcement do their jobs. I realize everyone feels anger toward the NSF, but I assure you that law enforcement is taking care of the situation."

Behind his computer monitor, Maggie gave Charlie two thumbs up and a big smile.

"At this point, things are very fluid. What we do know is that Air Force One, with the president and close supporters, has left Edwards Air Force base. The word is that President Barakat has been offered asylum in Iran. They can have him. A state of emergency will be in effect for forty-eight hours, so don't panic if you see the National Guard or militia members in your area. They're the good guys and will be the ones preventing looting and establishing safety for everyone. An interim government in Washington is working with our French and British friends, and citizens in some cities may run into these peacekeepers. They won't be hard to miss because they wear baby blue helmets and armbands, and they will all speak with an accent. Please be respectful and courteous to them and don't make fun of the way they talk. They are our welcome guests."

"So to wrap this up, things are slowly getting back to normal. Your phones, cell service, and the Internet are back up and running, and all television stations are back on the air. There is important news being broadcast on the major channels, and I am pleased to announce you can also catch your favorite movie channel or reality show again."

"Getting back to our ordinary life will not happen overnight. I am sure everyone who is listening, well, you are likely as shell-shocked as I am. It will get better. So if you are a store owner, please stock your shelves and open your doors. It is now safe for everyone to go back to work. It is time we all resume a normal life, free and unafraid."

"This is Charlie Ashman, and God Bless America."

Maggie leaned over the computer monitor and clicked a key, turning off the camera. She came around and as Charlie rose from his chair, Maggie gave him a big hug.

"Great job, Charlie. You even made me feel safe," Maggie said smiling.

"Let's put a podcast together after we gather more information. We can put it on the Internet for viewers who missed the live broadcast."

Maggie nodded as they began walking toward the doorway of the small room. A flat screen television was airing a CNN special report. One clip showed a street in a restaurant area filled with laughing and cheering people. Almost all held drinks or beer bottles and were chanting at the camera, "USA! USA! USA!" The report switched to a National Guard officer at the Miami airport shaking hands with a uniformed man wearing a blue beret. A line of troops in the same uniform were hopping out of a large white helicopter behind them. Suddenly, the news report flashed to a mob scene where people were beating and pummeling an unarmed black uniformed NSF agent. A ticker at the bottom of the screen said the man had been caught after throwing a grenade at a crowd of celebrating civilians.

Maggie was reaching for the remote control when her father's voice suddenly bellowed from outside in the main garage.

"Charlie! Front and center!"

He and Maggie exchanged a look of surprise before quickly walking out of the office.

Entering the main area of the garage, Charlie saw a dozen camouflaged men, Major Mueller, and Russ standing around a figure sitting on a steel folding chair. At first Charlie thought someone had rescued a homeless person. The person just didn't look like a homeless person, Charlie thought to himself, but something like a seventh-degree homeless person. As he got closer, the wraith stood, dropping a green army blanket that had been draped over its shoulders. It took Charlie a moment to realize that the dirty, grinning figure coming toward him was his sister, Shade.

The two grabbed one another and stood silently for a moment. Charlie looked at Shade and reaching out, pushed the hoodie off her head, exposing Shade's bruised and swollen face. She looked at him through one eye, the other puffed closed.

"You look like hell, Sis."

"Think I look bad, you should see the other guy," Shade responded with a laugh, playfully punching Charlie in the stomach.

Chapter 43

Air Force One cruised at 30,000 feet over the Mediterranean Sea. A crew member had stuck his head into the president's office informing him they were between Greece and Turkey. President Barakat had been thinking, plotting, planning. His anger had been seething inside him like something brewing in a cauldron. He began to formulate a plan in his mind. First he would get settled and established in his host country where he would offer any and every bit of assistance to the Iranian cause. Barakat would feel no guilt at disclosing every piece of intelligence he could about America's military secrets and how to defeat them. After a while he would persuade the Iranian government to let him lead an invasion of its surrounding Arab countries. In his twisted mind Barakat thought his new Iranian friends would jump at the opportunity of reestablishing the might and splendor of the Persian Empire. Barakat knew that with the chaos he had left in the U.S., America wouldn't respond to a military movement by the Iranian army anytime soon. America's allies would be so tied up helping clean up the mess he had created, they wouldn't be able to make a move either. The only problem would be the Israelis. They had a powerful military as they had demonstrated in destroying the Iranian naval group. Barakat began to put the pieces of the puzzle together in a methodical manner. He had to first capture the Arab countries. Then he would blame everything on the Americans and the Jews. Finally, he would amass together the forces of every Arab country and drive the Israelis into the sea. Afterwards, he would point his dagger at Europe and America, his newest, greatest enemies. Barakat figured that losses in the invasion of Israel would be high and the small nation would fight to the last man, maybe even use some of its nuclear weapons. But that didn't matter. Any means to achieve the end, Barakat thought to himself.

There was a sudden knock on the door and an air force major with Andy Chaet at his heels pushed into the room.

"We have a problem, Mr. President," the major said.

"What would that be?"

"We just picked up four unidentified aircraft on radar."

"What are these unidentified aircraft doing?"

"Circling around behind us."

President Barakat glared at the major with contempt.

"Then I guess you need to go do whatever it is that you do in a situation like this," Barakat said, in a belittling voice.

The officer quickly turned and left. Andy Chaet stood across from the president with a look of dread and fear on his face.

Barakat stood and slowly walked toward Chaet, until mere inches separated them and Chaet seemed to cower.

"You assured me, Mr. Chaet, that we wouldn't be intercepted and forced down at a foreign airport. Maybe you can tell me what's going on here? I seem to keep running out of advisers and you might be next on that list," Barakat growled.

"We're trying to contact them now, Mr. President. The aircraft could be an escort sent by Iran or another friendly nation to guide us in," Chaet stuttered, white specks appearing at the corners of his mouth. "You know . . . maybe even Syria or Egypt."

Ten miles behind Air Force One, the flight of fighter aircraft banked, the sun flashing off their wings as they took positions behind and slightly above the larger plane. They reduced speed, slowing their approach to the huge Boeing VC-25A.

The same air force major reappeared at the president's door.

"Mr. President, we're still not getting a response from the aircraft; however, they are slowing and it does seem as if they are assuming an escort formation."

The president seemed unmoved. Andy Chaet, however, let out a visible sigh as if he had been holding his breath for ten minutes.

"Try to contact them again to see what they want!" Barakat said angrily and dismissed the major with a wave.

The four intercepting aircraft had closed their formation enough that the leader could communicate with the others by hand signals. The 33-year-old veteran glanced at the other F-35 fighter jets of the Israeli Air Force. He made a circling motion with his hand and the other helmeted pilots nodded in understanding.

He triggered a button on the joystick between his legs and a red targeting circle appeared on his HUD. Inside Air Force One, alarms began to scream and crewmen began to busily work at their duty stations.

"We're being painted!" a female lieutenant screamed over a piercing buzz.

Another yelled into his headset, tense but professional. "Unidentified aircraft, this is United States Presidential Air Force One. Please respond. Repeat, this is Air Force One."

Inside the cockpit of the lead F-35, the flight leader was also hearing a buzz inside his helmet or what fighter pilots called a growl, signifying a missile lock on their target. Squeezing a button on his joystick, two fire-and-forget AMRAAM missiles streaked from under the wings of the Israeli fighter. The 335-pound missiles raced from his aircraft locking onto Air Force One. He glanced quickly right and left and saw practiced and timed twin missiles launch from the other three planes. The leader counted silently to himself and activated another switch, sending two AIM-9 heat-seeking Sidewinder missiles at his target. The other aircraft followed suit.

During their mission planning, they knew that Air Force One contained a state-of-the art anti-missile defense system, but they also knew the sheer number of radar and heat-seeking rockets would overwhelm them.

"MISSILES INBOUND!" screamed a crewman, leaning over his screen.

The pilot of Air Force One, a full-bird colonel, howled "EVASIVE MANEUVERS!" throwing Air Force One into a sudden turn and dropping altitude.

President Barakat, who had been standing berating Chaet, suddenly found himself thrown off his feet and slammed to the floor. Chaet crashed on top of the president pinning him to the floor. Both men struggled to untangle themselves, but the aircraft was suddenly bucking as if out of control.

Among the bedlam inside the cockpit of Air Force, crewmen activated their anti-missile systems and flares shot from Air Force One to decoy the heat seeking guidance systems of the AIM-9 Sidewinders. The pilot knew his plane was dead. He had neither the maneuverability nor the speed to escape.

Three of the eight AMRAAM missiles, confused by the electronic defenses of Air Force One went ballistic and corkscrewed harmlessly into the clouds. Five of the AIM-9s took the bait and went after the red-hot flares falling through the sky. The others homed in on their target.

The time between the missile's launch and its impact lasted fewer than forty-seconds. The first AMRAAM hit twelve feet forward of the tail section exploding in a blinding flash of light. Debris began raining from the gaping hole in the fuselage.

Inside Air Force One, alarms blasted and yellow oxygen masks fell from the ceiling. People screamed. Two of the heat-seeking AIM-9 missiles zeroed in on the starboard engine and detonated at the same time, blowing the wing in half and causing the narrow end piece to fall away. For a second, Air Force One continued on its path before suddenly rolling right and then upside down, out of control. The other four AMRAAM missiles added to the destruction of the aircraft.

Pushing his control stick downward, the Israeli flight leader followed the burning hulk of Air Force One as it spun out of control, a dark black cloud pouring from the shattered plane.

Shoved against one wall by the force of the plummeting aircraft, President Barakat lay pinned. Blood gushed from a cut in his head where a piece of furniture had struck him during the initial evasive maneuver. The last thing President Barakat saw before Air Force One slammed into the waters of the Mediterranean Sea was a large map of the Middle East hanging on the wall. A red X in magic marker was crossed over Israel.

The pilot of the Israeli F-35 keyed a button into his phone. Several hundred miles away, Moshe Kavitz, attending a lunch meeting in Jerusalem, felt his phone vibrate in his jacket pocket. He kept smiling and chatting and glanced at his phone. The message read, "OPERATION MASADA ACHIEVED." He calmly went back to his plate of food.

Chapter 44

Maggie reached the top of the stone stairs, her long sundress swinging above a pair of clogs. She drew a key from her purse, unlocked and pushed opened the door into Charlie's apartment. Technically, it wasn't Charlie's apartment, or a glorified man cave anymore. Now it was their home since they had moved in together. Stepping just inside the door, Maggie was met by a loud purr as her big calico cat began rubbing against her lower legs, purring and meowing.

"Give me a minute to put the groceries down, Puma cat," Maggie said, placing a brown paper sack down on the floor and sitting on a small bench where she kicked off her shoes while stroking the impatient cat.

"Where's daddy, Puma?" Maggie asked, standing up and walking out of the entryway and into the living room with the calico leading the way, his tail held high.

Keeping up a chorus of meows and cat chatter Puma closely followed Maggie down the hardwood floor of the hallway to an open door. Maggie stopped just outside and peeked in, her arms crossed. Puma bounced past her and across the room and onto a wooden desk where Charlie sat in front of his computer.

Charlie turned and smiled at Maggie.

"I see the doorman let you in," Charlie said with a grin, as Puma flopped himself down in the middle of his mouse pad and began rolling around.

"I had lunch with Shade today," Maggie said. "She's doing really good. The doctor gave her a clean bill of health and lifted her off light-duty status. She gets to go back to work full-time on Monday, just in time, I might add. She was going crazy staying at home. I was listening to the radio in the car and they said the last UN peacekeepers left for home today, and everything seems to be back to normal."

"It's getting that way," Charlie said looking into her eyes. "The

211

states are conducting emergency elections in forty-five days. Everyone that Barakat put into office after the big massacre was given the choice of resigning or facing charges for collusion. Now the states get to legally elect their own senators and representatives."

"I can't believe they haven't arrested every goon in the NSF and thrown them in jail," Maggie said, a frown crossing her face. "Especially after the atrocities they committed."

"It's not like they're all getting amnesty, Maggie. If there's proof an individual agent did something criminal, they get arrested and charged. Every night there's a report about another one surrendering or being turned in by neighbors. Hell, Mexico turned twenty of them over to the U.S. after they caught them sneaking across the border during Barakat's fall from power. The great news is that the NSF is gone and out of business. They're being brought to justice, Maggie, just not as quickly as some people would like."

Maggie moved to sit on Charlie's desk. Puma came to sit beside her while batting one of Charlie's pens off his desk.

"What's the hubbub in the UN today, Charlie?" Maggie said.

"Iran accused Israel of shooting down Air Force One. Israel accused Iran of shooting down Air Force One, claiming they were pissed at Barakat for betraying them. There are a dozen conspiracy theories being batted around, a couple of Discovery Channel programs in the works, and some overnight radio call-in show that says Barakat's plane was vaporized by an alien space craft."

Maggie batted her eyes. "A space ship?"

"Yup. Even ET is taking the rap for the demise of Barakat and his gang. It doesn't really matter. If Barakat had escaped, the World Court would have found him and brought him to trial. What's important now is that the military has reorganized and the police are back on the streets. People can go to bed at night without being terrified. Barakat's reign of terror is over."

Maggie stared at Charlie a moment, until a small smile came across her lips.

"What?" Charlie said, his eyes narrowing as if he were trying to read Maggie's mind.

"I'm afraid, my dear husband, that you and I are about to experience our own reign of terror that neither the militia, the United

Nations, nor the U.S. military can protect us from."

Maggie reached inside her bra and pulled out a small square photograph. She let out a giggle as she held it for Charlie to see.

Wrinkling his brow, Charlie looked at the black-and-white sonogram picture. A look of shock and recognition came across Charlie's face.

"Is this what I think it is, Maggie?" Charlie asked, his face now beaming as he stood and reached out to study the photograph.

"It's your baby, Charlie. I wasn't sure before but the doctor confirmed it today. We're going to have a baby," she said in a sing song voice.

Charlie grabbed Maggie and starting kissing and hugging her. Maggie dropped the sonogram image on the desk near Puma cat, who gave it a glance of annoyance.

"I can't wait to tell Shade and Daddy the news," Maggie giggled.

Charlie suddenly pushed away from her as a serious look came to his face.

"I remember your warning about your father when we were," Charlie cleared his throat, "you know . . . together. Something about execution without trial."

Maggie reached out and drew Charlie's face toward her, making him bend at the waist. She planted a small kiss on his forehead.

"Good news for you, Mr. Ashman. I think when Daddy finds out he has a grandson on the way, he'll countermand any execution of his son-in-law. You're safe."

www.ingramcontent.com/pod-product-compliance
Lightning Source LLC
Chambersburg PA
CBHW032144020726
47496CB00003B/714